CALLING THE CHANGE

MICHELLE DIENER

ECLIPSE

ACKNOWLEDGMENTS

Thank you to the team of awesome readers, editors and authors who help me make my books as good as they can be. This journey would be a lot more lonely without you. Thanks to Lana for the amazing cover.

ACKNOWLEDGEMENT

ONE

UP UNTIL LAST NIGHT, Aidan of Juli had been an ally.

Taya would have even said a friend.

Now he blocked their way, standing between Taya and Garek and their quickest way home.

Guards stood around the sky craft which sat on the castle's wide guard walk, ready to sound the alarm in case sky raiders were spotted. The sky raiders had already snatched back the other sky craft Garek had stolen from them two nights ago, but for now, this one was safe.

And inaccessible.

Juli's guard master, Vent, stood by Aidan's side, and he'd brought about ten guards to stand with him, forming a wall of leather breast plates and swords.

Garek set down the box of shadow ore he'd been carrying.

The guard holding the other end of it followed his lead and then groaned with relief as he straightened.

The boxes didn't have that much ore in them, but they were filled to the brim with water, and Taya knew from personal experience how heavy they were.

Behind them, the two guards carrying the other box did the same.

Neither side said anything, but movement caught her eye, and Taya looked over her shoulder to find the three guards who'd helped them with her boxes had stepped to the side, so they weren't standing toe to toe with their own, their gazes on Vent, waiting for orders.

She turned back, and stood with feet braced apart. Ready for anything.

Garek seemed relaxed; his arms loose at his sides, his gaze steady and calm on Aidan. Waiting.

Some of the guards began shifting in place, uncomfortable, and Vent looked sidelong at Aidan, impatience in the scowl on his face.

"The liege said—" Vent spoke loudly. Everyone had to, up here on the guard walk. The rage of the river below the castle wall, and the thunder of it as it fell down the cliffs to the lake below, made speaking quietly a losing strategy.

Aidan made a chopping motion with his hand, cutting the guard master off. "My father can barely stand up. So rather say Dartan said." Aidan held the Vent's gaze for a beat, and then lifted a brow. "And since when is the word of Dartan better than my own?"

Vent shut his mouth with a snap.

"Why allow your guards to help us bring our things up, and then prevent us from leaving?" Taya asked Aidan.

"Because the right hand doesn't know what the left hand is doing," Vent said, disgust in every word.

That, Taya could believe.

They had arrived in Juli two nights ago—in triumph, some would say.

They had brought the liege's son, Aidan, home.

They had rescued the Illy and the Kardanx taken by the sky raiders.

But even before the sky raiders had surprised them all as they were disembarking, had swooped down to wrest back one of the sky craft by force, she'd sensed the undercurrents here.

There was no clear leader.

The liege had been so drunk the night they'd arrived, he couldn't walk in a straight line, and his mind was confused.

Under those circumstances, she could easily see how conflicting orders could be given. Probably every day.

"So what does this mean?" Garek spoke for the first time, unruffled and steady. He shifted, the movement so subtle it was hard to even pinpoint what he'd done, but he was suddenly a little in front of Taya, standing between her and the guards ranged against them. "Do you really want to go this route, princeling?"

Aidan flicked him a nervous look, and Taya decided he hadn't lost his mind, after all. He would know almost better than anyone here that Garek could sound calm a moment before unleashing chaos.

"Dartan heard you were leaving, and wanted me to keep the sky craft here." He spoke reluctantly, as if he sympathized with his father's councilor, but wasn't fully behind him. "I didn't know which way you'd take to get to the craft, so I came here directly."

They'd planned to load the shadow ore and then send a messenger to let Aidan know they were leaving. They hadn't hidden their intentions, and they wouldn't have left without saying goodbye. Taya decided Aidan had let the strange tension and suspicion that permeated the castle like the stink of a dead levik affect him.

"The sky raiders know it's here, and they'll be back to take it, just like they took the other one." Garek looked up, almost as if he expected to see the sky raiders above them.

"I agree, but I've got an idea about where we can keep it." Aidan glanced up, too.

"We made a promise to Kas," Taya said, although she knew the princeling had been there when it was made. "We're going back to Pan Nuk. Today."

She couldn't wait to get out of here, away from the feeling of edgy disarray that had seeped into every corner of the water city.

She wanted to go home. Wanted to be among her own things.

She'd only had time for a quick reunion with everyone from Pan Nuk two nights ago, and she wanted to hold her nephew tight and hear all his news. She wanted to wear her own clothes, wanted see how much damage months of disuse had done to her dye machines.

She wanted to leave so badly, she had to force herself to take a deep breath and not react too aggressively to this nonsense Aidan was throwing their way.

"What do you plan to do against the sky raiders when they come for the sky craft in Pan Nuk, and possibly take the whole village you just rescued back to Shadow? What army will you use to stop them?" Aidan asked her, his voice low and intense.

"What will you do?" Garek challenged. "All your guards together couldn't stop them two nights ago."

"Neither could you." Aidan's voice rose.

And that was true, too. Garek had been the only one harmed, shot down by the sky raiders with a weapon that made white lightning, and felt like being boiled alive. Taya had been exposed to its full effects once, when she was first taken, and she never wanted to experience it again.

Garek paused a moment. Nodded. "I was taken by surprise."

"Why are you even arguing with them?" Vent asked Aidan, even though his gaze was fixed on Garek. "This craft needs to be under the liege's control. They can't take it, the idea's ridiculous."

Taya folded her arms, waiting to see what Aidan's reply would be.

He knew he was in a hard place, because he took his time.

"It's not that simple, Vent. We wouldn't have the craft at all if it weren't for Garek. And while I've watched him pilot it, I'm not confident I wouldn't crash it if I try. He's the only one who really knows what he's doing when it comes to flying the thing. It's worthless to us without him." He looked at Garek. "And his good will is worth a great deal, too."

"His good will?" Vent's snort was unequivocally disbelieving. "Who the hell is he, then?"

"My future general." Aidan spoke softly. He held Garek's gaze, and Taya knew he was trying desperately to keep Garek's cooperation, while following the edicts of his father's councilor.

"You're right." Taya realized everyone had forgotten about her, because every gaze jumped to her with surprise when she spoke. Only Garek seemed unaffected.

Because he never forgot about her. Ever.

She slid him a small smile, and while his face didn't change, she saw the warm laughter spark in his eyes. He wasn't worried about this confrontation, she realized, or there'd have been no humor in him at all. He'd be all business.

He must think that even if it came down to a physical confrontation, he'd win.

"What am I right about?" Aidan asked, snapping her back to the conversation.

"You're right that it's going to be difficult to safeguard the sky craft. The sky raiders know it's here, though, so moving it to Pan Nuk temporarily can't be a bad thing."

"I told you, I have an idea where to hide it—"

"That isn't going to work." Vent spoke stiffly, as if loath to say the words and give any ground to her and Garek. "I checked earlier. There's not enough room."

Aidan frowned. "How long do you plan on staying in Pan Nuk?"

His question drew an incredulous growl from Vent. "You're going to let him—?"

Garek ignored the guard master. "A few days."

Vent narrowed his eyes. "If it gets taken—"

"If it gets taken, you're no worse off than you were before." Taya didn't like his tone.

Vent looked at her with open hostility. "Where do you fit into all this, little girl? I heard some strange stories about you, about spears that float, but looking at you now, I tend to think that white light the sky raiders used made everyone see things."

Beside her, Garek went still.

Taya shrugged. "I may be little, but I'm no girl." She tilted her head at Aidan, eyebrows raised.

"Will you stop insulting these two, Vent? You don't understand anything."

Vent crossed beefy arms over his barrel chest. "So explain it to me. This one," he jerked his head at Garek, "at least looks like he'd be useful in a fight. But this one doesn't look old enough to go into a tavern by herself, let alone tell the liege's son what to do."

Aidan looked up, as if to find strength, and then suddenly took a step closer to her and Garek, bringing up a hand to shield his eyes against the glare of the morning sun off the bank of clouds to the west.

"Sky raiders?" Garek looked up too, and his mouth formed a grim line.

They must still be far out because Taya couldn't see them yet.

"Move out the way, Aidan." Garek's gaze switched back to the princeling.

"A few days? You promise?" Aidan moved without protest.

"A few days." Garek leapt onto the ladder up to the pilot's door. "Get those boxes loaded." He disappeared into the craft, and the door at the back of it lowered.

Aidan picked up one side of a box himself, and Taya followed him and the three guards as they ran up into the belly of the ship, making sure none of the water in the boxes leaked out.

If it did, they really would lose the sky craft—in a fiery crash. The only thing protecting the sky craft's systems from the shadow ore in the boxes was the water that surrounded it.

"Try to make my case to him." Aidan grabbed her hand as the other guards ran back out. "It was a mistake to confront you like this, but that's how things are done here and—"

"Here's a tip." Taya looked straight at him. "The way things are done here isn't working very well."

The ramp started to rise and Aidan swore and ran down it. He was forced to jump from at least a meter in the air to get back onto the castle wall.

Garek lifted the craft up before the door had fully closed, and Taya waited in the back to make sure it did before she stepped through to the pilot's deck.

"Which way are they coming from?" she asked him, going straight to the window and trying to look up.

"Nowhere."

She turned, surprised, and saw Garek was grinning.

"Aidan made that up?"

He shrugged. "Or was mistaken. I wasn't going to argue."

He lifted them high above the city, and she caught her breath at the sight of it, the light glinting off the water as it tumbled and foamed down on either side of buildings cleverly built in terraces from the top of the waterfall to the lake below, with the castle perched at the top.

Then he sent them into a steep dive, to fly low over the wide lake created by the river as it left Juli behind it and carved a gentle, curved path toward the sea.

Taya looked back at the city—the castle towers were all that were visible now—and smiled.

Maybe Aidan was still their ally, after all.

TWO

GAREK WASN'T USED to adulation.

When he'd been guard master of Pan Nuk, he'd been considered annoying and largely superfluous.

There had been no sky raiders in those days, so he *had* been largely superfluous.

It had given him time to woo Taya though, and long afternoons of free time to spend dallying with her in the meadows above the town.

He'd taken the general annoyance as an acceptable price for what he'd gained.

When he'd had to leave to do his guard service in Garamundo, he'd been just one more grunt in a sea of them, until his strength and abilities had been noticed. Then he'd been a tool to those in power, and considered a threat by his commander as he worried Garek would be offered his job.

In this new reality, though, one where he'd rescued all those in Pan Nuk who'd been taken by the sky raiders, he was now the hero of the hour.

Even Kas, Taya's brother, had warmed to him.

And he'd never thought he'd see that day.

He put the sky craft down outside Haret, and someone must have been watching for them, because they hadn't even climbed down the ladder before a mob seemed to sweep out of the gates, all smiles.

"No problems?" Kas asked as Garek dropped to the ground behind Taya.

"Some."

A lot of people must have been listening to him, because the noise died down.

"What problems?" Kas's eyes went to Taya, as if to check she hadn't been hurt.

"The sky raiders swooped down on us as soon as we arrived in Juli. They took back the other craft."

"Are the Kardanx safe?" Min had come up beside Kas, and her face was tense as she asked. She was half Kardanx, had grown up with them, and if Garek were to guess, still thought of them as her people.

"They were already out of the ship and safe when it was taken." Taya told her. "They shot Garek, and threatened to shoot him again and kill him if I tried to stop them, so we had no choice but to let them take it. At least it was empty."

"And you think . . ." Kas's voice trailed off, and he looked up.

"They'll be coming after this one, sooner or later." Eli spoke up, the big, burly farmer looking upward as well.

"Yes." No sense in softening the blow. After what most of the Pan Nuk villagers had been through, they didn't need coddling.

"So if we're going to move things and people back to Pan Nuk, it needs to be quick, and we need to think of a place to hide the craft while Taya and I are here. Preferably not near the village in case they decide to scoop you all up a second time."

The possibility of that sobered the crowd even more.

"We have the experience they need. They would much rather take us again than train a new lot of slaves." Jerilia's words were bitter. There was an anger beneath the surface with her that Garek hadn't seen when they were growing up. Being taken to Shadow had hardened her, and woken her fury.

But however honestly she'd come by her rage, her words upset some of the children and the elderly who'd been left behind. Faces of all hues drained of color, and he sent her a sharp look.

"That's why we're going to move quickly and think of a good hiding place." His look encompassed the crowd. "We all know what we're dealing with this time. We've beaten them once, we can beat them again. And this time we're on Barit, where we're a lot stronger."

"They won't be taking me again," Eli said, grim-faced, and there was a murmur of agreement.

"You heard Garek. Let's load up." Kas clapped his hands. "We'll need to do some repairs if we want to sleep in our own homes again, and the day is wasting."

Most people scattered back into Haret, to their temporary lodgings, or to the stables where a lot of their things had been stored by Haret's town master.

Eli, Kas, and Min didn't follow, though, and neither did Taya. She stood with her arms around her nephew Luca, murmuring to him.

Their hair was the exact same golden shade, Garek noticed. Like liquid light from the Star.

"We'll need to keep watch," Kas said, quietly. "Day and night."

Garek nodded. "And I can't be more than a few steps away from the craft at any time."

"You need to be able to get in and fly off, lead them away, if they're spotted," Eli agreed with a slow nod. "Makes sense. But I hope it doesn't come to that."

"I wish I understood how they knew we were in Juli to take the sky craft back." This was what weighed on Garek more than anything. "They could have caught sight of us and followed us to Juli after we'd dropped you off here. Or there could be some other way they know, something inside the craft that tells them where it is."

"Either way," Min said, "they know where to find Pan Nuk,

because they've been there before, and it's logical you'd bring everyone back home. They know it's possible the sky craft will be here."

Garek nodded. "That's why we need to hide it away from the village. The only thing I don't like is that I can't be watching the craft and the village at the same time."

Kas and Eli exchanged a look and he thought perhaps he'd insulted them.

"Everyone will help guard the village." Kas broke the silence.

"I'll help guard the village." Taya had stepped closer, Luca still glued to her side. "With watchers to help warn me when they're coming, I could take them by surprise."

There was another silence. Not hurt pride this time.

Shock.

And even he was guilty, Garek acknowledged. They kept forgetting Taya could call a Change now. Was, in fact, one of the most powerful weapons they had against the sky raiders.

She looked around at their expressions, even Luca's, because he didn't know yet about her new skill, and made a face.

"Shadow ore, remember?"

Garek tucked a long strand of Taya's hair behind her ear. "Sorry."

She gave him a sweet smile and shrugged. "I obviously look like someone who can't go into a tavern by herself, instead of someone who's at least useful in a fight."

He laughed at her repeat of Vent's judgment of her. If only the Juli guard master knew how wrong he was.

"What's that about?" Min asked.

Taya shook her head. "Just something Aidan's guard master said about me. In a way, it was a relief he thinks I'm so useless. When the sky raiders took the second sky craft back, I used two of the shadow ore spears, but they threatened to kill Garek if I used them. Aidan was unhappy I'd revealed what I could do, but if even his guard master has somehow discounted what some must have seen with their own eyes, it looks as though my secret is still safe."

"Aidan might have helped there. Downplayed what the guards saw," Garek said, thinking it through. It looked as if he owed the princeling.

"Where will you go after you help us move back to Pan Nuk?" Kas asked, and Garek didn't miss the way Taya squeezed Luca tighter to her, as if she didn't want to go anywhere.

His heart sank at the thought that she would want to stay here. He wasn't leaving her again.

"We should go back to Juli." He watched Taya as he said it, and she looked up and met his gaze. "At least for a little while. We need a permanent solution to hiding the sky craft, and there's the threat to West Lathor from Harven and a few other Illian states. You can be sure the Harven liege will be trying to cast doubt on what we did to help his people."

Kas tapped his chin. "He won't do anything until Luci and her people go back to their village. He'll need them gone before he can try to undermine their rescue."

Garek gave a nod at Kas's assessment.

Kas had always had a good grasp of politics. If Aidan wanted Garek as his general when he became West Lathor's liege, Garek didn't think he could go wrong with Kas as his advisor.

"If or when Habred does make a move, I know Aidan thinks the sky craft will be the deterrent that will make him turn tail and run."

"But he already knows we have it," Eli pointed out. "Wasn't the point of our dropping off Luci and her villagers at Harven's capital Aidan's way of letting their liege know we have more powerful resources than he does?"

"That was part of it, and partly to make the people of Harven grateful to us, so it will be harder for Habred to mobilize his forces against us. But it depends how far along the other states in collusion with him are with their plans to invade us and how many secret deals Habred has made. If he's committed to action with Fabre or Kadmine, or both, he might be forced to support them, even knowing we have a sky craft."

"He'd have to convince his allies it's useless to move against us, and that might be hard to do if they're already set on invasion, already dividing up West Lathor in their heads." Kas frowned. "It might be worth spending some time patrolling the skies around those three states, see if they're moving troops."

That was a good suggestion. Garek nodded. "I think Aidan would consider that an extremely useful exercise."

"His father, or rather, his father's advisor, may not." Taya lifted her head.

"Why not?" Min asked.

"He tried to stop us leaving this morning. Aidan distracted them so we could go against his orders, but they don't like Garek in control of what they see as West Lathor's property."

Eli snorted out a laugh. "They had nothing to do with it. It's Garek's sky craft. He wasn't even working for them as a guard when he took it."

Kas shook his head. "But he is a trained guard of West Lathor. And it is what could be considered a state asset. In fact, I'm sure it is. Which means technically, the liege can confiscate it."

"It makes me not want to return to Juli at all," Taya said. "Or if we do, we find a place to hide the sky craft nearby, and walk in on foot."

There were pros and cons to that, Garek acknowledged. The downside would be not having the sky craft near to hand, but the benefit was definitely keeping control of something he'd risked his life to obtain. The sky craft was a strategic advantage he was reluctant to hand over.

"We'll have to think about that." He'd been watching the gate into Haret, and saw the first few Pan Nuk villagers coming out loaded with furniture and baskets, and he climbed back up the ladder to open the ramp at the back.

The irony didn't escape him that they were going to use the very sky craft that had taken everything from Pan Nuk to put it all back.

THREE

IT WAS good to be home, but hard—harder than Taya would have thought—to see Pan Nuk looking like a dead place.

They'd worked through the afternoon and night the day before, in the end staying one last night in Haret and setting guards to watch for sky raiders while Garek snatched a few hours sleep on the floor of the sky craft.

They'd been up again at dawn, bringing a lifetime of things out of storage in Haret and putting them back in Pan Nuk.

The village was not a ruin, but it needed serious repairs.

The sight of broken clay bowls and ripped curtains flapping from broken windows brought back vivid memories of the day she'd been taken, the shock and the terror of it so real now she was back. On Shadow, it had been about surviving, dealing with whatever the sky raiders threw at them. Here, she could remember.

And she didn't like it.

She stood in the small shed that had been her dye workshop and poked a stick at the dried dye sitting at the bottom of one of the barrels.

It had originally been a deep blue liquid, but had dried to almost black since she had run out of here, on that terrible day, to see what the screaming was about. She'd barely gone five steps before the sky raiders had hit her with white lightning.

She'd woken in a sky craft, and her life had changed forever.

A spinner, almost the size of her palm, scuttled on ten legs across the floor in front of her, jerking her back to the present, and she took a breath to center herself.

The shed had become a haven for insects of every kind, and it would need a thorough clean.

She picked up a bucket and walked to the back where the water pump was located. She had to lean her whole body into pushing the handle down, and then strain to lift it up, it was so stiff with disuse.

It took long minutes of effort, but eventually, with the thump of pipes groaning under the strain, the water flowed sluggishly. It was brown and smelled of clay and she filled the bucket to the top and then walked outside and threw it out, repeating the process until the water gushed out, clear and sweet again.

She poured it into the barrels, hoping the dried residue would dissolve—not so she could start dyeing levik wool again—they had no leviks anymore—but so she could drain the barrels. She wanted to clean them so when she returned for longer than a few days, and when their herds had been replenished, she could start again.

They had promised Aidan they wouldn't be gone for long, and it wasn't fair to endanger the village by having the sky craft so close for any period of time, anyway.

She couldn't let herself get too attached to Pan Nuk just yet.

But it was going to be hard to walk away from the little business she'd built up. Of course, her clients—the wool merchants in Juli and Gara—would have already given up on her. She'd been gone for so long on Shadow, if they didn't know she'd been taken, they would think she was no longer taking orders. So she'd have to start again. But she'd done it before, and she could do it again.

She took a deep breath as she stepped out of the shed and looked down the length of the street that was the main thoroughfare in Pan Nuk. It had been home for all her life before the sky raiders came, with only a trip to Juli a year ago to expand her horizons.

Now she'd been to Luf, the capital of Harven, and Valian, the Dartalian capital. She'd been to the Endless Escarpment and flown over the Dartalian Range. She looked up at where Shadow loomed, high above the mountain peaks. She had been there, too. Further away than any on Barit could ever have imagined.

And while her life might have been altered forever, it hadn't been all bad. She'd found that she did have a Change to call. A type of earth change that was so specialized, she would have gone her whole life without knowing it if she hadn't been forced to dig for her element in a sky raider mine up on Shadow.

And it was deeply satisfying that the Change she called was particularly effective against the sky raiders. They'd forced her onto Shadow, awakened her Calling, and now she was a danger to them.

In the distance she heard the familiar rumble of the sky craft, and it made her chest constrict for a moment, remembering what it was like back on Shadow.

She'd become used to the sound of the transports as they flew in to take the prisoners to the camp or the mine, and she wondered what the elderly and the children of Pan Nuk who'd been left behind made of the noise.

With a blast of dust, Garek set the sky craft down at the end of the main street, and villagers began dragging the last of their things down the ramp.

Pan Nuk was coming back to life.

She walked toward the craft, pleased to see through open doors and windows that people had started making their cottages into homes again.

A flash of color caught her eye as she passed the narrow street that angled upward to the village water tank. The water it held came from the lake high above the village via aqueduct, and there was

Min in an orange dress standing beside it, her hand on the stone supports.

Calling her Change, Taya realized. Something must have blocked the flow of water, and Min was trying to fix it so they all had water tonight.

A small group of children watched her, transfixed.

Pan Nuk had never had someone who could call the water Change.

Taya hesitated, considered calling a hello, but eventually continued on her way without interrupting.

By the time she'd reached the sky craft there was a small group crowded around the ladder—Kas, Eli and Quardi, waiting on the ground as Opik helped Luca down.

Garek must have let them both ride with him in front.

Opik had helped Garek steal the sky craft Garek had used to reach Shadow, and she knew he'd been determined to have a chance to ride in one.

Garek swung out of the pilot's door, climbed down, and moved across to her, easy and relaxed, and pulled her close.

Having him back here in Pan Nuk, beside her, made her hands tremble as she slid an arm around his waist. She had imagined this so many times on Shadow, but some small part of her had wondered if it would ever happen.

"Have we got a hiding place for the sky craft?" She addressed her question to Eli.

"There're a few options," he said, "but they're quite far from the village."

She felt Garek's arms tighten around her. She didn't like the idea of him being far away, either.

"Do you think the sky craft would break if we hid it under water?" she asked.

"You think, because water is a buffer against the shadow ore and their equipment, it might prevent them sensing the sky craft some-how?" Kas looked at her in surprise.

17

She shrugged. "If they're tracking it using something inside the craft itself, it would hopefully put an end to that."

"The sky craft Garek and I stole from the Garamundo town master was there for months, ever since Garek brought it down, and they never swooped in and took it," Opik said.

Taya's gaze snapped to his. "That's a good point."

"A very good point," Garek agreed. "But they may have thought it was too damaged to save. They'd have risked their people to come in and get it, and all for a craft that possibly couldn't fly."

There was silence for a moment while everyone thought through the implications.

"Do we really want to risk damaging the craft by putting it in water, on the small chance they may be tracking it by some method we can't understand?" Eli said at last.

Everyone was quiet again.

"I don't think we can risk it." Garek broke the silence. "But is there somewhere we could put it that's close to water? It would be better than nothing."

Eli pointed to the right. "There's the marsh at the end of the valley. It's boggy, but if we built a wooden platform to put the sky craft on and then covered it with sod, it might look like a small bump in the landscape. There might be enough water in the sod to be help-ful, too."

"That could work, except we'll need time to put the wooden plat-form together." Kas let his gaze drift over the village, and she thought she could see his body droop at the thought of what they needed to do, and how much work they had ahead of them.

They were all worn out. Exhausted by their escape, and from the grinding, never-ending work they'd done for the sky raiders before that.

"We could use doors to make a platform," Luca said, and it was the first time since the conversation began that Taya remembered he was with them, listening avidly. "Some of them are off their hinges, anyway."

"Doors?" Opik frowned.

"Well, ask yourself this," Taya said. "Do you think having a door on your house, or hiding the sky craft, is more important?"

"Put like that . . ." Eli turned and looked down the main street. "Let's get some tools."

FOUR

IN THE END, it had taken more than the doors from every room in every house and barn in Pan Nuk to make a platform the sky craft could land on. They'd had to use wooden window shutters, too—but they'd put together something that Garek could land on in just a few hours.

Then they'd cut large bushes and set them around the base of the sky craft, and covered the roof with sod.

The way everyone worked, focused, tense, told Garek more than words how concerned everyone was about the sky raiders returning.

"Should Taya and I just go now?" he asked Kas, realizing he was speaking up a little late. Everyone had begun packing up.

"No." Kas shook his head. "You're both tired, and we've taken precautions. I don't like the idea of cowering from them. Not anymore."

There were a few murmurs of agreement around them, and Garek realized more people had been paying attention to their conversation than he'd realized.

He walked around the sky craft, mud squelching beneath his boots on the marshy ground, with a critical eye. It was a good job.

Hopefully, from above, it looked like a hillock.

He wasn't taking any chances, though. He'd stay close to it all night, which meant he wouldn't join the village in their first celebratory dinner since they'd been back home.

He and Kas organized a roster of watchers to keep their eyes on the sky, to give him as much warning as possible if the sky raiders appeared.

He hauled some pallets and blankets down, and made himself comfortable underneath the craft itself, hidden by the bushes but able to jump in and fly off at a moment's notice.

Taya crawled through the bushes to bring him dinner, muttering curses as she was forced to stop and untangle her hair.

She stayed to chat while he ate in the last, muted light of the day, made even dimmer because it had to filter through the camouflage to reach them.

When he finished, he leaned forward, cupping her cheek in his palm. "I know you're protecting the village tonight, but get some sleep. Let the watchers wake you if they spot something. They can sleep tomorrow, you have to be in Juli."

"All right." She bit her lip. "I know we promised, but is it a good idea to go back? The liege is volatile and things are out of control there. No one knows who's really in charge."

"Perfect conditions for Harven, Kadmine and Fabre to attack," he agreed. "With luck, I can persuade Aidan to let us patrol the border from the air and see what the other lieges are up to. That should get us out of Juli itself."

She relaxed a little under his hand, and he drew her down onto the pallet.

"What if Aidan can't control his father's advisor?"

"If he can't, he's not fit to be liege." And Garek would have to reassess his loyalty. But he didn't think that was the case. Aidan had proven himself on Shadow. He'd make a better liege than his father.

When Garek had raced from Garamundo to Pan Nuk—before he knew the whole village had been taken—it had been to fetch Taya and run. Run as far and as fast as he could from the Gara town master and his political machinations.

There would be no running for them now. Not with a real threat to West Lathor from other Illian states. He hadn't wanted to be caught up in whatever the Gara town master had planned, but he would help the liege's son protect West Lathor from attack. After all, he'd sworn the guard's oath.

"I'm sorry we can't stay in Pan Nuk longer." Not for himself. He'd always known Pan Nuk wasn't big enough for him, but Taya loved the people here. Had carved out a good life for herself.

"I know we have to go." She lifted up as he slid his arm under her and then turned so she was snug against his side, her head on his shoulder, her hand warm on his chest. "But it's good to be home. It finally makes me feel like we won. We wanted to go home so badly, for so long, and thanks to you, we managed it." She tightened her hold, lifted her head and kissed him lightly on the lips. "We beat them."

There was a wealth of satisfaction in her voice.

He ran a hand down the smooth fall of her hair, gave it a playful tug.

"So, how close are those watchers your brother set?" Because he'd been counting the hours until he had her to himself again. It had been days since they'd had any privacy, and now, here they were, in their own little cocoon under the sky craft.

He felt her smile against his neck.

"I should be walking back to the village. Standing guard."

"They can wait for a half hour more." He lifted up on an elbow, leaned over and kissed her, his hand trailing down her body.

She smiled against his lips, arched up into his touch, and then pulled him down, so there was not a sliver of space between them.

"Then we better get started," she whispered.

It was more than half an hour later when she crawled back out from under the ship, and he crawled out with her. They stood under the night sky, with Shadow in crescent above them, and he held her in his arms for another kiss before he made himself let her go.

He watched her walk away, watched her turn and wave a last goodbye before she disappeared over the hill. There were sounds of shuffling around him, and he was reminded there were four watchers on duty, although he hadn't see any sign of them. Which was a good choice on their part.

There was no possible way any of them could have misunderstood his and Taya's tryst, and he didn't want her embarrassed.

In the distance he could hear sounds of revelry from the village. The feast they were having to celebrate being back home, being reunited with parents and children, was well under way.

The shouting and singing drifted down the valley, and he felt a little pang for being on the outside of it.

"Sorry you're missing all the fun," he called out to the watchers, his gaze moving up to rest on Shadow.

"There'll be plenty more feasts to come, now we're home," Lynal called out from somewhere to his left, and Garek grinned.

"You'd already be out cold with the drink anyway," someone else called back to Lynal, and Garek heard the chuckles from all around.

Pan Nuk was a good place. It had just never felt like his place.

Something he and Taya would have to work out down the road. But not now.

He crawled back under the sky craft and settled back into blankets that smelled of her. It was already more—much more—than he once thought he would have.

WHEN HE EMERGED from underneath the sky craft at first light, shielding his eyes from the Star as it stabbed down into the valley with bright fingers, his gaze when straight upward.

The skies were clear though.

He called the watchers over to help him pull away the bushes and throw the sod off the sky craft's roof, then had them all climb into the sky craft and gave them a lift back to the village.

It was time he and Taya got going.

Aidan had stuck his neck out for them back in Juli, and he'd need them to keep their word for the sake of his own standing at the palace.

Garek landed the craft at the end of the main street, and as he, Lynal, and the other watchers climbed out, he saw most of the village had come out of their doorless homes to watch.

He left a new group of guards to stand beside the craft and sky-gaze for him, and walked down to the house Taya shared with Kas.

It had no doors either, and he walked straight in to find everyone in the kitchen. Taya stood and wrapped her arms around him, sleepy-eyed and ruffled, and Kas, Luca and Min all found their breakfast very interesting for a few moments.

"We going soon?" Taya's voice was husky and she gave a huge yawn.

"Yes." He leaned forward and accepted a warm hotcake from Min, who'd shared Taya's room last night, and would use it as her own while Taya was gone.

"I'll put some of my clothes in a bag and wash up, and then I'm ready." She reached out a hand and touched Luca's shoulder. "I'll have to bring you a present from Juli, Luca."

When she slipped out from under Garek's arm and disappeared to the back of the house, silence fell over the kitchen.

"She doesn't want to go." Luca's voice was quiet.

"No, she doesn't. But I can't leave her." Garek kept his voice as calm as he could.

"She doesn't want to leave us, but she doesn't want to leave Garek either." Kas was just as quiet as Luca had been. "She doesn't want to be apart from you, Luca, but she knows I'll keep you safe. And she and Garek made a promise to the liege's son."

"The liege doesn't need Taya. Not if he has Garek." He looked at Garek as he spoke, and his eyes were filled with tears.

Kas slid an arm along Luca's shoulder. "They do need Taya now. Remember how I told you she found out she could call a Change while we were on Shadow? A special change that helps against the sky raiders?"

"We need help against the sky raiders, too."

"Remember what I told you when I came to Haret, after I found Taya and your father had been taken." Garek crouched down in front of the boy.

He nodded.

"I risked everything to get Taya back. Went all the way up to Shadow to get her. I can't let her out of my sight yet. It's still too soon for me. It was just a few weeks ago I thought she was gone forever. Do you understand that?"

Luca's mouth formed a stubborn line, but eventually he dipped his head in agreement.

"We'll be back. I don't know when, but this is Taya's home. She'll never stay away."

Luca blew out a breath. "That's true. It's your home, too, although it doesn't feel like it because you were gone for so long."

He didn't set Luca straight, but he caught Kas's look. Knew Kas understood Pan Nuk hadn't been home for Garek for a long time.

"I'm ready." Taya was back, looking sleeker now with her hair tied in a braid down her back, wearing the guard uniform she'd found in the Stolen Store on Shadow. She was carrying a large bag over her shoulder and the small box of shadow ore needles cupped carefully in her hands, so as not to spill the water inside.

"You want Garek and I to carry the shadow ore boxes to the sky craft?" Kas asked her.

Taya shook her head. "I think I'll leave them here, nice and safe. I'm scared someone will steal them in Juli, and it's not safe for them to be in the sky craft for no good reason. If there's a water leak . . ." She trailed off, shrugged.

"Maybe take two spears," Kas said. "Just in case."

"We'd still have to cart them around in a heavy water box." Taya shook her head. "I'll take my needles, and if we need the spears, we can come back for them. But I'd feel happier knowing they're here."

Garek gave a reluctant nod.

The spears, knife, sword and disks his father and Taya had made on Shadow were all the shadow ore they had, other than the needles. With Juli as volatile as it was, perhaps it was better for the ore to be somewhere else.

"Let's go."

He led the way, although Luca ran past him and joined his friends standing beneath the sky craft.

Taya followed more slowly, and Min walked beside her, their heads tipped close together as they talked quietly to each other.

He nodded as his father rolled up in his clever chair with wheels.

"You look after her," Quardi told him.

He didn't bother to respond to that, and his father grinned at him.

Kas joined them. "Try to get word to us on what you're doing, let us know when you'll be back."

"I'll also try to get some aid sent your way, so you can start restocking the levik farms."

Kas's lips twisted. "You think that will happen?"

"We have Aidan in Juli. He'll try to make sure something is done." And if he didn't, Garek would make sure it did, anyway.

"All right. That would take a lot of the worry away." Kas's gaze went to the people standing in the street, looking at the sky craft, or looking up, watching for the sky raiders. He sighed. "We have a long way to go before we'll be back to the prosperous little village we once were."

Taya reached them; she'd been hugging friends goodbye, waving to others. Garek took her bag, climbed the ladder and stowed her things away.

When he looked out again, it was to see her running back toward the house, the tiny box of shadow ore needles clutched carefully in one hand.

"She forgot her coat," Min called up.

"Garek!" It was Eli, waving to him from the other end of the street. He was pointing up.

Garek lifted his head, saw, as Eli must have, the tell-tale glint of light reflecting off metal, high in the sky.

"Sky raiders!" he shouted, and the villagers scattered.

Kas grabbed Luca and started running. He looked over his shoulder at Garek as he swung his son up close to his chest. "Go!"

Garek ducked back inside, threw himself into the pilot's chair.

He had to get away. Had to draw them away from the village.

He'd never turned the craft off, so it was mere moments before he was airborne, skimming down the valley and then banking right, making himself as obvious as he could.

"Come after me. After me, you bastards." He slowed down, watching them, waiting for them to notice him.

He knew the moment they did. Saw them descend at a steep angle toward him, and he accelerated away.

"Catch me if you can."

FIVE

TAYA WATCHED the sky craft lift up and speed away and couldn't stop the cry that was ripped from her throat.

A forgetful moment—she had left her coat, folded over a kitchen chair, and had run back for it—and now Garek had been taken from her again.

"He'll be back. He's just leading them away." Kas shielded his eyes and watched the horizon.

She couldn't do the same, her eyes were clouded with tears.

"There was only one small fighter craft that we could see." Eli ran up, out of breath. "Just the one."

"Then they were after Garek's sky craft, not trying to grab us again." Kas kept his gaze upward. "We'll have to set a watch all around the village."

His words snapped Taya out of her shock. She ran inside, pried open one of the boxes containing her shadow ore, and pulled a dripping wet knife from the box.

She shoved it into her boot, grabbed up two spears and ran back outside, running behind the house and straight up the steep hill to the meadow above the village.

Eli fell into step with her, and by the time they reached the sloping field, Kas had joined them, too.

"Shouldn't you be down there, organizing?" she asked Kas, gasping as she got her breath back.

He nodded. "Just wanted to see how far you can see from up here. Eli, you're more useful on the other side of the valley." He turned to her. "You'll be all right here by yourself?"

She nodded, taking a seat on one of the smooth boulders that lay as if thrown in a giant game of skip stone on the hillside, one spear in her hand, the other lying beside her.

"I'll send someone to relieve you in four hours." Kas was already running back down, Eli following with his long-legged lope.

She hoped Garek would be back long before four hours was up. Long, long before.

She shaded her eyes against the bright morning sun, and let her gaze follow a careful pattern across the sky.

He would be back, and then they'd be on their way.

She just had to be patient.

FIVE HOURS LATER, she was too numb to feel the need for patience.

She tried to let the soft rustle of the breeze in the long, end-of-summer grass soothe her, and realized the buzz of unease just below her skin was due to the lack of noise from the levik herds.

They were all gone. Stolen by the sky raiders. Dead up on Shadow.

She hadn't realized how integral the sound of them was to her sensory memory of Pan Nuk.

She rubbed strained eyes, and bit into the warm flatbread Opik had brought up.

Her face stung a little, burned by the Star's light even while the sharp breeze chilled her cheeks.

29

She'd declined to take a break earlier when Pilar had come up to take her place, had offered to stay on watch. She was hardly going to relax at home with Garek still not back, but the food Opik had brought her was welcome.

And the company.

"He'll be here soon enough," Opik said. He'd lowered himself to the ground beside her, and they both had their heads tipped back, watching the clouds.

Taya closed her eyes and felt the burn of staring too long at the bright sky. Moisture leaked from the corners of her eyelids.

Maybe she did need a break.

"He'll try. But they have weapons we don't understand." It hurt her throat to even speak the words. And she knew she was being . . . unlike herself. She was the one who always saw a way forward, found a solution. Never gave up.

But she and Garek had just found each other again. It seemed like a blink of an eye between the evening when she'd walked up to the camp fire on Shadow and found him sitting next to her brother, and now.

It wasn't fair that the sky raiders would snatch him from her.

She made herself take a deep breath and opened her eyes.

"This is Garek you're talking about, don't forget." Opik pointed a finger up to where Shadow hung, white and gray, above them. "The man who fetched you in a rescue so unbelievable, he'll be a legend before the year's out, if he isn't one already."

Taya lifted a shoulder in half-hearted acknowledgment. "The thing is, legend or not, he's a person like everyone else. He can bleed, he can die. He can be captured." She thought back to just two days ago, when he lay, still and helpless on Juli's castle wall, after the sky raiders had shot him with their white lightning.

Perhaps that's why she was so afraid now. She'd seen him at his most vulnerable and had been helpless to save him.

"Whatever your man is, he's not like everyone else," Opik said.

"He is." She was tired of the way everyone here insisted on

treating him differently. Of setting him to a different standard. "He is *just* like everyone else."

"No." Opik's words were gentle. "He has always been bigger, stronger, more powerful." He held up a hand when she turned on him, hot with indignation. "If he'd been dumb with it, or slow, maybe you'd have a point, but he's sharp as any sword his father ever shaped. He is more . . . more than anyone I've ever known, and everyone else sees that, lass, but you."

"I see it," she disagreed. "I just know he doesn't like always being on the outside, resented or feared for being himself."

Opik stared at her for a beat, then looked up again. "Careful now, my Taya. You'll end up part of the legend yourself, you say things like that."

She gave a little snort of laughter.

"It's true." Opik snapped off a piece of grass and began to knot it. "Most see him as dangerous. But that's because he is. There's no getting around it. A dangerous beast is always going to be feared for what it is. I'm just glad he has someone like you, who loves him anyway."

"That's where everyone gets it wrong," Taya said. "He's not dangerous to those he cares about, he's a protector. A warrior and a protector. He risked his life to rescue us. What you said before, about him becoming a legend for managing the impossible? That was to protect. To rescue. How is that the act of a dangerous man?"

Opik sighed, shook his head. "So says the only person he truly cares about."

She frowned. Decided it wasn't worth fighting about now, and went back to eating the last of the flatbread.

"You look like you need a break." Opik's words startled her and she raised her head. She didn't remember resting it on her knees. She turned to him and blinked.

"You're right. I was almost asleep." And that was no good when she was supposed to be on watch.

"I'll go down, ask Kas to send someone up to relieve you." Opik rose and touched his fingers lightly to the crown of her head. "Garek made it to Shadow to get you. He's not going to let the little matter of a few sky raiders get in his way now."

She forced herself to smile, then watched him disappear down the side of the hill.

The Star was climbing to its zenith, and even though the heat of high summer was over, the cooling breeze had died down and in her guard uniform she was hot and uncomfortable under its glare.

She shuffled into the shade thrown by the rock she'd been sitting on, and pressed herself against its cool side, which was still untouched by the Star's light.

When she heard the murmur of voices, she thought it was the replacement Opik had gone off to fetch, and she frowned at how quickly they'd come up the hill.

Then she realized the soft conversation was coming from above her, from the path that wound down from the pass above the village.

She gathered herself into a crouch, making sure she was still deep in the shade, glad she had brought the spears off the hot rock with her.

She grabbed one in a loose fist, straining to hear.

A woman spoke, more clearly now the newcomers had moved closer. "I don't think you understand—"

"Stop."

The woman's sentence was cut off with a vicious hiss.

"No more talking, we must be getting close. And you're wrong, I understand perfectly."

"Do you, though?" A third voice asked, the tone dry and sarcastic. And weary, as if this wasn't the first time this argument had played out. "I've walked the walls with Garek, and so has Darla. Forgive us if we're a little concerned about forcing him to do something he doesn't want to do."

"He'll do it, or be branded a traitor." The hisser had the power of righteous zeal in his voice.

"Sure." The third person spoke again, a challenge in his voice. "A traitor to the liege of West Lathor, or a traitor to the liege of Harven?"

There was a beat of silence.

"What do you mean by that, Haz?"

"I think you know." Haz's voice maintained its low, clear volume. "What was that Harven ambassador doing coming out of the briefing room just before we were given our orders to come fetch Garek back? Who's the traitor here, Gaffri?"

There was the sound of a scuffle, and Taya risked looking around the rock to the path.

A man and a women, Haz and Darla, if she were to guess, were struggling against four others. One had to be the hisser, Gaffri, and it appeared he had three others willing to support him. They were all dressed as guards.

And they were obviously from Garamundo.

What had Haz said? He and Darla had walked the walls with Garek.

And those two at least were unhappy with whatever it was they had been ordered to do.

"What are you going to do? Cut your team by a third?" Darla tossed her head, and her long, dark braid flicked over her shoulder, striking one of the men holding her on the cheek. She was dressed in clothes similar to the ones Taya had on herself—thick trousers and a long-sleeved shirt with a leather waistcoat.

"Better a smaller team than a knife in the back," Gaffri told her. He was a big man, broad in the shoulders, with a barrel chest and dark red hair cut close to his head, like Garek wore his.

Darla shrugged. "I'm loyal to the liege." She waited a beat. "Of West Lathor."

Gaffri jerked back his head. "Then you'll have no trouble carrying out the order of the town master the liege of West Lathor appointed to Garamundo."

"I'd have no trouble with it, if it wasn't impossible to carry out, and if I didn't suspect it was more to do with the strange alliance the town master is openly forging with Harven," Haz said. He was much leaner than Gaffri, with light caramel skin and almost no hair at all.

"Impossible to carry out?" Gaffri laughed. "Garek's one man."

But the other three with him looked less certain, and Haz shook his head. "You've been listening to the guard master for too long. Utrel's made a hobby out of undermining Garek, of painting him as not quite as good as he seems."

"And why would he do that?" Gaffri flung a hand in front of him in derision.

"Because he's piss scared Garek will take his job." One of the three holding Haz said, and Gaffri frowned at him.

"It's the truth, captain." Another of the men shrugged, loosening his grip on Darla.

She jerked free, glaring at her team mate.

"You're blowing this out of proportion." Faced with more resistance now, Gaffri lifted up both hands, all reasonable and logical. "Why wouldn't Garek agree to come back with us at the town master's order?"

"Let go, Fek." Haz jerked his arm out of the hold Fek had on him. "He won't agree because he's not a Gara guard anymore, and the town master has no right to issue him with an order. He had to stay two years instead of one as it is. He won't come back."

Darla nodded. "Never."

"Why did you two come along then, if you thought this was such a useless waste of time?" Gaffri's hands were in fists.

"Because we were ordered to do it, and we *are* still Gara guards." Darla sounded like she was explaining things to a toddler.

"I bet you're wondering why two guards who aren't in the town master's pocket were sent with you?" Haz asked, and from where she crouched, Taya saw Gaffri's face darken.

"I caught a glimpse of the list, and two names had been struck off, and Darla and mine added. So my guess is there is more than one officer who has seen just as clearly as we have what's going on, and decided to level the playing field a little."

"Wish they'd had a quiet word with us first to warn us." Darla straightened her clothes.

"I have no idea what you're talking about." Gaffri turned back to face forward on the path, but Taya could see he was shaken, perhaps no longer as sure of himself as before.

"I'm guessing those who are worried about what's going on might even have sent word to the liege," Haz said, conversationally, as they all followed behind Gaffri. "It'll be interesting to see how long the town master hangs on to power after that."

"That's assuming he's doing something improper. He may be acting on the liege's orders, for all we know."

"Of course." Darla's voice was mocking. "You never know."

Gaffri turned to glare at her over his shoulder.

The sound of children laughing rose up from the valley below, and without another word, they suddenly all moved in a quieter, more stealthy way.

Like predators.

Opik would have found Kas by now, and a replacement might be on his or her way up. Taya was suddenly afraid for whoever it was, even though it sounded like these guards were here for Garek, not to cause trouble with the villagers.

She couldn't get down to Pan Nuk before them, the path was the fastest way.

But she couldn't let them go on alone, and enter the village without warning.

She looked down at the spear in her hand, and the one on the ground. No sense in looking dangerous. No sense giving away her secrets.

She patted the knife hidden in her boot. That would have to do.

She waited until the head of the last guard dipped below the horizon, then rose up, leaving the spears tucked against the rock, and moved onto the path, whistling a cheerful tune. She made no effort to walk quietly, and kicked a few stones for good measure.

The man at the back of the group was one of the ones aligned with Gaffri—Fek, she thought Haz had called him—and he stopped and turned toward her as she crested the hill, hand going to the sword hanging from his belt.

She made herself smile widely, and wave.

"Hello! Have you come to help us already? That's wonderful." She kept moving forward, forcing her expression into a look of open friendliness. She hoped.

She stopped in front of the man, and gave another cheerful smile. "Welcome to Pan Nuk. Not that it's looking its best at the moment, but you understand that, I'm sure. Did you bring any leviks with you, or are they coming later?"

Fek blinked. Said nothing.

"Who are you?" Gaffri shouldered Fek out the way, and Taya let herself frown at his rudeness.

"Perhaps the place for introductions is in the village." She didn't want to stand alone with them any longer than she had to. She stepped around Gaffri. "The town master will want to welcome you himself. I'll show you the way."

Her offer gave her an excuse to jog ahead of them, and she could sense their confusion and hesitation.

They didn't know how to deal with her, and they didn't want to give away their agenda. Not yet.

They must also be wondering who else the village could be expecting, given her greeting. She'd used it as a way to put them off balance, but perhaps it would also make them think more carefully about their actions, if they believed other guards were due here.

"Kas!" She hoped the relief in her voice wasn't obvious to the guards behind her as she rounded the last corner. Her brother was standing on the roof of their house, searching the skies. "We have visitors. The guards we were expecting!"

Kas turned, eyes going wide, and then he disappeared.

By the time she reached the end of the path behind their house, he was standing with Eli and Opik, but she had the sense everyone else was just out of sight, behind houses and sheds.

The children who'd been laughing earlier were nowhere to be seen.

There was a moment of silence. She tried to catch Kas's eye, but his full attention was on the guards behind her.

"You're not from Juli," he said. Kas had been a guard in Gara, of course he would know their uniform.

"You're expecting guards from Juli?" Gaffri asked, and he wasn't good enough to hide his shock.

"Yes." Kas's answer was curt and deeply suspicious.

He finally looked at Taya, and she gave a tiny shake of her head.

"If you're not the guards the liege is sending us from Juli, why are you here?" Eli asked. He shifted, and Taya realized just how tall he was. His time on Shadow had honed him, too, so that every muscle was defined. His hand was curled around something small, and she realized with a frisson of shock it was one of the small black devices Garek had stolen from the guards on Shadow that shot white lightning.

She shuffled a little further away from the Gara guards to get herself out of the line of fire and Gaffri frowned at her as he noticed. Neither he nor his team said anything and the silence stretched out.

"Is this to do with Garek?" Kas finally asked.

"And why would you think that?" Gaffri's voice was soft.

"Because you're from Garamundo, and Garek just finished two years' conscription there."

"Where *is* Garek?" Gaffri looked past Kas, as if trying to see behind him.

His question should have been unremarkable, but there was something so aggressive in the way he spoke, everyone straightened.

"Why do you ask?" Opik crossed his arms over his chest.

"We have an order for him, from the town master of Gara."

"He's doing something for the liege in Juli." Taya spoke for the first time since she'd brought the guards to the village.

There was a truly startled silence from the guards this time.

"Well, when will he be back?" Gaffri tried hard to look relaxed, his hand dropping from his sword for the first time since he'd seen Kas.

Eli shrugged. "We don't know. Perhaps with the guards from Juli later today or tomorrow morning; perhaps not. It depends what the liege's orders are."

"He left Gara less than three weeks ago. How has he gotten an offer from the liege already?" Darla's gaze was also straining beyond the house, trying to see more of the village, and Taya saw her interest at the state of disrepair.

"His many acts of bravery brought him to the liege's attention," Opik said.

Again, a startled silence.

"What did he do?" Haz asked.

"He flew to Shadow in a sky craft and rescued us from the prison camp where we were being held by the sky raiders." Eli's gaze flicked up to where Shadow hung above them.

Gaffri opened his mouth, and Taya thought he was going to laugh at the notion, but something stopped him.

"The sky craft that was stolen from Gara," he said softly. "That was Garek?" He looked at them all with more attention than he had before.

"You were held by the sky raiders?" Haz stared at them.

"Yes. For months. The liege is sending guards to help us repair our village from the damage the sky raiders caused when they took us, and from it lying abandoned while we were prisoners."

"You thought we were the guards from the liege." Darla looked across at Taya. "You're expecting them today?"

"At any moment." Opik smiled.

Gaffri muttered a curse under his breath.

"I can pass on whatever it is you were sent to ask Garek," Kas said.

"I'm afraid that won't work," Gaffri said. "We've been asked to put an important offer to him. I've been tasked with it personally. We have our own camping gear, so we won't be in your way, but we'll stay a few days and wait for him."

"What offer is that?" Opik asked.

"It's confidential." Gaffri spoke in a stiff, hard staccato, as if he wasn't used to explaining himself.

Darla had a smile in her voice, but her face was impassive. "Of course, knowing that he's working for the liege directly now does complicate things, as the liege comes before the town master of Gara. Doesn't he, Gaffri?"

"Yes." His answer was stiff. "But I'll wait to ask him, just the same."

"Well," Kas shrugged. "I certainly won't turn down the offer of help from Gara guards, if you have to stay anyway. Welcome."

Gaffri hadn't offered to help, but with Kas's hand extended in a bonding promise, he reluctantly hooked his thumb around Kas's and grasped his hand.

"I'll show you where you can pitch your tents," Opik offered. "Come with me."

He walked around the house, and Darla and Haz followed him. Fek and the other two hesitated, then did the same, and eventually, Gaffri tramped after them with ill grace.

"I heard them talking and hid. They're here to take Garek back to Garamundo, whether he wants to go or not." She spoke quietly, and Kas and Eli both bent their heads to hers so she could lower her voice even more. "Darla and Haz aren't convinced Garek will agree, and don't want to force him. The other three will listen to Gaffri, who thinks he's going to be able to take Garek back, willing or no."

"I thought he looked stupid," Eli said. "Because only a fool would think he could make Garek do anything against his will."

That was true, Taya told herself. But it would get ugly when Gaffri didn't get his way. And there had been enough ugliness in Pan Nuk already to last a lifetime.

SIX

"I HEAR you're Garek's intended, Taya." Gaffri set his plate aside and leaned forward.

He had to raise his voice to be heard over the conversations all around the camp fire, and for a moment there was silence from those directly around them.

Taya wondered who'd given it away. Or maybe no one had, and Gaffri or one of his men had been eavesdropping.

"Yes, I am," she said.

She looked around at the gathering, and felt a strange lurch in her chest to see everyone here, sitting around a fire together when they could be eating dinner in their houses, doorless or not.

Some part of the way things had been done up on Shadow had become a habit for them.

She wondered how long it would take for them to drift back to cooking dinner in their kitchens again.

One thing was certain, the children were loving it. Loving the party feel of it, and loving being able to see all their family together.

Perhaps that's why they'd done this for a second night in a row.

The joy of the children was precious enough to hold onto with tight, grateful hands after four months of being away from them.

"I didn't know Garek had an intended." If Gaffri realized the scrutiny he was getting from those around him, he didn't show it.

Taya shrugged. "Garek isn't known for sharing his private business."

"I knew," Darla said. She smiled at Taya. "All the women who walked the walls knew."

She wondered what Darla meant by that.

Gaffri swiveled his head to look at his fellow guard, and there was displeasure on his face. "You didn't mention this before."

"I didn't know what Taya looked like, or even her name. Just that Garek had an intended back in Pan Nuk." Darla held Gaffri's gaze, and didn't look away.

"What does it matter?" Eli asked. He was sitting between Taya and the Gara guards, and he leaned forward. "What business is it of yours, anyway?"

"If the Gara town master had known, perhaps he would have made allowances in his offer to Garek, so he could bring Taya with him." Gaffri gave a smooth smile. "As it is—"

"Guards approaching." Pilar burst from the Haret road. Gaffri and his unit had been put to work clearing it of undergrowth while everyone else concentrated on their houses, and the way was partly open and clear now.

"Guards from where?" Kas had been standing in the shadows— Taya'd noticed him watching the interplay between herself and Gaffri, but now he stepped forward.

"From Juli's my guess." Pilar shot a quick look at Gaffri, then back to Kas.

"Go back, lead them in," Kas nodded to him, and Pilar turned and ran back into the darkness.

"Eyes like a gool," Opik said admiringly as they heard the thump of his footfalls disappearing into the night.

Gaffri stood, almost to attention, and Taya didn't miss the way his hand went to where his sword would be hanging, if he'd been wearing it. But he and his unit had set their weapons aside earlier when they'd cleared the road, and hadn't put them back on.

Gaffri turned his head to look in the direction of their tents, and Taya imagined he was weighing up whether he had time to get his sword before the Juli guards arrived or not.

It interested her that guards from Juli made him that uneasy.

And then they appeared, Pilar leading the way with a woman striding beside him. Her hair was dark and pulled back from her face, her skin only a few tones lighter, and she sized them up with light gray eyes.

"Kas, this is—"

"Captain Nostra. Juli Day Command." Nostra stepped forward, and greeted Kas with the guard's grip, hand to elbow.

Day Command. That sounded important.

They had either ridden zanir to get here so fast, and left them down the track, or they'd really pushed themselves to get here after she and Garek had left Juli.

If that was the case, she wondered if Dartan, the liege's advisor, had sent someone less to help than to check up on Garek and his sky craft.

It was the only thing that made sense, given the general confusion and disorganization in Juli at the moment. No one had the time for a mercy mission. A mission to make sure the sky craft was safe, however, was a different thing altogether.

Nostra's gaze landed on Gaffri, and she drew herself up, and made a small movement with her fingers which Taya almost missed.

The signal had an electrifying effect on the eight guards who had come with her. They moved into a semi-circle behind her, and all conversation stopped for a moment.

In theory, both groups of guards represented the liege. They were fellow guards of West Lathor. Allies.

But it didn't feel like that. If felt like a nasty fight was about to break out.

Taya wished, as she had so often on Shadow, that Garek was here. She looked upward, and hoped with everything inside her that he was all right.

"State your name, rank and unit." Nostra's voice was cold as she addressed Gaffri for the first time.

Gaffri stepped forward. He was not used to being spoken to like that, Taya saw it in the way his nostrils flared, but he had no choice but to answer. Guards from Juli were the liege's own. They held seniority over the Gara units, particularly outside of Garamundo.

"Captain Gaffri, Garamundo Unit Ten." He spoke stiffly. "Is Garek in your group?"

Nostra said nothing for a beat, and then Kas stepped forward, speaking quietly in her ear.

She jerked her head back in surprise, and Taya guessed Kas had told her the sky raiders had come back, and Garek had led them away. She bent closer again, her face a picture of focus.

When Kas finished, she eased back, and her gaze went to Gaffri.

"You're here on the orders of the Garamundo town master?"

"We are." Haz answered when it was clear Gaffri wasn't going to. "He didn't realize Garek was already under contract to the liege."

"I'm surprised Gara hasn't heard the news yet, of Garek saving the liege's son and rescuing all the sky raiders' prisoners from Shadow. But then, the liege was surprised to know that Gara had a working sky craft and hadn't let him know about it. So it appears communication is bad in both direction."

Her comment was as subtle as an ax smashing a window, and all the Gara guards seemed to go still.

"The town master didn't tell the liege about the sky craft?" Darla breathed out the question in almost reverent awe.

Nostra glanced at her, and although her expression didn't change, Taya had the sense she relaxed a little.

She would know the guards would not have been responsible for what the Gara town master did or did not tell the liege.

"No," she said. "He didn't. So imagine our surprise when the liege's son arrived in one with Garek. I'm sure the town master had a good reason for his omission." Her tone made it clear she doubted that, and Gaffri looked down at his boots.

He knew the liege hadn't been informed.

The thought jumped into her head, and Taya's gaze sharpened on Gaffri. He'd said almost nothing since Nostra had arrived, although beforehand he had been loud, brash, and clearly in charge of his unit.

Of course, what Nostra didn't say was that while Garek's return in a sky raider ship forced the story into the open, the liege actually *had* known about the sky craft Garek had brought down over Garamundo and that the town master had hidden away. And the liege knew it because he'd put his own son, Aidan, into the Garamundo guard as a spy.

Or his advisor had.

Taya didn't know if the liege was capable of such a complex plan.

Either Dartan or the liege himself had been content to simply watch and wait, and give the Garamundo town master as much rope as he needed to hang himself with.

Maybe Nostra didn't know about that.

Taya shook her head. Secrets within secrets.

She was glad she had no part in it.

"You and your team must be hungry, please sit and eat before you set up your camp." Kas diffused the situation with his usual easy charm, and Nostra nodded, slowly sliding her pack off her shoulders and setting it at her feet.

Taya watched the Juli guards eat, trying to judge from the way they spoke and interacted with the villagers what their intentions were. Gaffri and the other Gara guards were much quieter than they had been before, but they didn't look like they were planning to turn in early.

She'd been sitting beside Min and she stood when the food was gone and talk turned to gossip and tall stories.

"Going to bed?" Min asked.

She nodded. "Got watch duty at four tomorrow morning."

44

"I'm on watch in fifteen minutes, so I'll stay here until then." Min looked upward. "Sleep well."

She waved goodbye and met Kas coming out of their house as she approached the door.

He grunted. "I just put Luca to bed. I'm going back to keep an eye on things."

"Make sure war doesn't break out between the Juli and Gara guards." She was joking, but he gave a grim nod.

"There's always been a rivalry between the two cities, it's only natural. But now there's outright suspicion, and from what I can see, Juli has every reason to be suspicious."

"I agree, but that's not the Gara guards' doing. It's the town master."

Kas sighed. Rubbed hands over his cheeks. He looked exhausted and she wondered how much time off he'd gotten, and how much watch duty he'd done today already.

"I agree it's not their fault, but Gaffri rubs me the wrong way, and I wouldn't be surprised if he didn't know more than a unit captain usually would. He's got that smug air about him."

Taya nodded. "He plans to try and force Garek back to Gara, so for that alone, he's no friend of mine."

"What about the others in his unit?" Kas put out a hand to stop her as she slid past him into the doorless entrance.

"From what I overheard, Darla and Haz sound like they were included by other senior officers to be the moral compass and common sense of the group."

"That's interesting. I thought there was some tension there." Kas released her and stepped back. "I better go keep an eye on the whole mess."

"Kas." She called to him as he turned away.

He looked back, and she didn't need to say anything else, he knew just by looking at her face.

"He'll be back, Taya. Nothing will keep him from you. I've learned that lesson very well. Garek sees no obstacle as insurmountable when it comes to you. My guess is that he hasn't come back because he doesn't think it's safe for you. That's what drives his every decision."

She nodded, eyes stinging, and as he disappeared into the darkness, she tried to convince herself he was right.

SEVEN

TAYA WAS on watch in the field again, looking up at a sky slowly lightening from indigo to a crystal blue.

She yawned widely and rubbed at her eyes, balancing uncomfortably on her haunches.

The rock she'd sat on yesterday was damp and cold, and she didn't want to sit on it.

Her foot nudged the spears lying on the ground beside her and they made a high-pitched ting as they knocked together.

She stood, restless and bone tired at the same time. The weight of worry on her shoulders felt like it was going to crush her.

"Where are you?" she said to the sky. "Where in the Star are you?"

Kas was right.

Garek wouldn't torture her like this. Wouldn't put off coming back unless he had no choice.

The sound of footsteps was a welcome distraction, coming up from the village.

She wondered if someone was bringing her breakfast, although it was only five, and a little early for that. She certainly wasn't in the mood for food.

Whoever was coming up stumbled in the last of the night's gloom and swore, and she felt the first prick of unease.

The voice was rough, the language more colorful than usual for Pan Nuk.

She considered crouching beside the rock again, waiting to see where the person was going, but it was too late.

The first rays of the Star's light found their way over the mountains, and the meadow went from mostly dark to gently lit with golden light.

She saw the newcomer clearly, and he saw her.

"Fek." She kept the suspicion out of her tone. "What are you doing up here so early?"

"They told me to bring this up to you," he said, extending something in his hand, and curious, she stepped closer and reached out for it.

He pounced, leaping at her and swinging around to clamp an arm around her chest and jerk her back hard against him.

She went limp, taking him by surprise so he loosened his hold as she became a deadweight.

She dropped into a crouch on the ground and then pushed off against his legs as she ran toward the village, shouting at the top of her voice as she went.

Over her own cries, she heard him yell and then the pounding of his feet.

An answering call came from the other side of the valley, and lights went on below her as she took the path at top speed, using her smaller size to jink left and right as Fek lumbered behind her.

She looked behind her as she turned the last corner, and slammed into two people coming the other way.

She fell back, winded, and then someone reached forward and hands grabbed her upper arms and yanked her to her feet, making no effort to be careful.

Shock bloomed in her belly as she realized it was Gaffri and another of his henchmen who had her in their grip.

"Kas!" she shouted as loud as she could, and almost as if surprised she had dared, it took Gaffri a moment before he let go of her arm and tried to muzzle her with a hand over her mouth.

She twisted away from him, but she had nowhere to go, trapped between him and his guard, and Fek, who was now right behind her.

She dropped to the ground as Fek grabbed for her again and rolled off the path, but there were too many thick bushes in the way, and Fek grabbed her ankle, and pulled her back.

She struggled, kicking out at him, and as he lifted her off the ground by her leg, she twisted, fighting, and caught a glimpse of Kas, face set in horror, as he ran up the path.

Fek hauled her up, clamped a hand around her waist and levered her upright. Then he put a knife to her throat.

She tried to catch her breath and get her bearings, dizziness forcing her to close her eyes for a beat. When she felt steady, she opened them and saw Gaffri and his helper were ranged beside Fek, and there was a big crowd facing them. Nostra and her guards, Kas, Eli, Min and a whole contingent of Pan Nukkers.

"What is going on?" Kas locked eyes with her, and Taya lifted her shoulders in a tiny shrug.

She honestly had no idea.

Gaffri said nothing, and Kas turned to look to the side, where Taya realized the third guard who was in Gaffri's camp was standing amongst the villagers and guards from Juli.

He looked stunned.

Eli was suddenly behind him, with a knife to his throat, mirroring Fek.

The guard jerked. "Captain?" His voice wavered as he tried to catch Gaffri's gaze.

"As your captain won't talk, you can do the honors." Kas walked closer to him. "What it going on? What do you want with my sister?"

The guard looked at Gaffri, his expression one of confusion and panic. "I don't—"

"Why not ask this one?" Nostra, the captain of the Juli guard stood just like Eli, but she had Darla's neck beneath her knife.

"I wish I could tell you," Darla said. "Neither Haz or I know. We were included on the team because one of the senior officers in Garamundo knew something about this mission was off, and they must have realized it was loaded with guards that Gaffri controlled, but whatever good they thought our presence would do to mitigate Gaffri's orders, it obviously hasn't worked. We were both asleep when we heard Taya shouting. They did this without our knowledge, and I really don't know what it's about." She looked over at the guard Eli was holding. "What's interesting is that I'd have said Darrin was part of it, but when we woke this morning, he was sleeping in his tent just like us. Gaffri, Fek and Janu were all packed up and gone. So whatever they decided, they chose to leave Darrin behind. My guess is he doesn't know as much as he thinks he does."

Nostra paused a moment, and then stepped back. She obviously believed Darla, which left all eyes to land on the man Eli still held.

Eli pressed the knife into the skin of his neck, and the first rivulet of blood began to flow.

Nostra walked right up to him. "Whatever you think, you're not going free. You either tell us what you know, and go to Juli with at least the fact that you cooperated to your name, or you go to Juli an unrepentant traitor." Her words seemed to make him shrink into himself.

"They said . . ." he cleared his throat.

"You don't know anything, Darrin." Gaffri's shout jerked everyone's attention to him. "We left you because you were too soft. Too slow." Gaffri's eyes were almost bulging from his head.

Darrin flinched, and then his expression hardened. "They said . . ." Darrin's hands loosened from the fists he'd formed, and he rubbed his thighs. "Back when we had our briefing, a secret one, without Darla and Haz, they said how Harven is going to take West Lathor, that the liege is too weak to hold it. They told us if we do this favor for them, grab Garek and a woman named Taya, then we'll be big men when the dust settles and West Lathor is under Harven control. We'll be top of the guard."

"Who is we?" Nostra asked, soft as a lover's endearment.

"The town master of Garamundo, the Harven ambassador to Gara, and Gaffri." Darrin nodded to his captain.

"They specifically included my sister in their orders?" Kas asked.

Taya wondered about that, too. But if someone had questioned Luci or her people—the Harven villagers who'd been taken by the sky raiders with the Pan Nuk villagers to Shadow—then they would have heard about how she found her calling, of how she could call the Change on shadow ore. Someone might find that interesting enough to want her under their control.

She didn't think any of the Harven villagers would have gossiped to cause her trouble. They were proud of her, grateful to Garek for rescuing them. They would be horrified to learn someone had used their stories to do Garek and Taya harm.

Darrin nodded. "I don't know why they said to take her. It was an added bonus, get Garek, and if you can get this woman, too, then get her. We didn't know she was Garek's intended. Only now . . ." He looked at Gaffri again, desolation in his eyes. "Gaffri said how the game is up. Darla and Haz being with us means there are officers in the Gara guard who aren't happy with what the town master is doing, and like Haz said, they've probably sent word to Juli.

"To top it off, Garek isn't even here, and he's working for the liege, which means we can't just take him and no one will notice, which is what the town master thought would happen." He rubbed at the blood pooling in the dip of his collarbone, painting himself rusty red.

"It's all gone wrong. That's what Gaffri said last night. He said we'd have to call it off and go home, tell the town master the bad news."

There was silence. Gaffri was looking at Darrin with such hate in his eyes, Taya was surprised he didn't cower.

"And grabbing Taya while she was on watch?" Kas turned back to her, and she could see he was searching for a way to get her back, but Fek had her held tight against him, and the knife had already nicked her three times while Darrin told his story.

Darrin shook his head. "Darla's right. I was asleep when the shouting started. I didn't know they were leaving."

"And where are you going?" Nostra asked Gaffri.

He jerked his head. "Up this path, and you won't follow or we'll slit her throat. If you let us go, we'll leave her at the top, and she can walk down to you. You try to follow before that happens, and we'll leave her to bleed out where we cut her. If she hadn't gotten in the way while we were trying to leave, we'd be gone by now, and none of this would have happened."

Something was wrong with what he was saying.

This whole standoff had been completely unnecessary if they didn't mean to take her with them. They could have passed her going up the path this morning, and Taya would have been happy to wave them goodbye.

They had deliberately come into the field to take her.

It was just possible they hadn't known there was someone on watch to see them slip away, but that seemed unlikely. They knew there was a watch roster, and they'd have to be stupid not to expect someone up here.

She could warn Kas not to believe them, but she felt an eagerness in Fek to hurt her, and this would be giving him an excuse. Even if they were lying, and weren't planning to let her go, she could hopefully find a way to get free later.

Fek started walking backward, up the path, dragging her with him. She struggled again, out of sheer instinct, and he simply lifted her off the ground, pinning her arms tightly to her sides and tightened his grip so hard, she felt her bones creak.

"You put one more mark on her, and you'll never be able to run far enough," Kas said to Gaffri as he backed away as well, sword out.

Gaffri stopped. "You want to ensure that we don't, you wait until she comes walking down the path. I'll kill her if we catch sight of anyone following us."

As the path twisted and she lost sight of the villagers, Fek turned to face forward, speeding up as he jogged with her still in an impossibly tight grip.

She hoped they were telling the truth.

But logic told her it would be a long time before she walked down this path again.

EIGHT

HE WAS TIRED.

Exhausted, really.

Garek rubbed at his eyes and then glanced back, saw the flash of blue light in the dark sky that told him the sky raiders were still following.

They had the advantage, because there was most likely more than one of them piloting their craft, whereas he had no one to share the flying with.

He'd been hunched over the controls and keeping his focus for almost a full day, and he knew he couldn't keep it up much longer.

He'd flown around the whole of Barit, he guessed, and had probably seen more in the last day than anyone else had seen in their lifetimes.

The sea was beneath him now. It seemed endless, but he caught the glimmer of lights from a city that sat on its shores, and because he knew he needed to find a place to hide and rest, he turned toward it, dropping lower so that the craft almost skimmed along the tops of the waves.

The city hunkered down right where the sea met the land, but beside it, to the left, was a cliff that seemed to rise up like a monument.

It was dark and so it was only when he was directly in front of it that he saw the waterfall coming over the cliff's pointed tip.

Taya thought hiding in water might make the sky craft invisible. Perhaps hiding behind it would work, too.

He looked back again, saw the sky raiders had gotten closer because he'd slowed as he'd made his pass of the city, and he accelerated away, rising over the cliff and skimming the peninsula beyond it. Then he turned left in a wide arc, going faster than he'd ever pushed the sky craft before, to come up behind the sky raiders, then drop until he almost touched the choppy sea. He paused in front of the pounding water of the fall and then nosed into it carefully, finding a deep cave beyond.

The cliff had been eroded, and the area behind the waterfall was substantial, a deep bite out of the land.

So close to a big city he expected to find some sign of habitation, but aside from a few empty huts built up against the back wall, there was nothing.

Rocks lay on the sand, fallen from the roof above, and he guessed any dwelling had been abandoned as too dangerous.

He landed, leaving the engine running, and kept watch, sitting ready to take off at the first sign the sky raiders had managed to find him.

After half an hour he realized he was losing the fight to stay awake, and shut everything down.

Then he lay on the floor, closed his eyes, and slept.

He dreamed of Taya, standing in the middle of the road in Pan Nuk, reaching out her hand as if to pull him back as he flew away.

He'd made a promise to himself not two days ago that he wouldn't leave her again.

And here he was. Half a world away. And with no idea how he was going to get safely back.

HE WOKE to the sound of something hitting the side of his craft. He stretched, started up the engine, and then walked to the window.

As soon as he'd started the engine, the banging stopped abruptly, and he saw three men and a woman running away, a hammer in the woman's hands.

There was a lot of light, dappled by the falling water, and Garek guessed it was at least early afternoon.

He felt thirsty and hungry, but rested.

He needed to find his way back to West Lathor, but he decided going back to Pan Nuk would just bring more trouble to their door.

Aidan would be getting nervous that he hadn't returned, so Juli was the best option.

And he didn't mind bringing trouble to Juli.

They'd sat nice and safe behind their wall while the villagers and merchants were targeted.

Decision made, he lifted off, slicing through the waterfall and then banking up to get above the cliff. The group who'd tried to damage the craft was standing defiantly on rocks to one side of the massive waterfall, and he couldn't help but admire their courage.

If he'd come across a sky craft, he'd have tried to destroy it, too.

They ducked as he passed overhead, and then stood and watched him accelerate away.

He could see no sign of the sky raiders, but he kept low as he reached the peninsula above the waterfall and followed the path of the river, south and inland.

He had no idea where he was, and wished he still had Zek as a guide. The merchant from Dartalia's capital, Valian, who Garek had rescued from Shadow, had seemed to know most of the places they'd flown over when they'd come back to Barit.

When Garek was far enough away from the coastal city he rose higher, hoping if the sky raiders were still patrolling the area they would stick to where they'd last seen him.

The altitude helped him orientate himself, because in the distance he saw what looked like the Dartalian Range and he realized he must have been flying over Nordra, and the city he'd hidden beside during the night must have been Turn.

He'd heard tales of its size and splendor, and had to admit what he'd seen of it last night seemed to indicate the stories were true.

As he reached the first peaks of the range, he turned west, keeping high and flying through clouds when he could.

He passed close to the peaks that surrounded Pan Nuk, and almost . . . almost, dipped down to quickly scoop up Taya.

But any stop meant the danger of attracting sky raider attention, and he refused to let that happen.

He rose up into the high layer of cloud that hovered just above the mountain peaks, and sped toward West Lathor's capital.

It was already dark by the time he reached Juli, and he dropped out of the cloud as soon as he saw the city lights, overshooting the castle perched between its waterfalls, and then turned, coming down to land at the same spot on the wall where he'd landed three nights ago.

He didn't shut down, he didn't trust the liege's advisor or Juli's guard master enough for that after what happened last time. And he didn't think it wise to leave the sky craft here, in open view.

It didn't take Aidan more than five minutes to emerge from the stairs and run toward him. There was a whole entourage of guards with him, but they must have been under orders to keep back, because Aidan was the only one who came up to the sky craft.

He let the princeling climb the ladder, open the door and climb in.

As soon as the door was closed, he took off.

Aidan shot him a sidelong look, but sat in the chair beside him.

"I can only assume the delay in your return was due to sky raiders?" he said.

"They tried to take the craft yesterday," Garek confirmed, and Aidan stood and went to the window, to keep watch.

"I was already in the craft, so I took off, and they chased me around the whole of Barit."

Aidan turned back to him, eyebrows raised. "You aren't exaggerating that, are you?"

Garek shook his head. "I found a place to hide close to Turn, managed to get some sleep, and then came straight here, once I worked out which direction to go."

"Turn?" Aidan almost choked out the word. "My mother's home city. And I've never even been there."

"It's impressive," Garek said. "Taya had an idea, about hiding the craft in water, because it masks the shadow ore from the sky raiders so well. We decided it was too risky to submerge it, but there's a big waterfall that falls into the sea next to Turn, and there was a deep overhang behind it where I was able to hide the sky craft. I think it made me invisible to them. So I thought, given we have a big waterfall here—" He hadn't flown away when Aidan had gotten into the sky craft, he'd been circling the city, but now he lowered the craft in line with the Right Plait of Corinnda's Hair, one of the two massive waterfalls that fell on either side of the city. Beside it, the roofs of the houses and shops that had been built into the cliff below the palace in a series of stepped terraces glistened green with moss, wet from the constant spray.

Aidan frowned and turned back to look out the window. "I don't think there's enough room behind it."

"Shall we see?" Garek moved the sky craft gently, felt the wobble as the front hit the force of the falling water, and concentrated on keeping the craft steady.

They drifted forward, and came up against a sheer rock face. He reversed and lifted up and over, to the other side, and nosed forward again on the Left Plait.

The water was stronger on this side, and he fought to keep the craft steady, aware that he was calling his Change as well as working the controls.

When they finally made it all the way in, he turned carefully so they were looking at the water falling directly in front on them, and Aidan could look down and see whether there was place to land.

"It's almost impossible to see, it's so dark, but I think there's a couple of rocks at the bottom you could put down on, but you'd be resting at an angle."

Garek lowered the craft, using a cushion of air as he called his Change again, so they settled on the highest of the three rocks, and then as he pulled back, the craft tilted backward and then to the side, and eventually went still, settling lightly down as Garek slowly withdrew the air cushion he'd created.

"How did you do that?" Aidan hadn't moved since he'd begun lowering the ship, and he was still frozen at the window, his legs spread wide to keep upright as the floor sloped at a steep angle.

"I called my Change." Garek stood carefully and moved across the floor with slow, controlled steps. "I'll probably need to call it again to lift off. But I don't think they'll be able to find it here."

"We need to talk." Aidan scrambled out of the door as soon as Garek opened it, and then negotiated the slick rocks and waited for Garek to close things up and join him where the curtain of water met the side of the cliff.

Talking here was useless. The sound of the water pounding down was overwhelming, and Garek edged to the left and hauled himself onto a steep bank at the bottom of the falls.

Aidan joined him, tiny beads of moisture twinkling in his hair and on the tips of his eyelashes like gems in the ambient light from the city above them.

Garek guessed he looked the same.

They eased sideways, making their way down to a thin crescent of rocks lapped by the lake waters. The rocky beach was created by a kink in the almost sheer green hills that plunged directly into the lake on either side of the city.

It wasn't a far swim to the central dock between the two Plaits, and they were halfway there when Garek heard the scream of sky craft engines. He flipped onto his back, still moving toward the dock, but more interested in watching the sky raiders above as they circled the city three times, and then shot straight up and disappeared into the white clouds.

"They knew it was here," Aidan said. "They wouldn't have circled three times if they didn't think it was somewhere near."

Garek nodded. "So we have to ask ourselves, how did they know? Were they following me because they have some way to track the sky craft without actually seeing it with their eyes? Or did they see me turn in this direction, and knowing I'd been here before, assumed I'd come here again?"

"How will we ever learn the answer to that without asking them?" Aidan shook his head, staying on his back for a moment longer.

"And why would they answer truthfully if we did?" Garek answered. It was what it was. But he'd love to find out.

At least it appeared that Taya was right. Water did shield the sky craft from them.

"Do you think anyone saw us hide it?" Aidan asked him.

"What if they did?" Garek said. "Only I can fly it out, and it's not as if anyone would tell the sky raiders where to find it."

"Good point." Aidan flipped back on his stomach and started swimming for the dock again, and with one last look at the falls, glittering in the diffuse light of both Shadow and Barit's moon, Lanora, Garek followed.

NINE

GAFFRI CALLED a halt after ten minutes of hard running from Pan Nuk. The path split three ways here, one led to Gara, the other two went north and northwest.

Taya groaned with relief as Fek swung her down and she crouched, head between her knees, when he dumped her on the ground.

"I'm strong, but I can't carry her the whole way," Fek said. "She'll have to walk."

Taya heartily agreed with that, but she kept her opinion to herself. She was already well aware that anything she wanted, these three would make sure she got the opposite.

"Hope you're up to it." Janu kicked at her, mostly missing, although the edge of his boot hit her thigh and unbalanced her, so she fell to the ground.

"Idiot." Gaffri shoved him. Then, in a fit of temper, shoved him again. "If she's injured, she slows us down, and her brother and her highness, Nostra, queen of the guard, will be coming after us any minute now."

Janu opened his mouth to answer back, and then closed it with a snap.

Gaffri hated Nostra, that was clear enough. But it seemed personal. She wondered what Nostra had done, or accomplished, that Gaffri was so jealous or angry about.

"So what's the plan?" Fek asked. His breathing was almost back to even now, and she had to admit that he was strong and fit.

"This," Gaffri said and leaned over her, grabbed some of her hair, and ripped it out.

The pain was blinding, like the white lightning the sky raiders used to knock them all unconscious when they were stolen, and she realized her cheeks were wet with tears.

She lifted a hand to her scalp, and her fingers came away bloody.

"And you shoved me—" Janu was complaining, but Gaffri ignored him, bent over her again, grabbed the collar of her shirt, and ripped that too, half-choking her in the process.

When he stepped back, holding her hair and a strip of fabric, she wiped her cheeks with the backs of her hands and breathed through the sinking of her heart.

Because while she'd guessed it, now she knew for sure. He had no intention of letting her go.

"Listen." Gaffri's snarl cut through Janu's whining. "You're going to take these," he held out her hair and torn collar, "and you're going to run like Nostra is on your heels—which she will be—to Gara."

"I thought we were going to Luf." Janu took a step back in surprise, but he took the hair and the collar when Gaffri shoved them at him.

"Fek and I are. You're going to Luf via Garamundo. You're the fastest of the three of us, and you're going to give us your pack so Garek's little intended has some food and equipment, and you're going to move your ass as fast as you can. You're going to put the hair in a bush along the way, and the collar at another point, and you're going to get to Gara, find out what the situation is, and then get yourself to Luf."

Janu stared at him. "I thought you said things have gone to hell in Gara. Why would I go there, put myself in danger? Not to mention the Juli guard will be right behind me, as you say."

"You'll do it because I'm giving you money for food and a place to sleep, and you're the fastest of us. A single guard, running without equipment, is going to beat Nostra and her crew, and you've had a head start, with no deadweight slowing you down." He glanced at Taya.

"I'm *guessing* things have gone to hell in Gara, but we don't know whose head's on the block, do we? Who we can trust, who's gone over to the liege's camp, whether that idiot town master has talked his way out of trouble or not. We need information, and you're the only one I trust to give it to me. I've got enough money for you to slip quietly into Gara, put your ear to the ground, and then get transport to Luf." He dumped his pack on the ground, pulled out a small leather pouch that jingled with coins, and handed it to Janu. "Now go. Nostra won't wait long."

Janu took the pouch, mulish and suspicious. "I don't know, Gaffri—"

"For Star's sake, get going, or we'll all be caught." Fek's low rumble seemed to galvanize Janu. He threw his pack down, shot a hot, furious look at Gaffri, and ran down the Gara path.

Gaffri kicked the pack in her direction. "Let's go."

Her head was still so painful, it felt as if metal spikes were being jabbed into her brain with every thump of her heart.

She got to her feet, picked up the heavy pack, and then saw Gaffri was taking the Gara path, as well.

"I thought we were going that way," Fek pointed to the northern path.

"We are, but we'll make sure there's a trail for a short bit toward Gara, then we'll cut across. Carefully."

Gaffri tipped his head toward her. "Get ready for a long walk. And if you try to slow us down, or do something to set Nostra on us, a hunk of hair will be the least of what you'll lose."

TAYA DID TRY to find a way to mark their path for Kas to follow, but Gaffri and Fek watched her like the sharp-eyed hovers coasting the updrafts in the sky above, waiting for a meal to break cover.

They forced her to take the lead, physically pushing her when she went too slowly. They were careful not to hurt her, although she had a strong feeling Gaffri would have done so if he could have done it without slowing them down.

As it was, she was already deadweight. Much smaller than them, needing two steps to their every one, she also downplayed her fitness.

She'd become strong on Shadow. She'd dug tunnels and then carried rocks for four months, and she had the muscles to show for it, hidden beneath her clothes.

They assumed she was weak, and she was happy to keep giving them that impression.

Every now and then, she'd look upward, hoping to see the glint of a sky craft. Because Garek would be back—she had to believe he'd managed to lose the sky raiders he'd lured away—and when he came, it would be in a storm of fury and violence.

As Fek shoved her between the shoulders again, making her stumble, she enjoyed the thought of what Garek would do to them. She'd like to participate.

"So, what happens when we get to Luf?" she asked as they climbed the tight, narrow path up the first mountain that stood between West Lathor and Harven.

She knew it was just the beginning of the difficult terrain. There were round, green hills and valleys beyond this mountain, which comprised the last easy stretch, and then they'd hit the Dartalian Range, sharp spikes of sheer gray rock which started in Dartalia and curved like a scythe between West Lathor and Harven.

Fek grunted, and gave her another shove. Her temper snapped as she stumbled again and she pretended exhaustion, stopping, hands on knees, as if to catch her breath.

Slowing them down was the plan. Slowing them down at every turn, at every opportunity.

"You think the Harven liege really wants me? Do you even know what for?" She made her voice breathless and faint.

If she was right, what the Harven liege would have heard about her from Luci and her people was reason enough for his interest, but she wondered if he'd shared the information with the Gara town master, and whether that had been passed on to Gaffri and Fek.

"Move." Fek shoved her again, and she let his push take her over, and she lay, collapsed and panting, on the hard, rocky ground.

"Get up." Gaffri loomed over her.

She blinked at him, and then closed her eyes, trying to keep her body loose, although she wanted to brace for a kick. It felt good, even with a few rocks digging into her back, to just lie for a moment. To rest.

"Has she passed out?" Fek asked. There was no emotion in his voice whatsoever except mild curiosity.

"If she has, then it's because you pushed her over."

"Barely."

She felt the toe of his boot nudge her side.

"Carry her, then." Gaffri's voice sounded closer, as if he were crouched down.

"Are you crazy? I can barely get in enough air to breathe myself. And I'm already carrying her pack because it was slowing us down too much with her carrying it. Maybe you can take a turn."

She heard Gaffri grunt, and wasn't sure if that was a yes or a no.

"Air's getting thinner the higher we go." He nudged her again. "Probably what's wrong with her, too."

Interesting.

She'd been on Shadow for the last four months, and she was used to thin air. Since she'd been back on Barit, she'd barely been able to get over how easy it was to breathe.

So she had another advantage over them. That was good. As good as the knife that was still hidden in her boot.

She hadn't used it yet, but they had to sleep sometime. She couldn't take them both, but she could probably take one. And she could use her newly expanded lungs to run as far away from them as she could.

"We might as well have a break," Gaffri said from somewhere to her left. "Hey." He shook her. "Wake up. Get something to drink and eat, because when we go again, we're not stopping until nightfall."

She lay still for another beat, and he shook her again, harder.

She let her eyes flutter open.

He dropped Janu's pack next to her. "Eat. Drink. Or go without."

She struggled up on her elbows, and then pulled herself up to a seated position and leaned against a rock protruding from the mountain side.

She got out a canteen, sipped from it, and saw Fek and Gaffri were occupied with their own canteens, their own food.

They were getting used to her obeying. Being under their control.

That was good.

Because it wasn't going to last.

TEN

THE LIEGE'S ADVISOR, Hector Dartan, was a tall, imposing figure. Garek watched from the edge of the room as he strode into the sitting area of Aidan's chambers just as the first Star light of the day bathed everything in rose gold.

His dark hair was pulled back severely, and his dark eyes flicked to Vent in a way that told Garek there was no love lost between him and the guard master.

Vent had straightened from his guard's slouch against the wall when Dartan came in, and he rubbed a hand over a dark-skinned jaw stubbled with gray. There were deep creases around the guard master's eyes, and he had the thickset body of an aging warrior, but he was considerably bigger, and wider, than the liege's advisor. He yawned, a deep, noisy sound that seemed to involve his whole body.

It was the first time he'd done so, which made Garek sure it had been deliberately timed to coincide with Dartan's entrance.

These two probably tried to find ways undermine each other daily.

No wonder Vent said the right hand didn't know what the left was doing in Juli. What Vent had forgotten to mention was that he was part of the problem.

"Now we have the sky craft back," Aidan said before either Dartan or Vent could speak, "we have to decide what to do with it."

Garek lifted a brow, annoyed with even having to be here. It had been too late to leave for Pan Nuk last night, and he'd known he wouldn't get far in the dark. Better to save his strength and get going early and fast in the morning. Aidan had convinced him they needed this dawn meeting before he left, but his patience was already wearing thin at the posturing, and Vent and Dartan had only been here a few minutes.

"Before we do anything with the sky craft, I need to go back to Pan Nuk and get Taya. Then, perhaps it would be a good idea for us to fly over Harven, Fabre and Kadmine and see what they're up to."

"Spy on them from the air?" Vent sounded intrigued. "That would be . . . useful."

"And the best part is, they'd think you were a sky raider, and simply be grateful you didn't attack them or try to steal anything. They'd never suspect it was us." Aidan nodded, although Garek had already outlined the idea to him last night and he'd approved it. Just another reason why this meeting was a waste of time.

Dartan cleared his throat. "There seems to be no downside to that. Except wasting time to go and get your intended is out of the question."

Garek smiled at him, a quick flash of amusement, and said nothing.

Aidan cleared his throat. "Garek won't fly the sky craft until he has Taya. He was forced to leave her behind in order to keep the sky craft out of sky raider hands. But now he's shaken them off, he's going to get her."

The liege's son and the liege's advisor stared each other down.

"There must be someone else who can fly it," Dartan said.

"There isn't. Besides working the controls, which I could probably do because I've watched him, Garek doesn't just fly it. He calls his Change to help him with it, more than I think he even realizes himself. And there is no one who can call the air Change better than Garek."

Garek shifted impatiently and Aidan sent him a sideways glance of admonishment, then focused back on Dartan.

"We're hardly under imminent attack, Dartan. Unless you know something I don't?" Aidan gestured with his arms, hands palm up. "We can afford to wait the five or so days it'll take Garek to get Taya and bring her back here."

"What about that scientist you've sent for from Gara? Doesn't he know how to fly the craft?" Dartan wouldn't look at Garek now.

"You've sent for Falk?" Garek leaned back against the table behind him, and crossed his arms over his chest, his eyes narrowed as he looked over at Aidan.

"I didn't tell him about the sky craft. I sent a message to him, offering him a job here, and he accepted. With alacrity, which tells me things haven't been all that good for him in Garamundo since you stole the sky craft from his laboratory."

"No." Garek rocked back against the table. "The town master wouldn't have been happy with him about that. But also, he knows you flew off with me in the sky craft, so my guess is it's more about finding out what we did, and how the craft worked, than feeling under pressure from the town master. Also, I bet he guesses we still have the craft, so he probably thinks he'll have access to it again."

Aidan grunted in acknowledgment. "Didn't think of that, but you're right."

"Let's hope he keeps his mouth shut about what he knows." Dartan's frown deepened.

"Well, now we've had this nice chat, I'm off." Garek had requested a travel pack from the guard master, and Vent had brought it with him to the meeting. He handed it over.

Garek nodded in thanks, and then went still as Dartan grabbed his arm.

He met the liege's advisor's gaze with a hard stare.

"I don't like your attitude." Dartan blinked and dropped his hand. "I don't like being forced to let you do whatever you feel like doing." His lip rose in a sneer. "You're a citizen of West Lathor, and the liege is your ruler."

"When my ruler can walk in a straight line and speak without slurring his words, I might even consider listening to him," Garek said softly. "But my whole village was taken, and he didn't even know, let alone try to help. I've sacrificed a lot of my life already to my obligations as a citizen." He stepped back. "You don't like me, don't want to use me, that's fine. Find someone to bring down another sky craft and learn to fly it."

Dartan's look should have been able to drop him dead on the floor. "I do have someone else who can fly it."

Garek frowned, then realized who he was talking about. "Dom." He gave a nod. "If he's still here in Juli, and not back in Kardai, then by all means. But he needs a sky craft to fly in, because he won't get mine out from where it's hidden. Until you can get him his own one, you'll have to put up with me and my unreasonable demands."

He shouldn't have felt angry when he walked out of the room, but he realized his hands were in tight fists.

He forced himself to relax, and then turned in surprise when he heard Aidan jogging to catch up to him.

"Where *is* Dom?" Garek asked.

"Still in Juli." Aidan gave an embarrassed shrug. "His mother chose to stay, and I've given both of them the right to remain."

"That's good." Dom wouldn't have an easy time if he returned to Kardai, and his mother wouldn't, either.

"I wish I could come with you," the princeling said. "This place is a mess."

"Take it over," Garek said, and readjusted the pack on his back. "You know it's time."

Aidan rubbed a hand over his recently cut hair, and sighed. "I'm starting to believe you're right about that."

GAREK PUSHED HIMSELF HARD, calling the Change and stepping into the inbetween for short, accelerated progressions on the road to Pan Nuk.

He had to choose empty stretches with no possibility of meeting anyone or anything, because if he hit something while he was in the inbetween, it was generally reduced to tiny pieces.

He also didn't want to tire himself too much, too worried about what he'd find in Pan Nuk. The secret fear the sky raiders had returned to take everyone back was a sick dread that had him balancing speed and energy on a brutal knife's edge.

He forced himself to stop for a break in the early afternoon when he came to a bridge that crossed a wide stream.

He climbed down to the water's edge and splashed its icy snow melt onto his face, then drank before he pulled himself onto a rock just below the bridge itself and found the rations Vent had packed for him.

He'd just finished eating, and was buckling his pack up again, when he heard the sound of running feet.

He pulled himself up until he was crouched beside the bridge but able to duck under it easily.

His eyes were level with the heavy wooden planks and he noticed the boots first.

Guard boots. Juli guard uniforms.

He wondered what they were doing here, but stood and stepped out to block their way when all ten of them were at least halfway across the bridge.

He heard the arrows being notched from the back, saw the hands go to swords at the front, but his gaze was drawn to the captain. She was in the lead, and unlike her guards, she already had her sword in her hand.

"Who are you?" Her voice was clipped.

"Garek of Pan Nuk."

He was surprised to see her mouth drop in surprise, and then her body relax.

There could be only one reason for that, although he couldn't understand why. "You've come from Pan Nuk?"

She nodded, walked toward him, with her team following warily behind her.

"My guard master sent us to Pan Nuk the night you landed in Juli."

Garek's eyebrows rose. "Why?"

"The princeling said you would be flying the sky craft there the day after, and although Vent was against that, he thought it best there was a guard there to keep watch over it in case you got your way."

Well, that made perfect sense. Garek simply hadn't credited Vent with that much tactical forethought.

"Well, the sky craft is back in Juli, so I won't stand in your way." Garek stepped to the side so they could pass him.

"You brought it back?"

"Last night."

Suddenly her blade was against his throat, and her eyes were hard as they locked with his. "Even if you left Juli as soon as you set down, you couldn't have come this far on the road yet."

"I only left this morning, but then I have an advantage." He called the Change, and slid backward into the thick, golden air of the inbetween, putting a few steps between himself and the captain's blade. He could have gone further, but staying in the inbetween too long would cost more than he could afford to pay just to make a point.

When he reappeared, he said nothing as he saw her come to grips with him no longer being within reach.

"You call the air Change. And are strong enough in your calling to find the place between the particles that no one can see." The captain looked at her sword, then slid it back into its scabbard. "My apologies. My name is Captain Nostra of Juli's Day Guard, and the reason we're returning is not purely because you were not in Pan

Nuk with the sky craft. Guards from Garamundo had arrived before us in Pan Nuk, looking for you."

That got his attention, and he walked back toward her.

There was a struggle from amongst the thick knot of her team, and belatedly he realized he'd given them barely a second glance.

Now he saw two guards push through, dressed in Gara uniforms.

"Haz," he said softly, "and Darla."

The Juli guards shifted a little more, and he saw another familiar face. He struggled for a moment to remember it. "Darrin."

"So you do know them?" Nostra asked.

He gave a brief nod. "These two, I'd trust. Him," he pointed to Darrin, "I wouldn't, but I see you've worked that out already." Because now he could see Darrin was loosely restrained.

"There were three others," Nostra said.

"Gaffri." Darla spoke for the first time.

"Gaffri was in Pan Nuk?"

"Gaffri, Fek, and Janu," Haz said.

So all of Utrel's bully boys.

If they'd been despatched to round him up and force him back, the Gara town master had truly lost all sense.

"You say part of the reason for your quick return was the presence of the Gara guards in Pan Nuk. Why was that?" Garek was starting to get a cold, sick feeling about this.

"It seems they were there to ask you to return with them to Garamundo at the town master's request."

So he was right.

"When they found you weren't there, and then heard you were working for the liege," Nostra's eyebrows lifted a little at Garek's startled look, but continued on, "they obligingly offered to wait for your return, and help the villagers restore Pan Nuk while they did so."

Garek was already shaking his head. "Gaffri wouldn't—"

"No. But he needed an excuse to hang around." Darla rubbed her upper arm with a nervous hand. "Neither Haz or I knew about it, but he was under orders to get you, and a woman named Taya. And according to Darrin here, it came as a request from Harven."

Garek went still, his eyes never leaving Darla's face.

"Gaffri insisted on waiting for you as cover so he could find out which one was Taya. And then . . ." She trailed off under his stare.

"Then early yesterday morning, while Taya was on watch duty, he, Janu and Fek grabbed her." Nostra filled in the silence. "We wouldn't have known about it for hours if they'd managed to do it quietly." A smile danced briefly across Nostra's lips. "But Taya can make a lot of noise, and there was a stand-off."

"You got her back?" He didn't know how he got the question out, but Nostra was already shaking her head.

"They threatened to kill her if we followed them, and I believed them. They were like trapped animals. They had a nasty surprise when they learned the liege was involved with Pan Nuk. With you. And when my unit arrived, I think it pushed Gaffri into coming up with a plan he thought would give him the most leverage."

"What happened to Taya?" That's really all he cared about. His gaze swung to Darrin, and the guard looked away.

"They had a knife to her throat. They said they'd let her go at the top of the pass and we were to wait for her to walk back down to us or they'd kill her."

"But she never walked back down." He made it a statement, because why would Gaffri let her go if she'd been part of his mission? She was the only bargaining chip Gaffri had left because Garek hadn't been there.

"No." Nostra swallowed. "Her brother ran up with some of the other men, as well as me and some of my team, and we tracked them to where the path splits three ways."

"And then?"

"Then Kas found some of her hair on the Gara path, and he and a few others from your village went after her. I decided it was vital my guard master know what's happening in Garamundo, so I lent them two of my team and we parted ways. We've been running ever since."

Garek stood for a moment, weighing up the options in his head.

Why would Gaffri go back to Gara if he thought things had gone bad there? Then again, why had he taken Taya if he didn't intend to return, because surely the only value she had in his eyes was as an object achieved in his mission?

He turned back to face the way he'd come. Back toward Juli.

"What are you going to do?" Darla asked.

"Go back, get the sky craft, and go hunting."

ELEVEN

TWO DAYS in the company of pigs, and Taya wondered how Garek had stood it for two whole years in Garamundo.

That Garek had known Fek and Gaffri personally was clear, and that they had not been friends was even clearer, given the sly comments and disparaging insults Gaffri threw at her.

He insulted Garek, he insulted her. Ridiculous insults that were nonsensical, and often contradictory.

Garek was a pathetic loser who couldn't get anyone better than her. But he had also slept his way through the whole Gara guard, because the thought of coming back to a hag like her was too much. She wanted to laugh a few times, but managed not to respond to any of it, which initially incensed him, but eventually he stopped bothering.

They had stopped physically pushing her around as much, too. Probably because they were getting used to her, and forgetting to do it.

She guessed they'd tried to use it as a means to keep her fearful and wary, but they were both too lazy to keep it up.

No wonder they'd been eager to be part of the town master's plan to betray the liege. They didn't have the drive to reach the senior ranks of the guard any other way but through stabbing their own people in the back.

Gaffri, in particular, was worried about the future he thought would be his. Fek didn't say much about it, and Taya had the sense he was more pragmatic. He would try to adapt.

Gaffri, on the other hand, didn't like his new reality.

He poured over every detail of their confrontation with Nostra, looking for a way to twist perception so he could come out of it without censure from the liege. Then Fek would remind him they had abducted Taya at knifepoint in front of the Juli Day Guard captain, and he would be silent for a few hours, before he tried to talk himself into believing he could still wrangle it to his advantage again.

He didn't like the idea of exile, she realized. He was afraid of the unknown, of what he'd find in Harven's capital, Luf, and he was desperately hoping that arriving with Taya in hand would still somehow get him the senior position of power he had already decided was his.

As light faded on the second day, Taya tripped on a small rock hidden by the shadows on the path and stumbled.

She wasn't hurt, but she used the moment to crouch down and curl herself around her bent knees. She used every opportunity to keep herself as rested and ready as she could.

Last night she'd been hedged in behind both men under a deep overhang off the path, with one of them always on watch.

They'd been nervous yesterday and through the night, but now another day had gone by without a hint they were being followed, and they were more relaxed, more confident their ruse to draw Kas and the others toward Garamundo had worked.

If they would only both sleep, she could finally pull her knife out of her boot, cut the rope they used to restrain her at night, and run as fast as she could back home.

"Get up." Fek stood beside her, his knees in line with her head.

She said nothing, tightening her grip around her shins.

He bent his knee so it hit her in the forehead and knocked her backward, and she landed in an inelegant sprawl across the path.

She looked up, straight into the bright blue sky, and saw the flash of Star light off silver metal.

A sky craft.

She leapt to her feet, darting past Gaffri, and waved her arms as she ran to the open area a little way up the path—one of the few places in full daylight, with no shadow.

She stood, jumping as she waved, even though she didn't know if the craft could see her, or even if Garek was piloting it.

Her attention was on the glint of silver, she never even sensed Gaffri until he shoved her down to the ground and pulled back his foot to kick her.

She rolled away from him, faster than her behavior until now had led him to believe she could, and she scrambled back into a crouch, with the sheer rock face of the mountain at her back.

The rock seemed to comfort her as she put a hand back to balance herself, and she had time for a quick zing of excitement at the thought that perhaps it contained traces of shadow ore, before she turned her attention back to Gaffri.

"You were waving to that sky craft." His voice, almost expressionless, revealed his shock.

"Yes." She chanced another quick look up, but the sky was clear again.

"Why?"

Had he not understood anything he'd been told in Pan Nuk? "Because Garek is flying one for the liege."

His mouth dropped open. "But maybe he isn't in that one."

Fek joined them, standing beside Gaffri, but his gaze was on the sky. "It's gone."

So she hadn't been seen, or it hadn't been Garek. Otherwise it would be hovering beside them right now. She slumped a little against the rock.

"Whether it was Garek or a sky raider, you tried to bring them down on us." Gaffri sounded as if he were sounding out the words for the first time.

"Yes. I was trying to escape." She kept her voice matter-of-fact.

Gaffri breathed in, a quick, sharp sound, and Taya knew the time for being passive had passed. She could have slid her index and middle fingers into the top of her boot to get her knife, but she *pulled* with her mind instead and felt the quick, bright leap of joy as she connected with the ore, as the hilt of her knife slid out of its sheath and into her waiting hand. It was like touching pure happiness.

She rose slowly to her feet. Gaffri's face was wild, and she felt the first real fear since they'd abducted her. He looked prepared to kill her.

"You think the Harven liege will be pleased if you bring me to him hurt?" She kept her voice soothing. "You think hurting me will make your journey faster? Your reward better? Or worse?"

"She's right." Fek looked away from the sky at last and turned to them. "There's no time for this, Gaffri. We need to make good time. Hurt her, and you'll slow us down."

"She's already slowing us down. Tripping, walking too slowly."

"She's half our size. If she could keep up, I'd be more surprised."

She'd got the sense over the last two days that Fek was the less volatile of the two, but now he seemed to be the more intelligent, too. She wondered how Gaffri had become the leader.

"I don't care. She tried to bring a sky craft down on us!" He took a step closer, and Fek put a hand on his arm.

"No. We're in enough trouble as it is, and if we get there and find your harming her has ruined whatever plan the Harven liege has for her, then we've thrown everything away for what? Your lack of control?"

Gaffri shook his arm free. "She tried to get us killed or taken! And if I hurt her, I hurt Garek. That bastard was offered everything, and he didn't even care about it. He walked away and didn't look back. And now he works for the liege? He's some big shot in Juli? I want him to hurt."

Gaffri pushed Fek away and grabbed her, hands biting into her upper arms, maneuvering them both so that his back was to Fek, and at last the path home was at her back and open.

"Wait." She raised a hand and placed it on his chest, levering back with her upper body. She lifted her face to his, not needing to pretend the fear in her eyes, and then used her other hand to stab the knife into his side.

She saw his eyes open, his jaw drop, and felt his grip loosen in shock and she shoved him as hard as she could, spun on her heel, and ran.

She heard him scream, more in rage than pain, and then start after her, and she made herself run faster.

She'd barely gotten ten strides away when she felt the hard slap of air between her shoulder blades. She was running downhill and the strength of it was just enough to make her stumble, and then two unsteady steps later, she tripped on the small furrow of earth that had risen up on the path.

She had forgotten.

She lay flat on her face, winded and struggling for breath, and cursed her idiocy. Fek and Gaffri were in the Gara guard. That meant they could call a Change. And she would bet Gaffri was the one who could call the air Change. It would explain his hatred of Garek more than anything else.

Fek was on her before she managed her first real breath, pressing her neck down with one of his huge hands, choking her.

When she fell, her knife had flown out of her hand and landed ahead of her on the path, and as she struggled against Fek's hold she considered calling it to her and impaling him, too. But if she missed, or even if she didn't, but he was still able to hold her, then her secret was out.

Gaffri limped past her, kicking out at her while he held his side with a bloody hand. He missed, staggering instead, and when he snatched the knife up he looked close to apoplectic with rage.

His eyes bulged from his face, and he gripped the knife and

turned to examine it in the last of the fading light. "Just biding your time, were you?"

He took a threatening step toward her, hand coming up above his head and suddenly the pressure on her neck eased. Fek picked her up as easily as if she were a child and set her behind him, putting himself between her and Gaffri.

"You won't touch her again. This is your fault, Gaff. You should have left her alone. You hurt her now, you'll slow us down even more." He leaned forward and tried to snatch the knife from Gaffri's hand, but Gaffri moved back, and Taya felt the hard slap of an air punch that forced Fek backward so he stumbled into her. The strength of it whipped her hair back and blew grit into her eyes.

"Get out of my way." Gaffri's gaze was still fixed on her, and her heart gave a hard, painful knock in her chest at the promise of pain she saw there.

"Are you crazy?" Fek seemed to grow bigger; he flexed his arms and slammed his fists together and the ground under Gaffri's feet rumbled.

The vibrations rattled Taya bones, too, but Gaffri was in the epicenter, and he dropped to a knee until the tiny earthquake died away.

The two guards stared at each other, and Taya took a slow step back.

The men blocked her escape, and there was no benefit in running toward Harven, but she had the sense it would be wise to be out of range when these two went at each other.

"What is your problem, Fek?" Gaffri slowly rose up, his grip on her knife even tighter.

"My problem is that your great plan to get ahead and be the big man in Gara wasn't quite as great as you made out. Now it looks like we're finished, not just in Garamundo, but in West Lathor itself, and I'm not sure we're going to be all that welcome in Luf, either. But the one thing that will at least get our foot in the door—the one thing—is that we've managed to grab the girl. We don't know why they want her, we don't know anything because we're too low down the ladder, no matter what grand ideas you have in your head, so it makes sense we deliver her unharmed. And you want to fuck even *that* up?"

Gaffri stared at him, then he slapped his chest with an open palm. "You think you're in charge now? Is that it?"

A wind came up and a swirl of dust and debris enveloped Taya, who'd managed to edge four or five steps back, and Fek.

It didn't last long, though, and Taya guessed Gaffri couldn't hold it.

The bleeding from his wound seemed to have stopped, but it must have weakened him, even if she hadn't hit anything vital.

"Fuck you," Fek said. "I'll leave you, take the girl, and you can limp into Luf on your own, with no leverage at all." He took a step back, toward Taya.

He could do it, she realized. He had her pack and his own over his shoulders, and together they could probably go faster than a wounded Gaffri.

It would be easier to escape from just one of them, although she'd have to worry about meeting Gaffri on the path behind them if she did manage to get away.

"You'd take off, after everything I've done for you?" Another, weaker, gust of wind slapped at them.

Fek nodded. "Even after everything you've done for me." The sarcasm in his tone was evident. Another rumble seemed to grow out of the ground, shaking everything, and Taya crouched down, unsure where to run.

A rock bounced off the cliff just beyond them, in the direction of Pan Nuk, and slammed into the ground.

The rumble intensified, vibrating through her chest and growing to a roar, and a large slice of the cliff seemed to sheer off from the mountain in a slow, graceful slide and slump across the path.

Gaffri had gone still at the first sound of the earthquake, then he turned and looked behind him before he was wrenched off his feet.

Taya saw her knife fly from his hand before she, too, pitched forward as the ground beneath her bucked and buckled.

She called her Change, looking for the knife with her new, extra sense, but she lost her focus as Fek grabbed her and threw her to safety up the path.

She landed hard, the air forced from her lungs, and as she struggled up she saw Fek lunge, take hold of the top of Gaffri's pack, and use it to drag him back as another rock bounced off the cliff, hit the path, and then disappeared down the drop on the other side.

The rumble died away, and then the sound of small pebbles skittering died away, too. There was silence except for the audible breathing of all three of them.

Taya stared at the massive piece of rock blocking off the path home. There was no way around it.

She tried to reach for her knife again, found herself bombarded with multiple pulls on her Change. There was definitely shadow ore in these rocks, small amounts spread evenly through the granite.

It acted like a crescendo of sound, making it impossible to find the one strand she needed.

She pulled back, focused on Gaffri and Fek, who were both looking upward with anxious faces.

Fek shook his head. "I must have destabilized a fault that was already there."

Gaffri gave him a quick, nasty look. "At least it'll make it harder for anyone to follow us when they work out we tricked them down the Gara path."

Fek nodded slowly. "True."

They both shouldered their packs more securely, Gaffri wincing as he did it and shooting her a look of pure hatred.

The shock of the earthquake, the close call with death, seemed to have forced their problems aside for the moment.

Gaffri stood stiff and slightly turned away from both her and Fek, and Fek seemed content to ignore his former captain.

She slowly pulled herself to her feet, and Fek turned to her, narrowed his eyes and gave her a push up the path. "We walk until it's fully dark. Get going."

She loosened her shoulders, stiff and aching from her falls, and then felt a tremor under her feet again.

Fek gave a shout and she looked over at him, eyes wide.

It was the last thing she remembered.

TWELVE

AIDAN MET Garek at the dock, warned most likely by the guards at the gate that he was coming in, hot and fast.

It was near dawn, the sky just starting to lighten to indigo.

Garek had made his way back to Juli balanced on the fine edge again between using his energy to call the Change, and being awake enough to fly the sky craft when he got there.

He'd left Nostra and her team far behind him almost straight away, and when he wasn't calling the Change, he'd run full tilt.

"What is it?" Aidan held a row boat docked at the far end of the pier steady for him to climb into, and then leapt in himself.

"I met Nostra and her team on the way back. Thanks for letting me know about them, by the way."

Aidan winced. "That was Vent's deal. He only told me after you left the first time, and when you came back with the sky craft there was so much happening, I forgot. I honestly forgot."

Garek pulled hard on the oars and brushed the apology off. "She said a team from Gara came for me in Pan Nuk, on the town master's orders. The ambassador from Harven is also involved somehow. She has the full details and is probably a day behind me."

"Who was sent from Gara?"

"Gaffri and a crew of his favorites, except for Haz and Darla. Again, Nostra has the information, and Haz and Darla are with her. The thing that had me running back was that the order was to take me and Taya, and seeing as I wasn't there, they just took Taya."

Aidan looked up at him, eyes wide. "Where did they take her to?"

"Kas thinks Gara, which makes sense. They found some of her hair on the path."

"Why would they do something so stupid? They must know you'll come after them. That Kas would come after them."

"If the town master and Utrel have taken control of the senior guard, what am I or Kas going to do about it? Take on the whole city?" Garek heaved on the oars again, looking over his shoulder to line the boat up with the Left Plait. "They don't know my connection to you. If I'd come to you as a normal citizen with a complaint about it, how quickly would Juli have investigated? Would anyone here have investigated at all?"

Aidan gave a wry twist of his lips. "Point taken."

"It's not all going the town master's way, though. Some senior officers put Darla and Haz in the team for a reason. If you're quick about it, you could crush the little coup going on there and wrest control back for your father. You'd obviously have some internal Gara support."

"I should hope I'd have a lot." Aidan grimaced, his eyes going to the palace high above them.

If he was waiting for support from his father, Garek thought he'd be waiting forever. There was none coming.

Valtor's mind was too clouded by mugs of firebrand and bitterness. If he ever gained his former clarity, it would only be after months of staying away from the drink. And West Lathor didn't have the luxury of that kind of time.

He said nothing though. Aidan should know this.

The scrape of rocks on the bottom of the boat signaled they'd arrived at the small beach beside the waterfall, and Aidan jumped out with him and helped him drag it clear of the waterline.

It was only just getting light, but despite the deep shadows, Garek could see immediately that someone had been here.

The bushes that clung to the side of the steep hill, which he and Aidan had used to ease their way down to the lake when he'd hidden the sky craft, had broken branches and crushed leaves that showed the passage of at least one interloper to the waterfall.

"You do this?" he asked Aidan.

"No." The princeling's answer was hard to hear over the sound of the falls. "I decided to keep quiet about it, but anyone could have seen us if they were keeping watch and been curious."

Maybe. Garek edged his way behind the curtain of water and moved to the side to let Aidan in, waiting for his eyes to adjust before he moved deeper into the cave behind the waterfall.

The sky craft sat precariously on its rocks, overbalanced and looking as if it had crash landed, rather than been put there on purpose. He carefully found handholds on the wet, slick rocks and worked his way to it, climbing up to the door and looking it over carefully.

"Looks like someone used a rock to scrape or bash it." He had to shout over the sound of the water, and Aidan bent his head close as he pulled himself up behind Garek, and then nodded when Garek pointed out the damage.

Whoever had come here had been looking for a way in. They hadn't found it.

Garek raised himself a little higher, and pulled himself onto the roof, walked around on it, noting the scuff marks from boots and the smudge of moss and dirt from footprints that told him whoever had been here had swum across rather than using a boat, and their boots had been soaked through.

He resented the intrusion because it forced him to waste time, but he wanted to make sure he and Aidan were alone before he opened up the craft and gave away where the button to open it was.

He let his gaze drift from one side of the cave to the other, the lightening sky behind the waterfall causing ripples of green and gold to dance on the rocks all around him.

There was a quick, furtive movement in the shadows, and he dived across the roof, sliding on his side and going airborne as he shot off the edge and landed lightly with a pull of his Change on the rocks below.

Someone scrabbled higher up, and small stones and showers of dirt rained down.

Garek caught the outline of someone as they reached the edge of the cave and pulled themselves onto the hill using the vegetation again.

"Go after them?" Aidan shouted.

"No time." And maybe they'd see who it was when they got the sky craft out.

Garek pulled himself back up to the pilot's door, opened it and started the craft up before Aidan was even inside. As soon as the door was closed, he lifted it up, and thought maybe Aidan was right, and he did call his Change more than he'd consciously realized when he flew the craft. Maybe had done from the very start.

Now that he was tired, had called his Change a lot over the last day, it was easier to notice the drain on his energy when he flew.

He shot out of the waterfall directly into the rising sun.

He spun the craft around as soon as they were free of the pounding water, lifting up and back, his gaze going to the hill and the rocky beach.

The boat was still there, untouched, but someone was crouched beneath a thick bush. He could see part of their leg.

They were wearing a guard uniform.

"Spy?" Garek wondered.

"Who for?" Aidan asked, but he didn't sound outraged by Garek's question.

"Take your pick." Garek sent him a quick grin. "From your father's advisor, to Vent, to Harven's liege, or any of the other states.

Even Kardai." As he thought of Kardai, he thought about Dom, the Kardanx he'd taught to fly the second sky craft they'd used in the rescue, the one the sky raiders had stolen back.

"You should keep a guard on Dom," he said. "Not because he's untrustworthy, but because someone might get it into their head to use him to fly a sky craft, just like Dartan has already threatened to do."

"Already done," Aidan said, and Garek sent him an appreciative look.

"Straight to Gara?" Aidan asked him.

"You want to come with me?" Garek had thought he'd drop Aidan back on the wall before he left.

The princeling nodded. "I think it's time I asserted myself a bit, and what better way than bringing Gara to heel?"

"You want to bring a few guard units along?" It would take time he didn't want to waste to organize extra guards to accompany them, but Garek didn't think getting Taya back from a hostile Gara guard would be easy. A cohort of Juli guards to back them up might make the difference.

Aidan nodded, and Garek landed the sky craft back on the palace wall.

"Make it quick." He realized his voice was shaking.

Aidan swung down the ladder, and then stopped. "You'll find her. You did it before, you'll do it again."

As he disappeared below, Garek slid long fingers through his short cropped hair and rubbed hard in frustration. He didn't know how he could have played the events of the last two days differently, but he'd promised himself and Taya he would never leave her again.

And he'd broken his word.

"DO you have to go so fast?"

Garek looked over at Vent with cool eyes and the Juli guard

master turned back to the window of the sky craft with a hunch of his shoulders, his grip on his sword hilt white-knuckled.

Garek was still unsure Vent should have come along, although there was no doubt the Juli guard master would command respect with the Garamundo guard, and he would cut through most of the nonsense they were sure to encounter.

Nostra stood beside him. She was handling the speed and the idea of being in the sky craft better than her boss, and Garek was glad he'd taken the half hour extra to fetch her, Darla, and Haz.

They'd left the rest of her unit, to the unit's considerable relief, to continue on to Juli with Darrin as their prisoner, but Garek had persuaded Vent and Aidan that Nostra knew the most about the supposed plot in Gara, and with her as witness, they would be able to get to the bottom of things faster.

Darla and Haz could hopefully also point out who to trust. They'd need all the loyal officers they could find.

But first—he dipped west when he reached the halfway point between Juli and Gara, curving around until he found the narrow backroad from Pan Nuk to Gara that ran through the mountains.

He skimmed close to the ground, and almost three quarters of the way to Gara, with the city walls rising up in the distance, he found Kas, Lynal, and the two guards Nostra had lent Kas for the search.

They'd been running but when they heard the sky craft they stopped and looked up.

He put down up ahead of them, opened the back of the craft, and then took off again as soon as they ran up the ramp.

"Thank the Star." Kas stumbled into the pilot area, face streaked with dust and eyes red from exhaustion. His gaze flicked to Aidan, widened with surprise at the sight of Nostra, and then sank into the co-pilot chair beside Garek.

"They took her, Garek. Right in front of me. Knife to her throat." His hands trembled on his thighs, and Garek didn't think it was just from exhaustion.

"Nostra told me. I was on my way on foot from Juli back home, so I ran back for the sky craft."

Kas processed that, gave another nod. He pulled a piece of fabric from his pocket, together with golden hair that was bloody at the roots. "Taya's shirt collar, or part of it. Her hair. We found them along the path. Not sure if they're careless, Taya dropped them to help us, or if it's all a ruse."

"Where else would Gaffri go?" Garek asked.

"Luf," Nostra said.

Everyone looked at her.

She shrugged. "Unlikely, because it's a long way. But don't forget, we don't know all the details of the deal with Harven, and our only information is from Darrin, who was clearly not included in everything. If Gaffri thinks the deal he has with the Gara town master has been compromised, he may have decided Luf is the safer bet."

"Then who left these?" Kas asked, lifting Taya's shirt collar and hair again.

"They could have split up." Garek felt his chest seize up, like it had done over and over since Nostra had told him Taya had been taken. He forced a careful breath out. Then in.

"And if they have?" Aidan asked.

"Then I fly the road to Luf. They won't have had time to reach the Dartalian Range yet."

Kas slumped into his chair and closed his eyes. "She knew. I didn't understand at the time, but she knew they weren't going to let her go, it was in her eyes. And there was nothing any of us could do."

"We're doing something now," Garek said.

He increased the speed of the sky craft, so the engines screamed as he shot toward Gara.

He intended to do a lot.

THIRTEEN

WHEN TAYA WOKE, it was to blackest night.

She came to slowly. Pain had woken her, along with the dryness of her throat.

She could barely swallow, it felt so parched.

Some of the dehydration would be from her proximity to a fire that burned low, but still threw off enough heat to make her want to turn away, to find cooler air.

She tried to do that, shifting on what she realized was the pallet from Janu's pack, and then holding still as the relentless thumping in her head became as sharp as mine picks.

She managed to swallow, and swallow again. She lifted a hand, hoping Fek would see it—even Gaffri would do—and give her something to drink, but it simply flopped down, and she couldn't hold her eyes open any longer.

They closed, no matter that she fought to stay awake, and she was pulled back under into the darkness.

When she woke again, it was to Fek putting her down on the hard, sharp rocks on the bank of a swift flowing mountain stream. The light was the muted gold and orange of early morning, and she

92

closed her eyes against the brightness of it as it danced and glinted on the water.

Fek shook her, and she squinted up at him. He stopped when he noticed her eyes had opened, and stepped back.

"Good. Was getting worried there. Clean up."

He walked away—she had the impression of him climbing up a steep incline—leaving her lying where she was, blinking in confusion.

She struggled up, tears streaming down her cheeks at the pain in her head, and then just managed to lean over the bank in time to throw up a thin stream of bile into the water.

She coughed, cleared her throat, then lowered her face into the tumbling river, choking as the icy snow-melt shocked her into breathing in a little water.

She managed to wriggle forward enough to scoop up handfuls of water and drink.

She drank for a while, tears still running down her cheeks and into the water at the agony and relief of it, and then lifted her hand to gently probe her head.

There was a large bump high behind her left ear, and from the matting around it, she guessed it had bled profusely.

She caught a whiff of her own body, and made a face. She smelled foul. No wonder Fek had decided she needed to clean up.

Forcing herself up on her hands and knees, she swaying for a bit, and then pushed back into a crouch, and looked around for Fek and Gaffri.

They were nowhere to be seen, and she realized she didn't have it in her to care that much about her privacy, anyway.

She pulled off her jacket, her shirt and tight undershirt.

She found a low rock, sat and pulled off her boots, then her trousers and underwear.

She was shaking, like she'd been sick in bed for days. Her muscles were like jelly, and her stomach was concave. She could barely stand as she rose up and took the few steps to the stream.

Almost impossible to believe how strong she'd felt when they'd first taken her.

She stepped carefully into the freezing water, biting her lip to stop herself making a sound.

The air was warming up, though, and she thought it would dry the clothes on her body before nightfall, so she pulled her shirt and underwear in with her and rubbed them as she lowered herself into the water, then spread them on the warm, Star-touched rocks before steeling herself against the cold and submerging herself completely.

When she was as clean as she could get, she rose up and out, her legs shaking even more than before. Her mind was sharper, though, her listlessness gone.

She had to brace herself to pull on the clinging, icy clothes, had to lower her head to her knees to get her equilibrium.

She crouched down one last time to drink, and when she lifted her head, she saw Fek and Gaffri standing on the rock above her.

Her teeth were chattering, she realized.

She also felt off-balance, with her body twisted, her head raised, and she fell sideways, just putting a hand out to stop herself in time.

"And you thought I'd slow her down." Gaffri's lips drew back from his teeth as he looked over at Fek. "She can't even sit up straight, let alone walk."

Fek flicked him a look of contempt and then ignored him, coming down, and hoisting her up into his arms.

Nausea gripped her again as he swung her up and carried her in big, jerky moves as he hauled them both up the rocks. Spikes poked at her closed eyes and she breathed carefully, trying to keep herself from vomiting, and then almost cried again in relief as Fek set her down on something with some give on the path above the stream.

He'd made a stretcher, she realized, using the thin, flexible wood from the bushes that lined the path.

She closed her eyes, exhausted, and only became aware they were moving a little while later, although she understood that she'd been pulled along for some time, the sway and bump as Fek dragged her behind him was almost familiar.

She was warmer, now, too, so she guessed the Star was higher in the sky.

She should be walking. Should be working out how to get away.

But not right now, she accepted.

Garek would be coming for her, she didn't doubt that for a moment, and she would help.

But not right now.

GAREK LANDED the sky craft in front of the Four Towers, the stronghold that would have served as a palace had Garamundo had a liege of its own. Instead, it was disrespectfully called the Pie Hole by the less wealthy citizens of Gara, an allusion to the fact that it sat exactly in the middle of a circular city with each sector divided into wedges.

As Garek powered the sky craft down, he was surprised to see only a few guards had come running, standing with arrows notched and swords drawn. He'd have expected a massive mobilization for the arrival of a sky craft in Gara.

As the Juli guard walked cautiously down the ramp with Vent in the lead, those guards stood open-mouthed.

Garek made his way to the back and caught up with Aidan and Kas as they followed behind Vent, and caught the shocked recognition on his old colleagues' faces.

As soon as they all stood on the lush grass of the lawn, Utrel shouldered his way through the thin line of defense.

He was one of the worst guards to ever walk the walls; lazy, brutish and incompetent. It didn't escape Garek's notice that he'd only shown his face when he thought the situation was safe.

He smiled.

He'd show Utrel just how wrong that assumption was.

The guard master stumbled to a stop when he caught sight of Garek, and when their gazes clashed, Garek's smile faded, and his vision went dark.

From everything Kas and Nostra had told him, Taya's abduction had been violent and brutal.

And Utrel had been the one who assembled the team that carried it out.

Garek didn't realize he was choking his old boss until Utrel started scratching at his neck, his eyes panicked.

"We need him alive, if only to tell us where Taya is," Aidan warned him, putting a hand on his shoulder as Utrel fell to his knees.

Garek pulled back reluctantly, and stood over the Gara guard master, watching him gasp for breath on his hands and knees.

"Where is my intended?" He saw, from the widening of Utrel's eyes, that of all the questions he'd thought Garek would ask, this was the last one he expected.

"Your intended?" Utrel's voice was husky as he twisted his neck to look up. "How should I know where she is?"

"You sent a unit to my village, with orders to bring me and my intended back to Gara. I wasn't there when Gaffri arrived, so they took my intended without me." Garek bent down, grabbed hold of the front of Utrel's tunic, and half-lifted him. "Now where. Is. She?"

"I don't know!" Utrel's voice rose, and Garek clenched his fist in the tunic's fabric, and twisted.

"I didn't hear anything about your intended, only someone called Taya." As Utrel spoke, words tumbling over each other in his haste, Garek saw the moment he put together that the woman named Taya and Garek's intended were one and the same.

"Utrel sent Gaffri to abduct your intended?" One of the archers Utrel had stationed around the sky craft lowered his bow. "Why?"

"You would need to ask him. To me, it's inexplicable."

"To me, too." Aidan said.

Utrel's gaze fixed on the princeling, and Garek gestured toward him.

"I think you know the liege's son, Aidan of Juli?" He watched Utrel's eyes widen. "And the guard master of Juli, Vent?"

Utrel's expression shifted from one to the other, and Garek bet he was recalculating the hundreds of conversations and meetings he'd had with Aidan. A hundred clashes with his liege's son, who at the time he'd thought of as merely a rich boy who was sulky at being forced to walk the walls.

Aidan had fooled them all, taking up his position as guard without ever letting on who he was, and his clashes with Utrel had been legendary.

"Tell Garek where Taya is," Aidan said to him. "Now."

"I don't know." It came out as a whine and Garek yanked on the air in Utrel's lungs and stared at him impassively as he choked and gagged. Then eased back.

"I promise. I promise." Utrel's voice was a hoarse whisper. "I'd forgotten about the girl, but they're not back yet, anyway."

Taya was *incidental* to him? Garek took a deep breath. It shouldn't surprise him. It was, in fact, completely in character.

There was a shift and a murmur from the Gara guards around him at the admission.

The rules of walking the walls were that when it was your turn, you kept family separate. You did not correspond, you truly gave yourself to your duty for that time, because it was finite and you would go home. But equally, family was respected. There was an understanding that communities and families were sacrificing to send their strongest to walk the walls, and they were honored for that.

"They were just there to offer you a job, not force you back." Utrel's gaze flicked from Vent, to Aidan, to Garek. He wet his lips.

That was a lie, but Garek didn't expect anything else from Utrel. "If that's so, why did they drag Taya away with a knife to her throat?"

The light breeze that had been blowing since they'd arrived died at that moment, so even though he didn't raise his voice everyone heard him.

"Did you see them do it yourself?"

Garek raised a brow. "Very good, Utrel. You know I'd never stand by and let that happen. No. I was assisting the liege in Juli at the time. But there are several witnesses here who did."

"Like me," Kas said.

"And us," Nostra said, and Garek realized Darla and Haz were standing right behind her. Utrel's gaze flicked to her, over her shoulder to his own two guards, and then back to her.

"Who are you?" he asked.

"The commander of Juli's Day Guard." Nostra met his gaze. "Your men abducted Taya of Pan Nuk in front of an entire Juli guard unit."

Utrel swallowed.

"The time for stalling is over." Garek lifted him a little higher, then let him go in disgust. "Give me some useful information, or I will take Gara apart until I find her."

FOURTEEN

TAYA DRIFTED in and out of consciousness, aware on some visceral level that the day wore on, time passed, and that she was being pulled and dragged, rattled and jostled. Sometimes she came out of the darkness suddenly, with her head clear, her senses sharp, even if only for a short while, other times she was hardly able to stay in the moment.

There was one consistent thread, though.

Pain.

It stabbed at her head, it tightened its grip on her muscles, until she felt like her whole body throbbed with it.

Nausea was also a constant, but she wondered after the third or fourth time she fluttered awake whether some of that might be hunger.

She put an open palm on her belly, and thought back to when she'd last eaten.

She couldn't remember.

She couldn't hold on to the thought, though, and drifted off again.

The next time she woke, it was to a feeling of lightness, of flying rather than the scraping, jittering movement of the stretcher dragged over the hard, uneven ground.

She was careful to keep her eyes closed, to look through her eyelashes first.

Gaffri was holding the end of the stretcher by her feet, and she realized Fek must be holding the front. She wasn't being dragged anymore but carried.

She wondered if that meant they had made it to the foothills of the Dartalian Range, and the terrain had become too difficult.

She felt the prick of tears behind her eyelids at the pleasure of not having her bones rattled, and her throat tightened in fury. What was wrong with her?

She hadn't cried when she'd been abducted and taken to Shadow, or when she thought she'd never see Garek again. Now it seemed she couldn't stop.

Gaffri shifted his grip, and she focused on him again almost with relief. He looked pale, tinged gray, and sweat gleamed on his forehead and his cheeks.

"I don't feel well." He wasn't looking at her, his eyes were fixed on what she assumed was the back of Fek's head.

There was a slight rocking of the stretcher and she guessed Fek turned slightly to look back at him.

"You don't look good. I can hear water up ahead, let's get there, take a break."

Gaffri made a sound of agreement, but it was bitter and surly.

They hadn't reconciled, obviously, and she wondered if that was to her advantage or not.

While they went at each other, they'd leave her alone.

There was no doubt she owed a lot to Fek's sense of self-preservation, but she refused to give him any more credit than that. If he thought it would be better for him if she died or was hurt, he'd kill her or injure her himself, and without a second thought.

Gaffri was the one who was motivated more by ego and hubris. He wanted to be the big man.

It still puzzled her how he'd made captain in the guard, and not Fek. Kissed the right asses, probably.

They slowed and she sensed them turning. Before they came to a complete stop, Gaffri dropped his end of the stretcher with a vicious downward shove.

Taya didn't have time to brace herself or grab the sides. She slid off the stretcher, hit the ground, and bounced, crying out as sharp rocks dug into her and she sucked in dust.

"What is *wrong* with you?" There was a chill in Fek's voice, high above her head. The sound of it was almost tinny. "You're like a child."

"What's it to you if she has a few more bruises?" Gaffri challenged. "You put the biggest ones on her. I'm just adding a few small ones."

"If we've got this wrong, if there's a reason the Harven liege wants her for herself, not something to do with Garek, then it *will* matter because she will have been deliberately hurt, whereas the other injury was genuinely an accident. Why is that hard for you to understand?"

Gaffri scoffed. "She can't call a Change. She's not a guard or even the town master. Her only value is as Garek's intended."

"That we know of." Fek crossed his arms. "We wouldn't be running toward Luf, with no idea what's going on, if we were trusted with all the secrets."

"Relax." Gaffri smirked. "I'm not going to kill her. And this is a hard journey. Not to be taken lightly by little girls from country villages. Who will even raise an eyebrow if she comes out of it a little battered? That logic should cover your own ass, as well."

Fek's lips thinned. "Understand this—if you're capable. I'm not going down for a single one of your mistakes."

Tired of them, sick to death of the whole thing, and done with spitting grit out of her mouth, Taya pulled herself up in small, careful movements.

Fek looked down at her, and so did Gaffri. Despite Gaffri's bravado, there was a little edge of fear in his eyes as he studied her.

She must look close to death.

She felt it.

"Can I have some water?" she whispered to Fek.

He dropped Janu's pack to the ground, rummaged around inside and handed her a water pouch, and she sipped at it in tiny little swallows until she could drink without feeling like she had splinters in her throat.

When she was done, she took the food Fek offered her, dried berries and nuts, and some small pieces of dried meat, all mixed together.

She ate it carefully, one piece at a time, chewing carefully.

She only managed to get a handful down, but she felt less nauseous afterward, and took a small pouch filled with the mixture from Fek to nibble on later.

Gaffri lifted his shirt and rinsed his side with water from the tiny spring that gushed out of the mountain side. It looked inflamed and bruised, but it seemed to be healing. He spread it carefully with ointment from his pack and then turned his head, catching her watching him.

"West Lathor is finished," he said, with a nasty smile. "You and yours will be under the Harven boot soon enough."

"Harven doesn't have a boot," she said, her voice calm, although her heart was thumping, because he looked so gleeful at the prospect of his own people being harmed. "They're Illian, just like us. There may be a skirmish, a fight between guards for dominance, but no matter who wins, why would they deliberately be cruel to their fellow citizens?"

He shot her a sidelong look, ripe with condescension, as if he knew more than she ever could.

"I'll tell you what I think," she said settling herself back on the stretcher. "I think there are two, maybe three states who see an opportunity to take more land because our liege hasn't held together well since the death of his wife. And maybe they're right. Maybe we do need a better leader. But even if they send in an army, I can't think of a single good reason to hurt us, to make it harder for us to live."

"Maybe before the sky raiders came, that was true. But now the weak are protection for the strong, because the sky raiders can pick off the weak so much easier." It was as if he couldn't hold the words back, spitting them out at her.

She shook her head. "The sky raiders don't care about our borders or who is who. They see us as indistinguishable from each other." She had heard that from the mouth of a sky raider herself, back on Shadow.

"The weak are never indistinguishable from the strong."

She lifted her head at that, but Gaffri looked away, ignoring her, and he took the front of the stretcher this time, and didn't talk again.

FIFTEEN

KUAN VAAR, Garamundo's town master, was sweating.

Garek could only tell because the light from the window of his office fell at just the right angle, glinting off the beads of perspiration on his upper lip.

For those not looking as closely, he appeared calm but affronted as Vent and Aidan shouldered their way in to his inner sanctum and tossed Utrel on the floor at his feet.

Garek lounged just inside the room, leaning against the wall and looking around curiously.

He'd never been inside.

Judging by the interest from the crowd of guards and curious onlookers who'd followed them in from outside the Towers and had gathered in the annex, he wasn't the only one. Vaar's aide tried to block the mob, wringing his hands in panic.

Vaar had always been careful to come across as well-heeled but not opulent. In a place like Gara, where at least half of the city's inhabitants were struggling to make ends meet, he would never have survived long any other way. His office, though, showed what a carefully cultivated lie that version of himself was.

There was something slightly obscene about the luxury of it.

In fact, it was more a sumptuous hideaway than an office, with its thick rugs and ornate carved furniture. There was a desk, but it was very much to one side of the room, not at all the central focus.

That prize went to the low couch beside an even lower table, covered with tiny bowls of delicacies. It seemed Vaar made himself very comfortable while he attended to his duties.

"And what is this?" Vaar's voice faltered just slightly, before he strengthened it. He cleared his throat, catching sight of Garek. "Aren't you—?"

"Quiet." Aidan made sure his voice carried as he cut Vaar off, and Garek knew he was playing to the crowd watching from the wings as much as he was to Kuan Vaar. "You stand accused of treason."

Vaar drew himself taller as he recognized Aidan. "You're one of my guards."

"I did do some time walking the walls," Aidan agreed. "But I think I may have forgotten to mention I'm Aidan of Juli, the liege's son."

There was an audible gasp from the spectators, but it was Vaar Garek he was watching, and the town master froze. He took just the smallest step back, and then hardened his face, his gaze flicking to the side of the room in such a calculated way, Garek guessed it contained a secret escape route.

"Enough." Garek pushed away from the wall, walking so that he was between Vaar and whatever it was the town master wanted so badly behind the thick wall hanging.

None of this was getting them any closer to finding Taya.

"You sent a guard unit to my village, with instructions to bring me back. You also told them to bring back a woman named Taya. Where is she?"

"This is about my . . . my offer of a job?" Vaar seemed stumped. He looked down at Utrel for the first time. The guard master was still prone, with Vent's boot resting on his back. "If Gaffri was a little overzealous, I apologize, but I don't understand why you would involve the liege's son and . . ." He deigned to notice Kas, Vent and Nostra for the first time.

"Vent, guard master of Juli, and my Day Guard commander, Nostra," Vent introduced himself with a polite smile.

"Kas. Town master of Pan Nuk." Kas paused. "Brother of Taya of Pan Nuk."

Vaar looked from face to face, considering, cool. "Gaffri hasn't returned yet, so I have no idea whether your accusations are true or not. I don't have any information on what's going on."

"We don't either." Aidan lifted his brows. "What does the Harven liege want with Garek and Taya, and why would you help him get them?"

"I . . ." Vaar looked at Utrel again, and for the first time, Garek saw some genuine fear flicker in his eyes. "That is an outrageous accusation."

"Nevertheless, it is the truth." Garek spoke quietly, and he held Vaar's gaze until the town master looked away.

"There was some mention that Garek had . . . done the Harven a . . . favor?" Vaar tried to sound as if he were struggling to remember something of little consequence to him, but he had begun to to look genuinely panicked. "I think they wished to thank you?"

"By sending a unit to abduct me? By carrying Taya away with a knife to her throat?"

"I don't know anything about that?" Every sentence Vaar issued sounded like a question, and he cleared his throat again.

"Where is Gaffri taking Taya?" Garek's voice was so harsh, Vaar flinched.

"They won't be back until tomorrow at the earliest. And the ambassador never said why he wanted the woman." Utrel spoke for the first time, and there was an edge to his voice, as if he was trying to claw back some pride.

Must be humiliating, Garek acknowledged, lying face down on the floor when you were used to being the big man.

"And when they do come back, where will they bring Taya? I'm assuming not here. Wouldn't want the town master implicated in the kidnap of a West Lathorian citizen on the orders of another state."

Vaar's eyebrows rose. "I must protest these baseless accusations—"

Tired of hearing his lying voice, Garek created an airless bubble around Vaar's head, and watched him frown in puzzlement, and then wave his arms in panic. He eased back a little, his gaze direct. He was getting tired of asking this. "Where. Is. She?"

Vaar sucked in air. "That was you? You can do—"

He did it again. Let it go on a little longer this time. Then released Vaar again. "I will not ask nicely again."

Vaar stared at him as if he were both a monster, and a chest of gold. "They were going to bring both of you to the cells. In the older section we don't use anymore. But they really aren't back yet. They couldn't have gotten back so fast."

Garek looked at Vent, and he nodded in turn to Nostra. She stepped out of the room.

Might as well check the cells, although Garek was inclined to believe they hadn't made it to Gara yet. Even running flat out, Kas hadn't managed to reach Garamundo by the time Garek had caught up with him. They'd seen no sign of Gaffri and Taya on the way in, but he and his thugs could have hidden and waited for the sky craft to pass. They might only be approaching the gates in the next few hours.

"Now that the pretense that you're a loyal West Lathorian is over," Aidan said over Vaar's silence, "you can tell us what Habred of Luf wants with Garek and Taya."

Vaar tried to outstare him, and then grimaced. "He didn't say."

"So even with no explanation, you were happy to do his bidding?" Aidan asked lightly.

"Not happy, no." Vaar bared his teeth. "I spent a year keeping Habred unaware of Garek, hoping he didn't hear about him, hoping to keep him my little secret, but we have a deal." Vaar's lips formed a thin line. "The deal is when Habred and his cronies in Fabre and Kadmine take West Lathor, I keep my job, as long as I follow orders."

This was the first direct confirmation they'd had that Fabre and Kadmine were in league with Harven. It was good to know who they were going up against.

"So you were promised protection for helping three other states take Garamundo and the rest of West Lathor?" Garek raised his voice this time, learning from Aidan, wanting to kill any remaining sympathy the crowd might have for their town master.

Vaar opened his mouth to refute, realized there was no unsaying what he'd just said, and at the sound of the angry muttering from outside, eventually said nothing. Utrel scoffed out a laugh and then silence settled over everyone, including the spectators.

Eventually, Vaar made a face, lifted his shoulders in a way that said he didn't understand the fuss. "I was just trying to survive."

"Yes, I can see things are difficult for you." Aidan looked deliberately around the opulent room as he spoke, and while he couldn't very well talk, princeling that he was, his words hit home with the crowd anyway.

Garek could hear the whispers and mutters gaining a violent edge.

"Kuan Vaar, town master of Garamundo, you are formally taken in by the Guard of West Lathor on the charge of treason." Vent obviously knew the tricks, too, because his voice was clear and succinct, and pitched to carry.

Garek watched Vaar's lip lift in a sneer. He'd been a slippery leader, hard to pin down, never ready with a straight answer, but he'd been diplomatic enough to skate through, always giving just enough to appease the factions around him.

Garek had never liked him, and had known Vaar had seen him as a game piece, to be moved around for his own benefit. So it was quite satisfying to watch Vaar leap past him, aiming for the wall, and to beat him there and stand directly in his way.

Vaar bounced off his chest.

He felt the impact, but it was muted by the leather armor Vent had given him to wear over the fine levik wool shirt Taya had made him.

Garek bent to help Vent lift the town master up and shackle his wrists.

"I could have made you great. A rich man, if you'd agreed to work for me," Vaar hissed at him as Vent motioned two of his guards to move the town master to the other side of the room.

Garek ignored him, his eyes going to the wall Vaar had been aiming for.

He tried to care about the possibility of a secret passage, about the greed and the graft obviously going on here, even about the treason. But he just wanted to find Taya.

At a shout outside the office, he turned.

Nostra was pushing her way back through the crowd, and for a moment, his heart lifted at the thought she might have found Taya in the cells she'd gone to investigate, but the person she was dragging behind her was someone else entirely.

"Falk," he said.

The town master's scientist, who'd been trying to work out how to fly the sky craft when Garek had stolen it to go looking for Taya.

"You know him?" Nostra shoved him into the room. "He was trying to sneak onto the sky craft. The guards caught him."

Typical.

"Garek. You're alive." Falk sounded unhappy about that. "What did you do with my sky craft?"

"I swopped it for a larger model, as you must surely have seen."

Falk chewed on his lower lip. "How? How did you get it?"

"I took the small craft up, found the mother ship, stole onto a craft going to Shadow, where the prisoners were being kept, and engineered an escape with them and Aidan. We came home in the sky craft you were just trying to break in to."

Behind him, Vaar gasped and Garek turned around, eyebrows

raised. He'd thought Vaar had been lying earlier when he claimed he didn't know why the Harven wanted himself and Taya. "The Harven ambassador didn't tell you? Some of the prisoners were Harven and I took them home to Luf. I even spoke to Habred, Harven's liege, for an hour or so."

Despite his circumstances, the look in Vaar's eyes was of fury. "You flew a sky craft to Shadow? And that bastard wanted you for himself?"

Aidan laughed at him. "It doesn't matter what Habred wants, what you want. Even what I want. Garek suits himself."

Garek turned his back on them all and walked to the wall Vaar had been so interested in, pushed the wall hanging aside, and found a narrow passageway behind it.

Aidan came to peer inside it with him. "What now?"

Garek turned to look out the window, saw the light was fading. "The evening opening of the gates must nearly be over. I'll go wait at the cells Vaar said they would use, and if they don't come by tonight, I'll go hunting again."

Aidan nodded. Then turned sharply as Nostra shoved Falk in their direction.

"What do I do with him? He says he works for you." She looked disbelieving.

"I offered him a job," Aidan admitted.

"And I accepted. I was packing up when the sky craft landed." Falk shrugged out of Nostra's hold.

Aidan nodded at her, and after a hard look, she turned back to see where she could be of assistance.

"Nostra." Garek reached out a hand, and she turned back to him. He knew she would have said straight away if there had been any sign of Taya, but . . .

"She wasn't there," she said simply. "But others had been in those cells recently. Given the location, and the effort to make it look like the area isn't in use, I'd say whoever was kept there wasn't charged under Illian law."

Aidan rubbed a frustrated hand through his hair. "You didn't see anyone there at all?"

"There were no guards on duty, and I thought it would be best to slip in quietly so I didn't spook anyone. We want them to think all is still well so they bring her there, don't we?"

Garek nodded. "Find someone called Esme. She's run the cells, the legitimate cells, for a long time, and I think she's trustworthy. She can keep her mouth shut, too, and she's no friend of either Utrel or Vaar. She can tell you which guards have been wandering down that way, maybe even who's been kept there. Tell her I sent you."

Nostra nodded, looking suddenly animated, and she whistled a little tune as she strode out the room.

Because Garek watched her go, he noticed the slim guard, loose golden brown curls pulled back from the warm bronze of her face, hovering uncertainly just outside. Her gaze was fixed on him as if willing him to notice her.

"Cara?"

"Garek." She blew out a breath in relief, motioned him over.

He motioned her in, instead, to get her out of the crush of onlookers. "You were looking for me?"

She walked into the room nervously, as if intimidated by the people inside, although only Aidan was paying them any attention, and she knew Aidan as well as she knew him. "I heard secondhand from some of the guards that you'd landed in a sky craft, that you were looking for your intended. That Utrel had sent Gaffri to take her."

He felt the hunter's instinct rise at the hint of a scent. "Yes."

"I was on gate duty when Gaffri left, and I know Janu was with him. The thing is," she wet her lips nervously. "I've just come off gate duty now, and I thought you might be interested to know I saw Janu slip in through the gate at the start of the evening opening." There was no mistaking the dislike for Janu on her face as she spoke.

"Who was with him?" Garek gripped her shoulders. "Did you see Taya?"

She shook her head. "I saw Janu waiting at the front of the line and kept an eye on him until the gates opened and he walked in. I'm sorry, Garek. He was alone."

SIXTEEN

THEY HAD DEFINITELY REACHED the Dartalian Range.

If the cooler air and steeper paths hadn't given it away, Taya had started to catch glimpses of The Finger.

She'd seen it before, flying in the sky craft when they'd taken Luci and her villagers to the Harven capital of Luf.

She closed her eyes and turned away from it. Before, it was a wonder she had never seen, another interesting footnote on her adventure. Now, it meant they were moving closer to Luf, and the Harven liege.

She had a good idea what he wanted from her, and she wasn't prepared to give it.

Luci and her people would have shared the stories of their rescue with the citizens of Luf, and there was every chance the liege's spies and informants had reported back to him.

In normal times, Taya knew her particular ability would be prized by any state, but it was even more valuable now, because the element she called was so effective at bringing down sky craft.

No one could physically force her to do it, though.

Habred would really have only one way to get her cooperation, and that was to blackmail her, holding the safety of her family, or of Garek, over her head.

He would have to take West Lathor first, of course, and he was far from doing that. And she would not help him.

So there would be uncomfortable times ahead for her.

Not that she was living a life of luxury right now.

The very thought of that made her fight back a smile.

She was still being carried, and thankfully both men were holding an end each, so she wasn't being dragged.

The pain in her head had softened to a dull ache, but she still felt nauseous and dizzy if she stood.

It had been nearly two days since she'd been struck, and she knew they'd made excellent time.

Fek and Gaffri may be traitors and scum, but they were fit and well-trained scum.

Perhaps their growing dislike of each other contributed to it, as well, pushing them to show the other up.

Gaffri, who was in front, stumbled, jolting her and forcing her to grab the sides of her stretcher to stop herself falling.

She opened her eyes, and while she was looking straight up, she saw a sky craft, high above.

Fek must have noticed her sudden focus, because his gaze went from glaring at Gaffri's back to looking straight up.

"Sky craft," he called.

Gaffri stopped, and they set her down, both crouching, heads tipped back.

"It's high. It can't see us." Gaffri didn't sound convinced of his own statement.

Taya tried to make out which kind it was, whether it was the larger transport Garek had stolen on Shadow, or the smaller, nimble fighters that raided the merchant trains and villages to provide for their prisoners.

"What do we do if it flies lower?" Fek asked, deferring to Gaffri for the first time since the earthquake he'd caused.

"What can we do?" Gaffri kept his gaze on the sky.

The sky craft that she'd hoped Garek had been piloting had flown high, too, Taya remembered.

She hadn't tried to call her Change since her accident, but now she did, and sensed again the small but well-spread presence of shadow ore in the rocks all around them.

They couldn't come lower, she suddenly realized. It was too dangerous. Shadow ore interfered with the systems that ran their craft. She didn't understand how the systems worked, but she knew that if too much shadow ore got too close, it burnt out or broke.

She scanned again, looking for a bigger deposit, because she knew it would be better for her to find more shadow ore—her current stocks were meagre.

Again, the sense she had was of tiny flecks of it, mixed through the granite, and then she caught hold of something bigger.

She latched on to it, the urge more instinct than deliberate action, and realized it was right beside her.

Gaffri's pack, which he'd set by his foot when he'd crouched down, fell over toward her.

It was inside his pack.

She tried to hold back a gasp, failed. Her knife. He still had her knife!

She'd thought it had been lost in the earthquake but it hadn't. Gaffri had had it all this time.

Gaffri's hand reached out, grabbed his pack and pulled it back toward him, his gaze going to her. "What is it?"

She stared at him blankly.

"Why did you make that sound? What did you see?"

Oh. She shook her head. Said nothing.

He watched her suspiciously, but the sky craft had gone, and they had to move.

She watched the sky after that, not hoping to see a craft this time, but hoping she didn't. While the spread of shadow ore she could feel was thin, it was all around them, the mass of it significant, and she didn't know what effect it would have on a sky craft.

Garek wouldn't know about the shadow ore, and he wouldn't hesitate to come down to get her, even if he did.

She gave a bitter smile. They didn't know it, but suddenly not being seen by the sky craft was just as much her objective as it was Fek and Gaffri's. There would be no running into the open, waving her arms again, no matter what the cost to herself.

THE HUNT WAS ON.

It felt good to move, to act. Garek had thought he'd chase Janu down on his own, but Kas, standing to one side of Vaar's office, watching on with impatience and bemusement, had insisted on coming. So too had Lynal, as well as Lorn, one of the guards Nostra had lent Kas at the start of their race to Gara.

Noticing Garek's surprise at her offer to help, Lorn had shrugged. "I don't know Taya, but I'm invested now. I want to bring them down as much as you do."

Cara joined them, too, leading them through the streets to the West Gate where Janu had come in, and then to the left, toward the Eighth Wedge, the darkest, poorest slice of Garamundo's pie.

Cara stopped when they came to a small square that was used as a food market during the day. "This is where he dropped out of sight. This is as far as you can see to from the gate towers."

It was almost fully night now, but Garek could see the top of the gate tower was just visible. "You were really keeping an eye on him," he said.

Cara's lips twisted. "Darla and I are friends. I knew she'd gone out with his unit. It made me wonder why he was coming back on his own. I was worried about her."

"I'm grateful you were, or we wouldn't even know he was here, let alone where to start looking for him." Garek took stock of their position. They were standing on the border of the First Wedge and the Eighth, on the main road that divided the two.

The tenements stretched high, but they were better kept than their neighbors just a few streets away.

"Do you think he went to ground here, or deeper into the Eighth?" he asked Cara.

She tipped her head from side to side, considering. "I'd say he'd stick close to the First, just because it's safer and cleaner, but I'm not sure. He strikes me as someone who'd have connections in the Eighth, and he knows it would be harder to find him there."

"Well, if you heard we were looking for him, he's probably heard the same thing by now," Kas pointed out.

That was true. If Janu had spoken to one of his friends in the guard, he'd have heard the news of Utrel and Vaar's arrests.

"We all know what he looks like," Lynal said. "Why don't we split up and wander around, keeping our eyes open. Unless he's holed up in a room somewhere, we'll find him." There was a suppressed excitement about Lynal, and Garek realized it was probably his first time in Gara, that he saw this as an adventure.

His suggestion made sense, though. "All right. We'll meet back here to report in an hour. Try not to draw attention to yourself. We don't want him to realize how close we are, because if he does hole up somewhere in fright, it will be even harder to find him."

Harder but not impossible. Because Garek was not going to admit defeat.

He waited while everyone chose a direction, then started out himself, heading straight for the heart of the Eighth.

He knew the whole of Gara well, he'd patrolled it all in the two years he'd spent walking the walls, but he'd kept out of the Eighth if he could.

There were plenty of inhabitants living in the Eighth Wedge through no choice of their own, but others made their place here because of its narrow, twisting alleys and crowded, hostile tenements.

It was hard to chase a criminal into the Eighth and have any luck catching them.

The windows all around him lit up one by one, as the last light of the day faded, illuminating the streets below. The street lamps in the Eighth were no longer lit at night. Most of them were smashed, and would be smashed again as soon as they were repaired. The gangs and criminals who lived here made sure of it.

He wandered in and then out of a few small eateries and taverns, careful not to leave too quickly, and always buying something.

He picked up a few followers after the second tavern, but one small push of air against their faces had them scurrying off.

It may be hard to run someone to ground here, but they knew better than to poke at the Gara guard on purpose, either.

Up ahead, a door swung open and light and noise spilled out into the night.

This tavern was already in full swing.

Garek looked up, but there was no sign over the door. Like a lot of businesses in the Eighth, it preferred to remain nameless.

As he stepped inside, he sensed the quick, furtive looks of those closest to the entrance.

He knew he looked at least as disreputable as they did.

He hadn't slept in over a day, he hadn't shaved or bathed in even longer and his clothes were dirty and stiff with sweat.

There was perhaps a longer pause than he'd have liked, but the patrons went back to their conversations.

Garek moved through the room toward what those from Gara called the central spin, the circular bar from where the staff took and filled orders.

He saw Janu almost right away.

The guard was leaning close to a woman in a tiny booth toward the back of the room.

She was shaking her head, and he obviously didn't like what she was saying. He leaned back with a scowl on his face.

Garek looked down, noticed his hands were shaking, then he started across the room, pulling his Change to him.

A man grunted in surprise as he passed his table, and he guessed he was flickering in and out of view.

Janu looked away from his companion, temper souring his features, and then saw Garek coming toward him.

He half-rose from his seat, and Garek used the air above him to shove him down.

It took Garek a moment to notice the wind rattling and whistling around the room, the stricken and fearful faces of the patrons, and he pulled back just a little.

"How is this going to go?" he asked.

Janu's mouth was slack. "Weren't you . . ." He shook his head. "Weren't you in Juli?"

"I was. When I heard what you'd done, I came here." He settled the air completely, and silence fell in the once-noisy tavern. "Where is she, Janu?"

"Gaffri's taking her to Luf." Janu laid both hands on the table, head bowed. "I'll tell you everything I know."

The woman opposite Janu shook her head. She didn't say anything to him but Garek thought he saw anger and pity in her eyes.

Unfortunately for him, Janu would get no pity from Garek.

No pity at all.

SEVENTEEN

"I'VE NEVER FELT SO TORN." Kas leaned against the window of the sky craft, looking down as Pan Nuk came into view in the early morning light.

Garek held his gaze. "Luca needs you. So does Pan Nuk. You know I won't rest until she's safe."

Kas nodded, looked down again, and then gave a wide, relieved smile when Luca had come into view, waving his hands wildly in welcome.

Garek paused only long enough for Kas and Lynal to disembark, and then rose again.

"This is your village?" Falk asked.

He'd been quiet since they'd lifted off from Garamundo as dawn was breaking.

The night before, after he'd brought Janu in to the Tower, Garek had had to get some sleep. He was useless to Taya without it.

He'd eaten a meal in the Towers and washed up, found a bed for himself, while Falk had followed him around, arguing for the right to come along.

Sometime between closing his bedroom door in Falk's face and getting up this morning to collect Kas and Lynal and leave, Falk had persuaded Aidan that he should go.

They both knew Garek wasn't happy about it, but also that he was in too much of a hurry to argue any more, and Falk had wisely keep his mouth shut from the moment he'd stepped into the sky craft until now.

Garek took the question for what it was, an effort to ease the tension, and ignored it, tipped the left wing, and flew as slowly as he could over the path below.

"You owe me, you know." Falk looked back briefly at him, then plastered himself to the window again, childlike in his excitement of flying.

"How so?"

"For showing you how to mix the air in the sky craft so that we can breathe right now."

Garek leaned back in the pilot's chair. That was actually true. He'd never have made it to Shadow without Falk showing him how to change the mix of air in the sky craft so that everyone could breathe it safely. Maybe Falk had earned inclusion in this trip.

"Just don't slow me down, and I won't leave you behind."

Falk sent him a hot look, turned back to the window. "What are we looking for?"

"The path to Luf goes over the Crag, then down through the low foothills leading up to the Dartalian Range. If they've made good time, they've probably reached the Range by now, but if Taya was injured, they may be slower than that, so I want to follow the path carefully." He didn't want to consider how or why Taya might be injured, but Kas's worry told him the abduction had been violent, and the hair and piece of clothing they'd found on the path to Gara backed up that impression.

"Looks like there was an earthquake," Falk said, and Garek tipped the sky craft forward a little, to give himself a better view. He was high above the path, and as he came down, a high-pitched note sounded, repeating over and over.

He frowned, rose up, and when he'd reached his former height, it shut off.

He and Falk exchanged a look.

"A warning of some kind?" Falk asked.

"The controls did feel different." Garek looked down at the control lights built into the arm of the chair.

"It didn't feel any different to me," Falk said.

Garek shrugged. "Aidan has pointed out a couple of times I call my Change more than I realize while I'm flying this. I think I compensated for the problem automatically."

Falk's eyes widened. "You're calling your Change?" He was silent for a moment. "I never could understand how you just worked out how to fly it so quickly. But if you were calling your Change, someone of your strength . . ." He shook his head in disgust. "This explains so much. I never even thought to get someone who calls the air Change to try to fly it. Now you say it, I can't believe I didn't." He frowned. "But didn't a Kardanx fly the other one, the one the sky raiders took back?"

Garek nodded. "When we were flying between Shadow and Barit, I wasn't calling my Change. There is no air between the two planets."

Falk looked stunned. "No air at all?"

"No. But when we got into the air of Barit, I flew beside Dom the whole way. I think perhaps I was helping him, too." He remembered how tired he'd been afterwards. He usually knew when he was calling his Change, but there were some things he had begun to realize he was doing automatically. Perhaps stabilizing the sky craft fell into that category.

It was only when he attacked or moved into the inbetween that he had to consciously work to call his Change. It was something to think about later, when he had Taya safe.

"Why do you think there's a problem going lower here, when there wasn't one landing in Pan Nuk?" Falk asked.

Garek could think of only one answer. "There's shadow ore in this mountain."

"The ore the sky raiders are mining? You think the sound is there to help them know where to look for deposits?"

"No. Shadow ore confuses the parts that make the sky craft fly. If we got too close, we could crash." He wondered if Taya had felt the shadow ore as she'd moved along the path.

From their high vantage point, he tried to make out what had happened on the path below. He would go down if he saw Taya, warning siren or not, but there was no way he was risking the sky craft before he found her. It was the fastest way to get her back.

"It looks like part of the cliff gave, and fell down onto the path." Falk was pressed up against the window.

There was a cold knot in Garek's stomach at the thought of it coming down while Taya was there, but the chances were slim that she would have been there at exactly the same time.

"I can't tell how old the rock fall is." Falk turned to him. "If it happened before they came this way, they wouldn't have been able to take the path."

"Or," Garek remembered now that Fek called the earth Change, "Fek did it deliberately, to stop anyone following after them."

It was a clever ploy, almost too clever for Gaffri and Fek, but very effective.

"Is Fek strong enough to have done something like that?" Falk asked.

That was a good question. "I don't know."

Garek had brought a map with the route to Luf with him, and he gave it to Falk to call out directions, following it from the air, taking it slowly.

The path widened on the other side of the Crag and twisted lazily between the low hills until it reached the Dartalian Range.

Garek was able to fly as low as he wanted to over the lush green, but there was no sign of anyone on the path, let alone Taya.

The mountains rose in a jagged line from the green hills, gray and sheer, some of them white-topped with snow.

He headed straight for them, but as soon as he got too close the ear-splitting noise forced him higher.

"More shadow ore." In a way, it was a good discovery, especially if there was a rich vein of it. Taya would eventually run through the stocks they brought back from Shadow, and would need more.

The thought of her at the mercy of Gaffri and Fek made him slow even more, until they were almost hovering in place as they searched the path far below them.

It disappeared from time to time, impossible to see from above because the shape of the mountains cut off their view, then it would appear again, bathed in midday Star light.

"So. This Taya we're looking for. She's the one you stole the sky craft to rescue?" Falk leaned a shoulder against the window and looked at Garek with interest.

"Yes."

Falk pursed his lips. "Why didn't you tell me?"

Garek took his eyes off the path for a moment. "Would it have made any difference? Would you have helped me if I had?"

Falk hesitated. "I don't know. Probably not." He turned back to the window. "I would never have believed you could do what you did. I would have tried to stop you if I'd known your plans."

"More than you already did try to stop me, you mean," Garek said, but there was no heat in it.

Falk grinned. "You weren't exactly gentle with me."

Garek snorted a laugh. "Aw, did I hurt you, Falk?"

Falk shook his head in disgust. "You did, actually. My ears were ringing for days. But I got over it." His lips twitched. "You got me into a lot of trouble with the town master, too."

"That's going to improve your standing in Juli, not hinder it."

"The one thing that worries me about this," Falk waved his arm to include the interior of the cabin, "is how does it keep going? There is no fuel that I can see, and you've never felt it lose power, have you?"

Garek shook his head. "I think it works on light, although I don't know how the light is collected or used. The sky raiders' big mother ship seemed to use light to power things, and we have a lot of light on Barit from the Star. I don't think we have to worry about the sky craft running out of power. It'll fall to pieces with rust long before it runs out of fuel."

"Light." Falk looked blindsided. "The power of light." He stared around the cabin with new eyes.

Frustrated at the lack of visibility below, Garek maneuvered the craft around to face back the way they'd come, hoping to see more from a different angle.

"Nothing." Falk's voice was distracted. "What do we do?"

If they couldn't get lower, there was little chance of spotting Taya below. There were also multiple routes through the mountains, so Garek couldn't be sure of exactly where Gaffri and Fek would emerge.

Most likely, they would deliberately choose a lesser-used route to hide their passage.

"We know they're taking her to Luf. We go to Luf, and wait," he said.

"Won't that tip their hand?" Falk asked. "Make it more difficult to find her when they bring her in, because they'll be more careful to hide her?"

Garek thought about it, moving the sky craft over the range into Harven, following the foothills of the mountains on the other side over the thick forests and deep, wooded valleys.

He accepted that catching sight of anyone walking in the forests below was impossible.

"We can play this two ways," he said, thinking things through. "From what Nostra and Kas said, the decision to take Taya was a desperate, unplanned one on Gaffri's part. He was due to take her back to Gara, not over the mountains to Luf. He only chose to do that because there was a chance the town master had been exposed, that their treason had been revealed. Habred won't know Gaffri's on his way with Taya. So I can arrive, telling Habred I hear he's looking for me, with no indication that I know he's also after Taya."

"What will that accomplish?" Falk was looking at him with interest.

"We'll see what lies Habred is forced to come up with when I ask him publicly what he wants with me. And we can settle in for a few days, polite emissaries of West Lathor's liege, and have a good look around, do a bit of bribing, see what anyone there knows about Habred's motives. And we work out where Gaffri will go when he arrives. I don't think he's ever been to Luf, and the only point of contact he's ever had with the Harven liege would be through Harven's diplomats."

"What's the other way we can play it?" Falk asked.

"We can go in there and threaten Habred with death if he doesn't tell me what's going on, and threaten to level Luf if they don't produce Taya the moment she arrives."

Falk blew out a breath. "I think we might have more success with the first option."

Garek nodded. "Probably." But if it didn't work out, he would have no problem moving to the second.

EIGHTEEN

THE HARVEN CAPITAL of Luf was set on a low hill, its walls circling it from halfway up, so they looked like the crown on a head spiky with towers. At the very top of the hill sat the palace, and given it had been just over a week since Garek had been here before, he circled the city like he had the last time, in warning that he was coming down, and landed lightly in the middle of the open parkland in front of the palace.

The reception he got was considerably warmer this time than before, and after Falk opened the door and climbed out, he powered down and closed up behind him.

He would have to consider the possibility that the sky raiders might find it while he was here and try to take it back.

He hadn't seen any since the night he and Aidan had hidden the sky craft behind the waterfall, and he wondered where they were hiding.

He hadn't had the time or the energy to think of them while fear for Taya occupied his mind, but he would have to make time, because they hadn't gone away.

He didn't think they ever would, unless Barit could make things so bad for them, it wasn't worth staying.

They were met by the liege's general again, rather than the city's guard master, and General Faloni eyed him with as much dislike as he had the first time.

"What are you doing back here?" He eyed Falk with suspicion.

"You tell me," Garek said with an easy smile. "I had word your liege requested my presence, and my own liege gave me leave to attend in case you required West Lathor's help."

That didn't sit well with Faloni.

Garek knew it was because the bastard was planning to invade West Lathor, and the idea that the West Lathorians thought themselves the stronger of the two must truly rile him.

Garek's smile widened. "So, how can I assist the good people of Harven?"

Unable to respond, Faloni jerked his head at Falk. "Who's he?"

"Oh, this is Falk. He works for the liege and was the scientist who made considerable strides in working out how we could fly the sky craft." Garek looked back at the silver silhouette behind them. "I couldn't have reached Shadow and rescued everyone without his research."

Faloni went still. "How were you able to conduct this research?"

Falk had gone still himself as Garek sung his praises, but he shook off his surprise with remarkable ease. "Garek brought down a small sky craft some months ago and I worked on it at the Tower in Garamundo." He shrugged modestly.

"I thought Garek said you worked for the liege, but this happened in Garamundo?" Faloni asked.

"Oh, something as important as a sky craft, I'm sure you'll appreciate, was of interest to the liege. I was reporting to him right from the start. I sent regular updates to Juli." Falk beamed at him. "The liege was very interested in my work, and I had plenty of personal visits from his son."

"I . . . see."

No, you don't. Garek could tell the general's mind was racing as he worked through the implications of this information.

Followed to its logical conclusion, if the West Lathorian liege knew all about a secret sky craft housed in Garamundo, then Faloni had to wonder if Vaar hadn't been playing him for a fool all along.

"Well," Garek made his voice a touch impatient, "if you don't know why Habred wants me, I'd better go and ask him myself."

"Come with me." Faloni turned on his heel, still frowning, and strode away.

Garek started after him, felt a bump against his side.

He looked over at Falk, who had clearly worked out what had happened and was enjoying himself a little too much.

"I thought this would be stressful," Falk said. "I didn't realize it would also be fun."

But there was no fun for Garek. Not until he had Taya safe again.

HABRED MADE THEM WAIT.

Garek knew the Harven liege assumed they would take it as an insult, but he knew the real reason. Habred was in a panic.

His clandestine request to Kuan Vaar to quietly abduct Garek and Taya, drag them to a disused cell in Gara, and then get them over the border to Harven, perhaps in a covered cart in the middle of the night, had gone wrong.

Instead, Garek had arrived as if formally invited, with the permission of his liege and flying the new jewel in West Lathor's crown, the sky craft.

Habred and Faloni would be huddled together, wondering what had happened to Vaar, wondering whether perhaps Vaar had never been on their side, but rather loyal to the West Lathorian liege all along.

It was the reason Garek had not said anything about Vaar's arrest. He wanted them as unbalanced as possible.

Let them think Aidan's father had been aware of their plans for months. Now they'd be wondering if West Lathor wasn't in fact very prepared for an invasion.

"Faloni knew about the sky craft I was working on, didn't he?" Falk asked quietly as they waited in the liege's antechamber.

Garek nodded. "Knew, and thought, as did Vaar, that West Lathor's liege didn't know it was there."

"Which is why he choked out those questions about my reports to the liege." Falk smiled. "They must be trying to work out which way is up in there right now."

Garek rose. "Let's go get something to eat, find out where we're sleeping."

He was fine with the delay. It would give him time to find some informants, time to watch and pick up the rhythm of Habred's court. Let Habred come and find him when he'd gotten over his panic.

Falk stood as well. "That sounds good—"

"Sky raiders!" The guard that burst into the room was wild-eyed, and Garek shoved him aside as he raced out of the room. Falk was on his heels, keeping up better than Garek thought he would.

They burst out of a side entrance, and Garek's gaze went straight up.

"Yes, there it is." It was still high, a glint of silver in the late-afternoon light.

He scrambled up the side of the craft, leaving the door open for Falk as he powered up.

Falk had just made it inside when a woman peered in, all big brown eyes and long black hair, and Garek frowned, trying to work out where he'd seen her before.

"Deva of Juli. West Lathor's ambassador to Harven." She stepped in, and in too much of a hurry to argue, Garek closed up and lifted off, forced to go straight up to avoid the trees around the park, and then angled up steeply straight toward where the Star hung low in the sky.

"Why are you here?"

130

Garek could hear the deep suspicion in Falk's voice.

"I missed Garek last time he was here. By the time I'd heard a sky craft had landed, and had made my way through the crowds, you'd already gone. I have to admit, after you and Aidan arrived in dramatic style, I've had to bluff my way for the last week and a bit."

"The West Lathorian ambassador to Harven you say?" Garek sent her a quick look, and she lifted a single, arched brow in response.

"You're wondering how deeply I'm involved in Habred and Faloni's plan to invade West Lathor. Wondering whether I'm trustworthy at all."

"Exactly."

She blinked at his bluntness, as if she'd expected him to prevaricate.

Then she laughed. "I'm around politicians and diplomats too much. I didn't expect such an honest answer."

She started to wander around the pilot's chamber, looking at everything in it with avid interest.

"I know there's a plan to invade, I've got a set of eyes and ears inside the inner chamber, but you set that back a bit when you swooped in with a whole rescued Harven village last week. Habred and Faloni have kept their plans close, only a few trusted councilors know anything about it, the majority aren't aware, and their praise of West Lathor since last week is effusive. Habred knows how bad a move against us will look at the moment."

"That's why Aidan persuaded Luci that it would be best to deliver her and her villagers to Luf rather than back to their village. Not quite as much fanfare quietly dropping them off where no one could see."

Deva laughed, a rich, smooth chuckle that made him want to join in. "I should have realized that. I've sent enough dispatches back to Juli telling the liege what Habred is up to. Of course Aidan knew." She seemed to relax a bit at the idea.

"You thought no one was listening?" Garek asked.

She hesitated, then nodded. "I haven't had a single response to my notes. They were heavily encrypted, and I knew they were getting through, as other, more mundane parts of my requests and reports were being responded to, but nothing on the invasion. It's a relief to know someone was taking notice." Her face went tight—with worry, and with a touch of frustration. "The liege is still not himself."

No, the liege was most definitely no longer himself.

"So you were on the spot, you say, after Aidan and Garek came and went in a sky craft?" Falk prompted her. He was standing at the window, looking for any sign of the sky raiders, and she joined him nervously, tucking the sleek black hair framing her face behind her ears.

"They wanted to know how long we'd had the sky craft. Who Garek was. How had he learned to fly it. What did I know about the trip to Shadow to rescue the villagers."

"What did you say?" Garek hoped she'd said very little.

"What could I say?" She took a breath, and placed her hands on the window and leaned in a little to look down, and then up. "I was lucky enough to get to the palace before the crowds broke up, and I eavesdropped on the Cassinyan villagers as they told their stories. It sounded close to impossible, but it also sounded as if Harven was your first stop, that there wouldn't have been time for any word to have gone to Juli, let alone gone from Juli to Luf, so I pretended complete ignorance."

"They asked you about the sky craft, though?" Falk said, and she nodded.

"They seemed more interested in that than anything else. Well, Faloni and Habred were. The others were amazed at how you'd gone all the way to Shadow, and rescued everyone."

"They probably never saw the small one you brought down," Falk said. "They were trying to work out if this craft was the one we've had all along. Whether Vaar was double-crossing them by not telling them that we could fly it."

"Double-crossing them?" Deva turned to look at him, eyes wide in surprise. Then her mouth formed a thin line. "I thought so. I thought that little weasel, Vaar, had some kind of deal with Habred. The Harven ambassador and Vaar were just too cozy at the meeting I attended in Garamundo a while ago."

Garek remembered where he'd seen her, now.

While he was usually assigned to walk the walls, one evening he'd drawn a rare duty as guard at the meeting Deva was talking about. She'd sat to the left of the Harven ambassador, laughing and talking to him along with Gara's town master.

"You looked pretty cozy with the Harven ambassador yourself," he told her.

"You were there?" She turned to face him fully.

"I was guarding the hall."

She nodded. "I was being diplomatic, but if Vaar's been on Habred's payroll, then I can understand you'd be suspicious." She paused. "Does the liege know about Vaar? Or does Aidan, at least?"

"Vaar was arrested this morning, along with his guard master."

She stared at him, mouth open. "Arrested? Did you tell Faloni just now, when he escorted you in?"

"No."

She leaned back a little, expression invigorated. "It's going to be interesting to watch what happens when they get the news." She smiled, her mobile, lush mouth lifting at the corners. It was just a touch evil.

"You seem happy, ambassador." Garek tipped his head to the side.

"You don't know how hard it's been to smile and eat and drink with these people, knowing some of them are planning to invade your home." She blew out a breath.

"Do you know how deeply Kadmine and Fabre are involved?" Garek asked.

She pursed her lips. "I know about Fabre. I would not have said Kadmine, which means if they're involved they've been very secretive about it."

"Kadmine and Fabre were always the strongest possibilities, and when Vaar was arrested, he confirmed them as Harven's allies."

"Sorry to interrupt, but do you have a plan about where we're going?" Falk craned his neck. "They're still following, but they're keeping back.

Garek had deliberately flown toward the Star to make it hard for the sky raiders to see him, but now he needed a better plan. "Is there anywhere near Luf with a waterfall?" He turned to Deva. "Not a small one, something big with space behind it to fit the sky craft?"

She shook her head.

"Would it work if water was pouring equally over the whole craft?" Falk asked. "You could put it under a smaller waterfall, then."

Garek shrugged. "That would be better than nothing."

"I don't know of anything like that. But why? Why do you need a waterfall?"

"Water shields the sky craft from the sky raiders. They might be able to find it from afar by . . ." Garek paused. He didn't have the vocabulary to explain what they could be using to find it. He didn't even understand it. "With a special searching tool," he said eventually. "If they catch sight of it visually, they can find it anyway, but if I can hide it, and shield it with water, then they won't be able to use their other method . . . if they have one."

"Well, the West Lathorian ambassadorial residence in Luf has something that might help. The gardens at the back are extensive, and the former ambassador had a water feature installed to recreate the one he had at his ambassadorial residence in Baltar. It comprises a circle of metal pipes angled so that when water is pumped through them, the water arches up and meets in the middle. You could put the sky craft under it."

"How is the pump operated?" Falk asked, eyes alight with interest.

"By treadmill," Deva said. "I could set my staff to operate it continually. "Usually we just run it for a few hours during embassy parties, but there is no reason why it can't be run all the time."

It would be very convenient to keep the craft in the city, and if it didn't work, he could always fly away again and try something else.

"Is there a way to hide the craft from above?" he asked.

Deva thought about it. "I could set up canopies. They won't cover it completely, but they may disguise it a bit."

Garek gave a nod. "Thank you, I accept."

He hunched over the pilot's chair and made the sky craft *move*, curving off to the Dartalian Range. If he could skim the edge of the safe zone there, to where the warning alarm just started wailing, loop back to Luf and land in the dark, maybe they would get lucky.

He was due a little luck.

NINETEEN

GAREK SPENT the night at Deva's, lying in her garden, comfortable enough on a mattress with warm blankets, with Falk snoring quietly nearby.

Deva trusted her staff, although he'd pointed out at least one of them had to be a spy for Habred.

She'd smiled, but she wouldn't tell him why. "You can trust them all. I swear it. No one will tell Habred or his guards the sky craft is here."

She had set her staff in two rotations. One group to keep the pump going, the others to stand watch, looking up at the skies, with orders to wake him the moment they saw a sky craft.

Despite the help, he slept lightly and woke often, checking all was well.

Falk didn't seem to stir.

He must have slept eventually, lulled by the sound of the water hitting the top of the sky craft and cascading off, because he was woken by the smell of hot galal, carried over by Deva herself, with a tray of warm bread and pastries carried by a shy girl, who placed her burden near him and then fled.

"My watchers tell me you didn't get much sleep," Deva said, handing him a clay mug.

He breathed in the spicy scent, and then took a long, grateful gulp. He hadn't had galal since the day he'd stolen the sky craft in Gara and started his journey to Shadow to rescue Taya.

"What?" Falk woke with an explosive jerk, looking at them wild-eyed.

"Morning," Deva said, holding out a mug, and he stared at her for a long moment before he took it, and then drank, closing his eyes.

"You think the fountain is helping?" Deva asked. Her gaze was on the sky craft, surrounded by white canopies, although none could be set directly over it because of the fountain.

The water poured off the edges of the craft like a diaphanous skirt.

"It seems to be. I'd like to stay out here a little longer, in the light of day, just to be sure."

"Word is, Habred is looking for you," she said, and there was that evil look in her eye again.

"He'll have to wait," Garek said, taking a pastry and biting into it between sips of galal. "And I have another favor to ask of you."

He had to trust someone, and so far, Deva hadn't let him down.

She'd been crouched in front of him, now she set the galal jug down and sat, cross-legged. "Name it."

"Part of Vaar and Habred's collaboration was that Vaar agreed to have some of the Gara guards grab me and my intended, Taya, and bring us here, to Luf."

Deva stared at him. "I've heard of Taya. The Cassinyans spoke of her. She calls a Change—something unusual. Something that helped you escape?"

"A new type of calling," Garek agreed. "One she discovered for the first time on Shadow."

"What?" Falk drew the word out. "A new type of calling? What is it?"

Garek ignored him. "Habred wants her because of those stories

Luci's people told, I'm sure. Anyway, I was in Juli when the Gara guards came for us in Pan Nuk, but Taya was home, and they took her."

"Took her to Gara?" Deva asked.

Garek shook his head. "They'd worked out by then that Vaar was in deep trouble, that his deal with Habred was either already known to the liege or about to come out, and they decided instead to bring her straight here, to Luf."

"That's why you're here." Deva leaned back, her head tilted up to lock gazes with him. "I wondered. You're waiting for her to arrive."

He nodded. "The two men who have her don't know anyone here. They're guards who were helping Vaar and his guard master with whatever deal they had with Habred, and they'll be low down on the ladder when it comes to information. But they know Habred wants Taya, and that their chances of making good in Gara are over. So they're coming here with her, looking to exchange her for either money or a position in the Luf guard."

"You want to know where they'll likely take her, who they'll talk to?" Deva poured herself a cup of galal and topped up his and Falk's mugs. "I have some ideas, but I know who to ask for more information."

"What new Change does she call?" Falk asked again. "Why does Habred want her for it?"

Garek looked over at him. Made his decision. "She calls shadow ore."

Falk gasped. "The element in the mountains that destroys the sky craft's ability to fly?"

He nodded. "She took down a sky craft with a spear made of it on the Endless Escarpment. Destroyed the suits the sky raiders use to breathe on Shadow with it, too."

"From the stories the Cassinyan villagers told, she's a formidable weapon against the sky raiders," Deva spoke quietly. "That is something Habred would want. Especially as you have the sky craft. It would be an equalizer, in his mind."

"He wanted us both, actually," Garek reminded her.

"And you came here anyway, knowing that?"

He smiled, and thought perhaps the evil he had seen in her eyes was now shining in his. "What is he going to do? Kidnap me while I'm here on West Lathorian business? By coming openly and making a production out of my arrival, I've tied his hands."

She nodded slowly. "Agreed. But watch your back. He's capable of arranging for an 'unfortunate' accident to happen to you."

"He wants me alive," Garek said, but she shook her head.

"If he thinks that having you under his control is unlikely to happen, he'd rather you be dead than alive to fly the sky craft against him for West Lathor."

He granted her the point with a nod. "I'll watch my back."

Falk snorted, and they both turned to look at him. "I feel sorry for whoever he sends against you, that's all." Falk rubbed at his ear with the hand not clutching his mug of galal. "The poor bastard has my sympathy."

GAREK HAD DODGED Habred for as long as he could, using Deva to find out the Harven liege's movements, waiting until he was out, and only then arriving to speak to him. When Garek was inevitably turned away, he'd then disappear for hours on end.

A few times he arrived when Habred was in a meeting with others, and after waiting for a little while, slipped out again.

He'd managed to draw it out for two days, but eventually he knew he'd need to meet Habred face to face.

This morning, on day three, he'd woken to a note delivered to Deva's with an unambiguous order to attend the liege immediately. He was obeying, but taking his time as he wandered through streets fragrant with the scents of baking on his way to the palace.

Taya was still not here. Or if she was, Gaffri and Fek were far more clever than he gave them credit for. It was now five days since she'd been taken, and if they were going quickly, with nothing holding them up, they were due soon. Most likely they were a day or more away still, because Taya would have fought at every opportunity. She would find ways to delay, he knew she would.

He only hoped they hadn't retaliated against her for that.

Deva had enlisted every source she had, and Garek had spent hours walking the city, talking to the guards, sharing stories of life walking the walls in Gara. As many as he could speak to knew he expected some of his fellow guards any day, and that he'd be grateful if someone sent him word of their arrival when they came through the gates.

Most asked him where the sky craft had gone, and he'd kept it vague, saying he was keeping it hidden from the sky raiders.

Falk stood constant watch in Deva's back garden, because the sky raiders had circled the city at least twice a day since he'd been here.

They didn't come down very low, and Garek guessed they were trying to find the sky craft by whatever mysterious means they had. Either they thought he'd returned, although he had no idea how they would know that, or they were simply going to the places they knew he'd been before on a regular basis. In which case the Nordren city of Turn, Pan Nuk and Juli were all receiving visits, too.

He was unsure enough of his theories, though, that he and Falk had decided it was best if one of them were beside the sky craft at all times.

Habred may well know where it was, if any of Deva's staff was a spy for the palace or had simply spoken out of turn, but there was nothing he could do about that.

"Garek."

He was just outside the palace gates, and he turned at the call to see Faloni walking toward him.

"Good morning, General."

"The liege has been looking for you." The words were short, the anger in them obvious.

"I know. I've been to speak to him no less than six times since I arrived. He's either been out or occupied with other things every time, so I assumed it wasn't urgent." He lifted his shoulders in a shrug. "But I do need to get back to West Lathor shortly, so perhaps you can tell me when he does have time to see me today, and we can finally meet."

Faloni stared at him. "He can see you now."

"Excellent." Garek gave a friendly smile.

Faloni sent him another flat stare and turned into the gate. He was shorter than Garek by a head, although he was still in good shape, stocky and muscular despite the gray threaded through his hair.

"Do you know how the villagers of Cassinya are doing?" Garek asked him, falling into step. "I would assume they've returned to their home by now."

Faloni shook his head. "They may be on their way back now, but the liege arranged for them to stop at one of his landholdings just outside Luf and gather livestock from his personal herds to replenish what was stolen from them by the sky raiders."

"That's generous of him." Garek kept his voice cheerful. Habred had had no choice but to be generous in light of his people being saved by West Lathor and returned home in a blaze of glory and spectacle in a sky craft. He'd been upstaged, and had had to come up with something to save face.

Garek was glad Luci and her people had benefited.

Entering the palace with Faloni had its benefits, too. The guards simply stepped aside as they made their way through the main doors and down toward the liege's chambers.

In the antechamber Garek had come to know well in the last few days, a small group of men and women stood, talking quietly to each other, a little apart from the aide who controlled the liege's appointments.

They looked up with a guilty start as he and Faloni entered, and Garek found himself giving his first genuine smile of the day.

"Zek!"

The Dartalian merchant, who Garek had dropped off in his home city of Valian after the rescue from Shadow, broke away from the huddle and drew Garek into a hug, patting him hard on the back. "Garek. What a wonderful surprise to see you here." He looked over his shoulder at his people, and Garek thought he caught a gleam of mischief and satisfaction in the wily merchant's eyes.

Faloni cleared his throat, and Garek saw, to his delight, that the general was unhappy. Of course, an openly friendly relationship between Dartalia and West Lathor was not in Habred's interests.

"Sorry, General, do you know Zek of Valian?" Garek made the introductions with a smile. "Zek, this is General Faloni."

"General." Zek gave Faloni a thin smile, then turned to face Garek again. "How long have you been here, my friend? When did you arrive?"

"Three days ago, in the sky craft," Garek told him. "I received a request from the Harven liege to talk, but unfortunately we haven't managed to do that yet. General Faloni was just escorting me to my audience now."

"Ah." Zek pretended it all made sense, but the look he sent Garek was full of questions. "When you're done, hopefully we can have a meal together like old times, eh?"

"Certainly." Garek had the sense far more was going on here than was obvious on the surface. "I have no commitments after my meeting, perhaps we can talk afterward?"

Zek smiled, his teeth showing. "Excellent. We've just been told the liege cannot see us until tomorrow. We were discussing what to do while we wait when you arrived, so that works well for us. Come to the Flinders Tavern just outside the palace gates when you're done. We'll wait for you there."

Zek put an arm around one of his colleagues, and physically urged him out of the room. The others caught on quickly, making a hasty exit.

Faloni looked after them with a dark look.

"Well, shall we?" Garek asked, indicating the door, and Faloni strode toward it without a word, and rapped sharply on the smooth wood.

He opened it and walked in without waiting for Garek, who gave the aide, who he'd come to know as a gossiping busybody in the few days he'd had to deal with him, a wide smile and then followed. He left the door open behind him, and noticed the aide did not close it completely.

Habred stood by a set of glass-paned doors, looking out into a private, walled garden.

He turned, eyes widening a little at the sight of Garek.

"Liege." Garek dipped his head, greeting him formally.

Faloni took up position beside a high-backed chair in front of the desk, gripping the backrest with both hands.

"Garek." Habred cleared his throat, sent a quick look to Faloni, and then crossed his arms over his chest.

"You asked the Garamundo town master to let me know you wished to see me in person?" Garek reminded him.

"Ah. Yes, I regret that was a slight miscommunication. I simply told Kuan Vaar that I was grateful for what you'd done for some of my people, and that you would be welcome in Luf, or anywhere in Harven for that matter, whenever you wished to come."

"Oh." Garek rocked back on his heels. It was as good a lie as any, he decided, and said with enough casual arrogance to dissuade anyone from complaining about having to wait three days to hear their journey had all been for nothing, merely the result of a 'miscommunication'.

Given he'd had more than a hand himself in the delay, he simply smiled. "Well, I'm honored to have the keys to Harven extended, of course, and that will only strengthen the friendship between our states. Thank you. I'll relay your words to my liege."

Habred blinked. He had obviously not considered his words would be interpreted that way. "Well . . ." At a loss, he looked again at

Faloni, who gave his liege the same blank stare he'd given Garek earlier.

Garek's smile widened. "I think I speak for my liege in saying it was our pleasure to save our fellow Illy from the sky raiders. We need to stand together in the face of the danger to us all."

"Quite." Habred watched him with dislike. "Well, if that's all . . ."

"Yes." Garek gave a tiny bow. "I have some meetings to attend, but will most likely be gone by tomorrow, so I'll bid you farewell. Perhaps I'll see you in Juli one of these days."

Habred's eyes widened at the ambiguity of that statement, and Garek turned to walked out.

"Wait." Faloni spoke for the first time since they'd entered the room.

Garek faced him, waiting patiently.

"Kuan Vaar, he told you my liege wanted to speak with you face to face?"

Garek dipped his head. "Yes. I was on personal business in Garamundo, and spoke to the town master in his chambers."

"When was this?"

Garek knew why Faloni was asking. The general assumed Vaar had double-crossed them, and he wanted to know the details. "The evening before I arrived here in Luf. I was all over before then, in Juli and . . . elsewhere, so it was the first opportunity he had to give me the message."

"And the message was incorrect." Faloni snapped it out.

Garek lifted his hands. "As you said. But no real harm done. Peace and prosperity to you." He gave the formal Illian farewell, and Habred, probably because of his upbringing and training, answered automatically.

"And to you."

Faloni said nothing, he turned his head deliberately away.

Garek pushed the door open. As he'd guessed, there were more than a few courtiers 'waiting' in the antechamber, and they would have heard every word.

He nodded to them in greeting, and then left the palace at an even pace.

He'd gotten one up on the man who had plans to invade his state, but he was still no closer to getting Taya back.

He walked to the Flinders Tavern with no real spring in his step. Without Taya, any victory he'd scored over Habred rang hollow.

TWENTY

"SO, you're here to back out of your deal with Habred?" Garek looked around the small table tucked into a dark corner of the tavern and the faces of the Dartalian diplomatic team stared back. One of them winced.

"Yes." Zek was sitting beside him, and he leaned in close. "I swear, Garek, I never knew about the deal when we were on Shadow, and Susa, my liege, told me she was never happy about it in the first place. It was an undertaking not to interfere if Harven, Kadmine and Fabre were to invade West Lathor. Susa agreed to it because of your liege's decline in the last few years. She decided it was inevitable someone would look toward West Lathor with greedy eyes. If Harven, Fabre and Kadmine didn't launch an offensive, someone else would."

Garek gave a nod. "And now that Aidan is stepping forward as a viable alternative to his father, and we have the sky craft, she's changed her mind."

There was a hesitation from everyone. Eventually Zek nodded. "You are right, and that embarrasses us. Honor dictates that your rescue of me and my friends, and your kindness in dropping us off at home, should be all that was needed. But the truth is, West Lathor's newfound strength did play a part in the liege and her advisors' decision."

"Better that we can defend ourselves," Garek told him. "Dartalia is not in a good position to do it for us."

Everyone relaxed, and Garek thought with amusement that they had worried he wouldn't understand their liege's strategy.

Zek smiled at him. "It's the way you look," he said. "So big and strong, so fierce, they don't understand that there is a sharp and focused mind behind those hard eyes."

Garek ignored that. "So, I could see you were happy I had an audience with Habred. You're hoping to use the publicly friendly relationship between West Lathor and Harven as a way to back out of your agreement?"

"Well," the woman Zek had introduced to him as Marin said, "it's a bad look for Habred to invite you to Luf and then in secret ask us to support Harven's invasion of West Lathor. Dartalia has never been underhanded in its diplomatic dealings, and our liege doesn't plan to start now. Their friendly overtures to you have voided the agreement between us." She gave a wicked grin. "Only Zek knew who you were, and why it was our good fortune you arrived when you did. We were just discussing how to get out of the deal without causing offense, and then you arrived. If Habred had given us an audience when he originally agreed to do so, we would have been in a much more difficult position."

"And that general knew it, too," Zek said. "That's why I got us out of there, before he could offer to get us in to Habred ahead of Garek as a 'favor'. He didn't want us speaking to Garek. Not at all." He leaned back in his seat and gave Garek a steady look. "Why are you really here, Garek? You wouldn't come running at Habred's call. So why did you?"

Garek hesitated. If Habred didn't have spies here, he wasn't the liege Garek thought he was, but the tavern was noisy and they were tucked neatly away.

The problem was he didn't want to talk about this to strangers.

He needed to move, to try to dislodge the dread that grew heavier over his heart every day that Taya was in danger, and he didn't know the people at the table well enough to spill all his secrets. He looked over at Zek. "Would you like to take a walk?"

Zek stood straightaway, his gaze on his colleagues. "Garek and I will catch up on old times. I'll see you later."

They all nodded and murmured their goodbyes and best wishes, their eyes full of questions.

As he stepped outside, Garek turned toward Deva's embassy. It wouldn't hurt for Zek to meet her. If he was any judge, there would be a closer relationship between West Lathor and Dartalia in the near future. And Deva and Zek were both experts in the language of trade.

"Habred didn't invite me here."

Zek looked at him sharply, eyebrows raised.

"He made a deal with the town master of Garamundo to have me and Taya abducted and brought here by force."

Zek inhaled. "How did you find that out?"

"They came for us, but I was in Juli. They took Taya. But they did a bad job of it, and spilled all sorts of secrets. And they also over-estimated their support in Gara. Most of the guard are loyal to the liege, and those who caught wind of what Habred was up to were deeply unhappy about it. Unhappy enough to try to interfere, and to send word to the liege. When the guards the town master had sent to take us realized they would most likely be imprisoned if they returned to Gara, not rewarded for abducting a fellow citizen, they decided to come straight here instead."

"And Garamundo's town master?"

"Arrested. So is the guard master. There is a thorough clean-up happening in Gara right now. Habred has lost one of his advantages."

"So, you're trying to find Taya, I take it?" Zek put a hand on his arm, and he allowed it, because the merchant and Taya had fought together on the Endless Escarpment, and he knew they liked and respected each other.

He gave a nod. "There's shadow ore in the Dartalian Range. Not a lot, but enough for it to be dangerous to go too low. There was a warning . . . bell, I suppose you'd call it, whenever I dipped down too far."

"It can't be through the whole Range. I was taken by the sky raiders on my way through the Range to Cassinya," Zek said, frowning. "Although, we were on the last pass before the foothills. There's a small escarpment that bridges the taller mountains and the last row of smaller peaks that border Harven. The sky raiders took us there. And it is far to the north of the path from West Lathor to Harven."

Garek gave a nod, storing the information away. "I followed the path as best I could, but I didn't see her, and I couldn't safely go low enough, so I decided to come here and wait."

Zek stopped. "You knew Habred wanted you abducted, and you came here and offered yourself up to him?" His voice rose a little as he spoke, and he slapped a hand over his mouth.

"I came on official West Lathorian business as instructed by my liege. Responding to a request from Habred to the town master of Garamundo that he needed to speak with me."

Zek stared at him, and then grinned, a wide, delighted grin. "Of course you did." He sobered. "No sign of Taya in Luf yet?"

Garek shook his head as he negotiated around a cart pulled by an old man. The streets this close to the city center were narrow and serpentine. "The West Lathorian ambassador here in Luf has been using her contacts to see what she can find out. And I have been talking to the guards. So far, nothing."

"What does he want with her, though?" Zek shook his head. "I mean, I know what he wants to use her for, but how can he force her to help him?"

"He wanted both of us, remember? Probably, he was hoping to threaten to harm one if the other wouldn't cooperate. My guess is, the guards who took her don't know why he wants her. They're just hoping arriving with her in hand will get them some reward."

Luf was built on a hill, with the palace and the main center at the very top and the rest of the city built down the slopes until the buildings fetched up against the high wall that surrounded the city about a third of the way up its base.

As he and Zek reached the stairs that led down the hill to Deva's, the Star's light spilled out from behind the clouds that had been blowing across the sky all morning, and Garek took a deep breath at the sight of the jewel colors of the houses set among tall, dark green trees, with the line of gray mountains in the distance. The Baby Teeth, the locals called them. Smaller than the massive giants of the Dartalian Range, they were the clear border into Harven.

The stairs were a steep slash of gray stone against the colorful houses terraced down the hill on either side, and as Garek put a foot on the first step, he sensed movement out of the corner of his eye.

He spun, caught sight of a figure lunging at him from the doorway of the house beside the stairs, and stepped into the inbetween.

He chose to move back down the empty street, not down the stairs, and he stepped out of the inbetween almost as soon as he stepped in, half a block from the stairs.

He would have to be careful. Using the inbetween out in the countryside was one thing, he tended to destroy buildings and gates when he used it in villages and towns.

A little way ahead of him, four guards—three men and a woman —stepped out from the dark alley between two houses, their focus on the top of stairs and the two other guards trying to subdue Zek.

None of them were in uniform, but he recognized one man from the conversations he'd had at the gate the day before, and he guessed from the way they moved and worked together, the others were guards, too.

The man who'd tried to attack him was looking around, confused, a long knife loose in his hand. A second man held Zek, and Garek caught the glint of a knife at the merchant's ribs. Everyone seemed unsure what to do, until his attacker finally saw him.

"How—?" He pointed.

The four guards spun around to face him.

Zek started laughing, and the two attackers beside him stared at him as if he were mad.

Garek felt the first burst of an air attack from one of the group of four guards facing him, a hard slap that pushed him back a few steps.

He smacked back, and three of them went down. The fourth had moved to one side, away from the group, and Garek lifted him up, throwing him high, and then letting him go.

The man fell hard and badly, but Garek heard him groaning, so he was still alive.

The other three had landed close together, and while he'd only ever done it on one person at a time, he tried to pull the air out of all three of their lungs.

From the choking sounds and desperate clutching at their throats, he guessed he'd mostly succeeded.

"Run," he said to them. "Or I'll keep going."

One started crawling away, and he loosened his hold, but he must have loosened it on the other two, as well, because they stumbled to their feet and shuffled to the alley they'd come from.

The guard who'd been crawling pulled himself up using a wall and ran after the other two.

The only noise to be heard for a long beat were the sounds of running feet and the groans of the guard he'd tossed up and dropped.

The injured guard stayed where he was, on his side, curled up, so Garek ignored him, and walked forward, toward Zek and the two guards holding him.

He waited for another attack. They were guards, so they could all call a Change. And he had no weapons on him save the ones nature had given him.

"Stay back." The guard holding a knife to Zek's side pressed it in a little, and Zek gave an involuntary cry.

"You have orders to murder the head of the Dartalian trade delegation?" Garek asked him. "Because that's who you're holding a knife to."

The man looked over at his accomplice. "What—?"

"Quiet." The first attacker stared at Garek. "You're strong."

"Haven't you heard the tales?" Zek asked him, breath coming in quick pants. "He flew to Shadow and rescued your people and my people, as well as his own."

"We heard them," the man said. "But stories are often exaggerated, are often embellished."

Garek wondered why they hadn't tried to call their Change and attack him yet. He decided not to question his luck, called his own Change and tossed the man up into the air, although he kept his eyes on Zek and the man holding a knife to his ribs.

His victim flailed and screamed as he fell down the stairs with a nasty thud.

"May I ask why you don't call your Change to attack?" Garek asked. "Just curious."

"We thought we could kill you without it. They didn't want anything to point back to the guard. We were told there would be an investigation when you died, and that it was best if there was no evidence of anyone calling a Change like earth or fire, or even water. Air is the only element that wouldn't leave much of a trace. And only one of us calls the air Change."

"Your job was to kill me?" He'd thought Habred wanted to abduct him, but it looked like Deva was right. Habred must have decided to cut his losses and make sure Garek wasn't alive to help West Lathor.

The man holding Zek nodded. "You seem fond of your friend, so I'll give you something to do other than come after me." He slashed across Zek's ribs, shoved him at Garek, and ran to the left.

Garek made it to Zek in a few steps. The merchant lay with his hands pressing against his side, blood darkening his light green jacket. His face was stark with fear.

"I know where we can get help," Garek said, hoping he was right. He scooped Zek up and ran down the stairs, jumping over the slumped body of their attacker without a second thought.

He couldn't quite believe this was the totality of the attack. It seemed so incompetent. But bumbling or not, Zek was in a serious condition.

Habred had just raised the stakes.

TWENTY-ONE

"HE'LL LIVE." Cantra, Deva's physician, washed her hands in a bowl of hot water and dried them on the soft white cloth her assistant handed to her. Garek was just relieved Deva kept a doctor on her staff.

"What would you like to do now?" Deva asked him as she walked over to where Zek lay, and handed him a mug of cool water.

"I don't think Habred intended for Zek to be caught up in that attack." And he felt a tug of guilt about it. He'd known an attack was a possibility, but his guard had been down after three days of safety. He'd thought Habred would let him go. "Habred won't know what I've told you, Zek, or what you believe and plan to report back to your liege. He may decide it would be easier if you're dead, so we need to consider your life in danger."

Zek's eyes were a little glassy, but he was sitting up, leaning against soft pillows. His wound was clean, stitched and bound, and he sipped delicately from the mug Deva had given him. "Even if Habred hadn't planned to include me in his attack, he did. And his guard sliced me, not in the heat of the moment, but deliberately. Susa, my liege, won't take this well."

"What I'm worried about is that the attack may have been a distraction for something else. They barely made an effort." It had been gnawing at him, a feeling of waiting for the real attack.

"To you, yes." Zek gave a chuckle, then winced, his hand going to his side. "They didn't realize how strong you are. You're used to dealing with the Gara guard, and they've had two years to get to know you, to see what you're capable of. But Garek, you're like nothing these guards would have ever seen. And no matter what they've heard or been told, they couldn't imagine the reality of it."

Garek looked over at Deva. "Vaar did say he'd tried to keep Habred unaware of me. But even so, Habred knew I'd flown to Shadow. If Luci and her people told anyone what happened there, he must have understood that I'm strong." How ironic, if Vaar's bid to keep Garek's abilities secret in order to hold more power was the reason Habred thought the attack this afternoon would be enough to best him.

"The reason you think the attack was incompetent was because as far as they were concerned, it was six against one, and there was no way you'd get away." Zek tried to find a more comfortable position. "And don't forget, Habred most likely only ordered the attack when you left his chambers. This wasn't well organized, it was thrown together at the last moment."

Perhaps. He still wasn't convinced. "Whatever the reason, I can't stay in Luf anymore. Walking around questioning guards is no longer possible. My guess is Habred was hoping to pass my death off as a criminal attack of some kind, that's why they were told not to use their Change. But if he decides he doesn't care as much about how suspicious my death looks in order to actually kill me, he could use his archers. No matter how strong I am, I can't stop an arrow aimed at my back."

He faced Deva. "I'm going to bring trouble to your door if I stay here, and I need you to be able to go about your business without watchers, and keep looking for signs of Taya. Falk and I will have to take to the skies. We might as well patrol the border and see what

Harven, Kadmine and Fabre are up to, because I won't go back to West Lathor without Taya."

"Is there room and time for a quick trip to Valian?" Zek asked. "I'd like to get home. I need to report to my liege, and I'm worried about the safety of my colleagues, too. Going in the sky craft will make my journey much more comfortable with this injury."

The request eased something in Garek. It was a good way to atone for the fact that Zek had been hurt in the first place. "Send a message to your friends and as soon as they can get here, I'll take you all home in the sky craft."

Zek smiled. "Get me a pen and paper and I'll write a note now."

Garek stepped out of the room while the merchant wrote his message, and Deva walked with him, down the stairs and out the back to where Falk stood a little way away from the sky craft, chatting to the woman on watch.

"What do you want me to do when I do get word of Taya?" Deva asked. "Try to rescue her myself?"

Garek shook his head. "I'll come back each night for an update." Garek tipped his head up to look at the sky. "Where is a good place to meet outside the city?"

Deva stood silent for a moment, then gave a decisive nod. "Land here at night. It'll be no more risky than sending a member of my staff off to meet you outside the walls, and there'd be no chance of the message being tampered with."

Garek tapped his lips with a long, blunt finger. "Why don't you put a light in the garden if you have news. If you don't, keep it dark and we won't come in."

She sent him a grin. "Good idea. That's a good idea." She looked back toward the house. "This has changed things, hasn't it?"

She was thinking of Zek, he realized. Of his clear importance in Dartalia, and the fact that he had his liege's ear. "I think Dartalia will be a firm ally after this, yes. West Lathor is clawing back its place among the Illy."

Deva rubbed the bridge of her nose, eyes closed. "All I can say to that is, thank the Star. We've been losing friends for far too long."

———

SUSA, the Dartalian liege, eyed Garek thoughtfully as he carried Zek down the ramp. She was a tall woman, her age difficult to guess as her warm skin was still smooth over the fine bones of her face, but her dark eyes spoke of age and experience.

The other members of Zek's group shuffled out and followed Garek down the ramp, still intimidated and awed at their ride in the sky craft.

Susa was surrounded by a twenty-strong guard, but their weapons were lowered, and there was no sense of aggression coming from them.

They were alert, but not belligerent.

Falk stayed back, keeping watch.

"I think you have an interesting story for me," Susa said when they got closer to her. "Can I ask if my guard master could have a look inside the sky craft? She has wanted to do so ever since you brought Zek back last week."

Garek's gaze landed on the guard master, a woman perhaps ten years older than himself, her light hair pulled back from her face, her gaze steady. "You are welcome. Falk is watching for sky raiders, but he can show you the inside."

They seemed surprised that he agreed, but the guard master didn't waste time. She nodded her thanks and approached the ramp, with some of her guards trailing in her wake.

They couldn't learn how to fly the craft by simply looking inside, and it would do good for them to see the extent of the wonders. The power of the craft.

It could only boost the respect for West Lathor in having such an advantage, by Garek's reckoning. And his agreement made them appear gracious, as well. Since Valtor, his liege, had descended into dark despair at his wife's death, grace had not been a trait associated with West Lathor overmuch.

Susa's gaze was back on his face, looking interested, as if she had some inkling of his thoughts, but as soon as they were a few steps away, her focus switched to the man he carried in his arms. "Zek, are you badly injured?"

"A knife wound in the side," Zek told her. "Garek got me to the West Lathorian ambassador's doctor quickly, and she did an excellent job."

"This happened in Luf?" Susa's eyes widened, and then she closed her mouth, lips in a thin line, and gestured them ahead of her. "We'll speak in comfort inside."

They were led into the liege's low, sprawling residence, perched haphazardly on the rocky hillside on which the town of Valian lay. Rooms were connected by stairs, by corridors, by open hallways—following the lay of the land, rather than overcoming it.

When they reached a large room with windows overlooking the valley below, the furnishings low and plush, Susa pointed to a cushioned couch, and Garek laid Zek down on it.

When he straightened, he saw the other four colleagues Zek had brought with him were in the room, too, as well as Susa, two guards, and two people Garek guessed were councilors.

Despite the crowd, the room was large enough to still feel spacious.

"You've brought my people home a second time." Susa tilted her head as she spoke.

"It wasn't safe for them in Luf, and with Zek's injury, it was much quicker and more comfortable for him to be flown home."

"And you are inclined to make my people's lives safer and more comfortable?"

"Zek's, certainly," Garek answered. "We walked the walls of Shadow together, in a sense. Those of you who are or were guards will know what I mean."

The two guards beside Susa gave a quick nod of acknowledgment. Susa nodded, too. "I have walked the walls myself. I know the truth of what you say. But it pleases me to see that you don't simply talk of loyalty. You show it. There are other things you could be doing in your sky craft, yet you are happy to play cart and zanir for my own, when they need it."

Garek looked down at Zek. "Zek was harmed because he was with me when Habred sent a team to kill me. Even if we hadn't escaped from Shadow together, I owed him for his being hurt because of his association with me."

Susa had gone still. "Habred tried to kill you? In Luf?"

Garek nodded.

"He wanted Garek abducted, but that went wrong for him." Zek spoke for the first time. "So he decided if he couldn't have Garek, West Lathor couldn't either."

"How did you come to be in Luf?"

Garek could see Susa understood the intricacies of the problem. How he arrived in Luf mattered. If he was an interloper, while the attack on him was unprecedented and probably illegal, Habred could say he was dealing with a spy.

"As far as the people of Luf are concerned, I was there at Habred's invitation."

Susa crossed her arms over her chest, her eyebrows raised. "And as far as Habred was concerned?"

"He was confused, thrown into panic, but outwardly confirmed my assertion that he'd invited me."

Susa's mobile mouth curved into a smile. "I see this is going to be very interesting. What was the impression of the Dartalian diplomatic team?"

Her gaze had gone to Zek and his four colleagues, and Marin, the woman Zek had introduced Garek to in the tavern, stepped forward. "We met Garek in Habred's antechamber. We'd just been told the liege couldn't see us as agreed that morning. Garek was accompanied by General Faloni, who was escorting him to a meeting with Habred. We had a brief discussion with Garek and the general, in which

Garek told us he'd been invited by Habred to Luf. This was not contradicted by the general. We later heard gossip that Habred had given Garek free entry to Harven in thanks for his rescue of their people."

Susa's smile widened as her gaze alighted back on Garek. "And what is the real story?"

Garek looked over at the two guards and the councilors.

Susa hesitated, and then nodded toward the door, and they reluctantly obeyed her.

When they were gone, Garek waited another beat for the door to close. "The real story is that Gara's town master was in collusion with Habred. He agreed to abduct my intended and me for Habred and bring us to Luf. I wasn't home when they came for us, so they decided to just take Taya. So I went to Luf, behaving as if Habred's plotting with the Gara town master was a formal invitation."

Now Susa laughed, a deep, belly laugh that made Garek want to smile in response. "Hence Habred's panic and confusion. You went there to look for your intended?"

"Yes, but they have to take her through the Dartalian Range, so they haven't arrived yet. I delayed meeting with Habred for days, just missing him, arriving at inconvenient times, but eventually I had to see him. He's desperate to learn how much I know, what the Gara town master told me, and how I could have misinterpreted his order for my abduction as a polite invitation. Of course, by arriving in the sky craft and spending my days walking around Luf, chatting to the people, it was extremely hard for him to do anything but back up my account."

"But eventually, he decided it was safer for him if you were dead." Susa looked down at Zek, and Garek saw genuine concern in her eyes.

Garek nodded. "Zek and I were walking to the West Lathorian embassy when we were attacked by six guards. They weren't in uniform, though, and there's no way to connect them with Habred. It couldn't be anyone else, though."

"No." Susa rocked back on her heels. "But hard to prove, as you say." She turned to Marin. "Did you take your leave officially?"

The diplomat shrugged. "Not in person. I wrote a formal letter to the liege, explaining the head of our mission had been badly injured in an attack on Luf's streets, and that we needed to get him home urgently. I said West Lathor had extended an offer of help and we had accepted it and would have to conclude the business we came for by letter, rather than in person, given he'd been unable to see us."

Susa sent her a pleased smile. "Well done. Very well done."

"You could write to him, saying you're pleased he's abandoned his ideas on invading West Lathor, given the new friendliness he's shown toward them, and that of course we're in the same position. Having had West Lathor come to our aid numerous times, we could no longer support any action against them." Zek's voice was stronger than it had been before, and Garek thought his color was better, too.

"Yes." Susa turned to Garek. "Your ruse to find your intended has worked very well for me. It's given Dartalia a very good excuse to withdraw from an agreement we never liked in the first place. But I have to ask. What is Valtor's mental state now? Is he behind these new moves, or is it his son?"

"It's his son, Aidan, and his advisor, Hector Dartan." There was no sense providing false hope of Valtor's recovery. Even if he did manage to regain his wits, he had lost the respect of too many to rule effectively again.

Susa gave a thoughtful nod. "I thought so. And it's better this way. Valtor has been too erratic for too long. It's best Aidan step up."

Garek nodded, but he knew Aidan wasn't in full control yet. The princeling had better make his move soon, or all the gains of the last few weeks would be for nothing.

He saw the sun was almost set, pouring thick pink light over the houses tumbled down the hill and into the valley below. "I need to go, but I'll be patrolling the skies for West Lathor, and I'll try to fly this way every few days. If you have a message for me, you can signal me to land by setting a light where I landed the sky craft."

Susa's gaze sharpened. "Patrolling?"

"Watching Kadmine, Fabre and Harven to see what is happening on their borders." Might as well start treating Dartalia as the ally they were clearly becoming.

"We would be interested in the information, also," Susa said.

Garek smiled. "I'm sure you would be. I'll share what I can." He gave a formal bow of farewell.

As he walked back to the sky craft, despite the weight of worry he carried over Taya, he sensed a glimmer of light for West Lathor.

As Deva said, they were finally making friends again. Gaining power.

It was about time.

TWENTY-TWO

SHE WAS ALMOST BACK to normal.

Taya turned her face to the midday light, keeping her body relaxed, her eyes closed, and soaked up the warmth as she listened to Gaffri moving around close by.

The stream they'd camped beside the night before was full, and the noise of it, gurgling and tumbling, soothed her and gave her some comfort.

She lay on the stretcher, although she'd been able to walk for short stretches at a time as they'd gone through the relatively gentle hills over the last two days.

She could probably walk completely on her own now, but she feigned dizziness and slowed her steps whenever she got tired, giving her body time heal.

As she'd done every few hours since she'd realized her knife was in Gaffri's pack, she reached out for it and felt the sweet zing of connection to the shadow ore.

The pack fell over, in her direction, and Gaffri muttered to himself as things spilled out and he was forced to crouch down and repack them.

One of those things was a piece of flexible metal, taken from a sky craft crash site they'd found in the rocky foothills of the mountains as they'd come into Harven.

They'd turned a corner and found it, smashed on the rocks, spread across a considerable area. It had clearly been there for some time, perhaps even from the first few months of the sky raider invasion, because moss grew on some parts of it, and bushes and trees that had obviously been damaged in the crash were already recovered and growing again.

She'd approached the wreck curiously, and only after she was crouched in front of a piece of debris did she realize Gaffri and Fek were hanging back, afraid.

She wondered how many other people had come across the site. They were on a little-used path, having turned north and taken the harder route to Luf to minimize their time on the open, busier roads to the capital city.

They hadn't met a single traveler since they'd entered the mountains, so it could be that only a few others had seen this, and most likely, they were up to something illegal themselves to be taking this harder, very obscure path, rather than the established routes.

It was possible no one in authority knew the sky craft was here.

That had occurred to Fek, too.

He'd taken out the map he'd referred to constantly on their journey, and made a mark on it to indicate where the wreck was.

Then he and Gaffri had hunted for a piece each that would fit into their packs as proof.

Taya left them to it and looked for the pilot.

There was no sign of one, nor of a body. But if the sky craft had come down because it got too close to the shadow ore in the mountain, perhaps before the sky raiders had a chance to pull up, it had obviously tumbled through the skies and landed far enough away from the mountains that another craft could have come in from the opposite direction and picked up the survivor, or the body.

There was no helmet. No thick, dark blue suit like the sky raiders had worn on Shadow. Nothing but the debris of the craft itself.

They had left the site faster than she would have liked, but Fek and Gaffri were nervous, wanting to get away from it, while at the same time excited and gleeful that they had another gift to present to the Harven liege in addition to herself.

That had been a day and a half ago, and they'd discussed it ever since.

Gaffri saw it as another way into the Harven's liege's favor, and he was already imagining the accolades. Fek was much more cautious, but Taya thought he also saw the find as something special, something that would bring him some benefit.

The birds in the trees around their camp site suddenly stopped calling and then, over the sound of the stream, she heard leaves crunching and branches being pushed aside. She turned her head warily, and Gaffri stopped moving completely.

Fek stepped into the small clearing.

He carried with him the whiff of violence, eyes a little wilder, fists clenched.

"Let's go," he said, and grabbed up his pack, along with her own. "We're leaving the stretcher, you'll have to walk."

Taya got slowly to her feet and realized somewhere, somehow, she'd missed out on a conversation between the two men, because Gaffri seemed to understand exactly what Fek was talking about.

While she'd been washing in the stream earlier this morning, she decided.

When she'd come back, Fek was gone, and Gaffri had been his usual taciturn self, so she had simply taken the opportunity to rest a little more, and warm herself after the cold dip in the stream by soaking up the Star's light.

She didn't ask questions as she followed Fek, she knew they would most likely not be answered.

That was all right. She was easily capable of working things out for herself.

Fek led them back the way he'd come, pushing ahead at a fast clip, with Gaffri breathing down her neck at her back, muttering about her slowness.

She hid the satisfaction she felt at his irritation, moving with care and an overly delicate sense of caution around branches, fallen trunks, and bushes.

As she emerged from a thick hedge, she stumbled over a man lying on the ground, falling forward and just getting her hands out in time to stop herself landing across his body.

He was breathing, she saw, but there was a trickle of blood running from his temple down his cheek, and his color was gray, rather than simply pale.

Gaffri grabbed her by the upper arm and hauled her up, his gaze on the burly victim. "Come on."

He dragged her out from the hedge, onto a wide road where Fek was standing beside a cart, checking the harness attached a zanir.

Now she understood why Fek had been gone so long. He'd been waiting for a cart to come along, and when it had, he'd attacked the driver and dragged him out of sight.

"Get in the back." Gaffri pushed her, and she made her way to the back of the cart and climbed in.

It was full of huncree, the hard, crisp fruit that was grown in Harven and traded with the other states. She took one, biting into it as she worked out how to make a comfortable place for herself.

Eventually, she curled up in a corner on a thick, folded tarpaulin. Fek shook the reins and they started moving.

Taya kept her gaze on the bush under which the man lay, but there was no movement, no sign there was even anyone there.

Outrage and a feeling of helplessness rose up in her that they would leave someone unconscious and alone.

She couldn't help him, and it made her sick. She couldn't run from her captors, either, she wasn't quite well enough yet, and so she had to accept that she was going to be handed over to the Harven liege, and that the man in the bush would lie there until he was able to pull himself back onto the road.

That Garek would come for her was not in doubt. But that might take time, and she would have to survive until he could rescue her, or she found a way to escape.

The thought was depressing, and she fought against the dark cloud that hovered over her. She needed to find her usual resilience.

On the horizon up ahead, a sky raider craft lifted high in the sky with a roar, then turned away, northward toward Dartalia.

Taya sat a little straighter, watching the glint before it disappeared.

Fek and Gaffri shifted uneasily in their seats.

Of course, sky craft often stole the goods from carts just like this one. She'd eaten huncree often enough on Shadow, and it would have been taken from farmers or traders just like the one Fek had knocked out.

"Scared?" she asked them. "The sky raiders are probably looking for new slaves for the mines up on Shadow, now that their old ones have escaped."

Fek grunted in response. Gaffri turned and gave her a dirty look.

"You're the one who should be scared. We're only three hours from Luf."

She held his gaze until he turned back. He sat easily on the seat, his wound almost completely healed. The cut had been clean and shallow, and because he was a guard, he'd had the medical kit and the knowledge to treat himself.

She supposed she should be grateful. Fek had a medical kit too, and he'd treated her wound and given her the best chance of recovery he could while still pushing through the mountains at a grueling pace.

And now they were three hours away from Luf.

She wriggled herself into a comfortable position and closed her eyes, enjoying the Star light, the fragrant, sweet smell of the huncree around her, and saved her energy for the confrontation to come.

THEY PULLED up to the gates at dusk.

Taya heard Gaffri and Fek lying to the guard, who were suspicious of West Lathorians driving a cart of huncree.

She was tied, gagged, and rolled tight in a sleeping bag, lying in the cart directly behind the driver's seat. They'd stopped to restrain her an hour from the city and she was trussed up and helpless.

She held her breath when one of the guards lifted the tarpaulin she'd lain on earlier, which Fek had taken and tied over the whole back of the cart, hoping he'd pull it off completely and discover her.

No matter that Habred was the liege here, he would be forced to deny involvement in having an Illian abducted, and the questions for Fek and Gaffri would be even more difficult.

"This is just a favor for a friend," Fek said, and she felt the rock of the cart as he jumped down from the front seat. "We walk the walls of Garamundo, and we're here on an errand for our town master, but the trader this cart belongs to fell ill, and asked us to take it in for him, seeing as we were going this way."

"Saved us a walk, too," Gaffri said.

"Ah, I heard you were coming." The guard dropped the tarpaulin. "Your friend Garek's been asking after you."

Taya froze for a moment, and then tried to throw herself from side to side. They'd wedged her in between the huncree and the wooden side of the cart, and she barely made the cart squeak.

Tears of frustration were streaming down her face by the time the guards let them in.

She heard them giving Fek a recommendation for a good value inn.

The cart moved forward and Fek and Gaffri were quiet. Frightened she guessed, with a fierce sense of satisfaction. She kicked out at the side of the cart, but couldn't even make contact.

It didn't matter. Garek was here somewhere, and he would find her. He wouldn't rest until he did.

The cart slowed, and she heard the two men whispering to each other.

She heard one of them call out, asking the way to the guard master's office, and blinked her eyes dry.

She would not be crying when they delivered her to Habred, not even tears of anger and frustration.

The cart rocked through the streets, climbing up, up, up toward the palace, and then turned and stopped.

She felt the squeak and tip of the cart as one of them got down, and then she waited.

It took a long time for anything to happen.

She was almost asleep when the cart started moving again, but they only traveled a short distance before the tarpaulin was pulled back, and she was lifted up like a sack of huncree.

She was passed down from the cart to someone on the ground, then tossed over his shoulder and carried up a set of stairs.

No one said anything, and from the echo of the footsteps, she guessed they were in a stone passage or room, and that it was mostly empty.

Breathing was difficult in the thick bag, so she forced herself to concentrate on getting enough air, on relaxing her body. It helped lessen her panic and the feeling of helplessness as she was manhandled.

There was a screech of a rusty hinge, and she was lifted and set down, and the sleeping bag pulled off her.

She blinked, although the light was dim she realized when she got used to it, just two lanterns on the wall opposite the cell she'd been placed in.

Fek loosened her gag, and it fell around her neck. It took him much longer to untie the rope around her hands and feet, and she sat breathing through the pain as they came off.

Gaffri stood near the metal grid door of her cell with two strangers. One looked at her with eyes that showed a great deal of discomfort. She locked gazes with him, and he looked down and away after a moment.

"You can leave your packs here for now, out of sight," the other man said to Gaffri. He held a lantern in one hand. "I know General Faloni will want to speak to you immediately."

Gaffri looked gratified, Fek less so, but they stacked the three packs against the wall outside her cell.

The cell she was in was one of two, separated by a stone wall about waist height, and then metal bars to the ceiling.

There was a corridor in front of both cells, running left and right, and there was a door a little way down on the right side. The corridor stretched on into darkness on the left, though, and Gaffri and Fek followed the man that way, without a backward glance at her.

The warden—she guessed he was the warden because there were keys in his hands—had finally looked up again, and they regarded each other in silence.

With a sigh, he stepped back, closed the door, which shrieked in protest again, and struggled a little to turn the lock.

"An old, disused cell?" she asked him.

He froze, his gaze going to her, eyes wide. "You're Illian."

"From West Lathor," she agreed.

He watched her for another long beat, his gaze going to the healing wound behind her ear. "Why do those two thugs from West Lathor think General Faloni will be pleased with them for bringing you here?"

"I was one of the captives on Shadow. I was here two weeks ago in the sky craft, returning the villagers of Cassinya to Luf. When I returned home, those two," she tipped her head in the direction Fek and Gaffri had gone, "came to my village and abducted me, they say on the order of your liege."

The man had frozen in place as she spoke, and he rubbed a hand down his face. "This is about sky raiders?"

"Some of it." She watched him as he shuffled uncomfortably.

"Who from Harven were among the prisoners? Tell me their names." He gripped the bars on the door, and she stepped closer to him, so they stood face to face.

"Luci, she was the town master of Cassinya." She watched his face, and gave a list of ten names without having to pause to think.

The fourth name, Bargat, meant something to him. He gripped the bars tighter as she mentioned it.

"You are the woman. The woman who calls the Change on the strange new metal."

His eyes were dark gray, and she held his gaze. "I am."

"My second cousin is Bargat. He told me about you. All of them spoke of you."

She nodded, looked down.

"The stories . . ." He drew in a sharp breath. "That's why Habred wants you, because of those stories."

"I think so." She waited a beat. "Fek and Gaffri tied me up and brought me into the city at the back of a cart, but I heard the guards at the gate say my intended, Garek, was asking after them. Is he here?"

He stepped back from the door. "The Garamundo guard who flies the sky craft? He's your intended?"

She nodded.

"He left two days ago."

She stared at him, all sound fading, her vision narrowing as black edged everything.

Garek was gone?

She tried to fight against the despair, because he would be back, he *would*.

She didn't even realize the warden had come back into the cell, or how she came to be kneeling on the floor, but suddenly he was there, pressing a mug full of cold, fresh water into her hands.

She took a sip, and then another, and finally lifted her head.

"My name is Gern Danaldi," the warden said, still crouched in front of her. He lifted a hand to where the rock had hit her and then pulled back. "I don't know what Habred has planned for you, but I give you my word, no one will harm you while you are under my watch."

TWENTY-THREE

GERN HAD FOUND A MATTRESS SOMEWHERE, one that was clean and smelled of soap and sunshine. Taya was comfortable and warm in the sleeping bag she'd arrived bundled up in, until the sounds of shouting and fighting woke her.

It was late in the night, and she blinked, trying to focus, trying to make sense of the chaos.

By the time she'd pulled herself up, Fek and Gaffri were in the cell next to her, and Gern was locking the door.

She looked across at him, and he gave a tiny shake of his head. He didn't know what was going on, either.

There were four guards outside the cells, three men and a woman, and from the bruises they were sporting, Taya guessed Fek and Gaffri had not gone quietly.

The woman opened up all three of the packs propped against the wall, and Taya was suddenly very focused on what she was doing.

She would find the knife. And that would be a disaster.

The guard pulled out the two pieces of sky craft debris, which were sitting on the top, patted the packs to see if there were any more, and then rose up.

Taya tried to let her breath out quietly.

"We were doing exactly what your liege asked us to," Gaffri said, his hands gripping the metal of the cell door.

The guard who'd dug in the packs gave a shrug. She glanced across at Gern. "We'll let you know what's happening with them later today."

Gern nodded, no sign of what he was thinking on his face.

With a grunt, the guard turned on her heel, the pieces of sky craft under her arm, and followed her colleagues out to the left.

Taya leaned back against the wall, still in the warm sleeping bag, and looked over at Gaffri and Fek.

She said nothing, but Gaffri came up to the bars that separated them, and shook them. He seemed beyond angry, his teeth clenched together as he tried to rip the bars apart.

She watched him for a long moment, satisfied that he couldn't get to her, and then turned her back on him, snuggled deep into her mattress, and closed her eyes to show him her utter contempt.

He let out a shout, and then she heard the sound of a fist hitting flesh.

She raised her head, saw Fek standing where Gaffri had been, looking down at the ground. He wore a look of fury and satisfaction, and she imagined he blamed Gaffri for the trouble they were in now.

"Shut up, or I'll punch you again," he said, and she couldn't fight the shiver that ran through her at his tone.

Gern stepped up to their door, looked in, and gave an irritated huff before he headed for the door to the right. He was carrying a lantern, and as the door swung shut behind him, the cells were plunged into pitch darkness.

Taya curled back on her mattress, listening to the two men shuffling around and then eventually go quiet.

She wondered what had happened between Gaffri and Habred, what was behind the Harven liege turning on the two men. She mulled it for a while, but too many days on the road, her injury, and the comfort of her bed all conspired to pull her under.

WHEN SHE WOKE AGAIN, dawn was breaking, its pale gray light falling through the thick, ugly glass of the window high on the wall opposite her cell.

She stirred, pulling herself up, and tried not to react when she saw Fek leaning against the bars that separated them, watching her.

"Why does the Harven liege want you?"

"Didn't he tell you?" Her voice was rough, and she cleared her throat as she snuggled deeper into the bag. She could hear Gaffri's light snoring, and realized she'd heard it all night.

Fek shook his head. "I could tell he was pleased we'd brought you here. But the general . . . the general was less pleased. And they both turned jittery when we told them about the crash site, and the debris we'd brought with us."

She frowned at that, wondering why an old crash site would cause alarm, then lifted her head as Gern opened the door and stepped through. He stood in the open area in front of the cells as the light above him changed from gray to pink, and looked between them. Then he unlocked her door, ignoring Fek's questions, and took her down the passage to the left to a tiny bathroom a little way away from the cells.

The passage continued on, though, and at the far end of it was a flight of stairs with a sturdy wooden door at the top of them. She stood staring at it until Gern gestured her into the bathroom.

It was no more than a toilet and sink, but Gern handed her soap and a cloth. She was used to cold water by now, and she felt very awake when she stepped back out.

"I forgot to say this last night, because too much was happening, but Fek and Gaffri attacked a farmer or trader who was bringing huncree to the city. They stole his cart so they could hide me from the guards at the gate. Fek knocked him out and left him under a bush about three hours from Luf. I don't know if you can do anything, let anyone know, but I wanted to tell someone, in case he's still there. He was breathing, but he looked in a bad state when I saw him."

Gern studied her for a long moment. "You're concerned for a Harven trader, even though the Harven have grabbed you and locked you up?"

"I was grabbed by two guards who are West Lathorian, like me. They walked the walls with my intended. I'm not blaming every single Harven for this anymore than I'm blaming every single Garamundo guard."

He gave a thoughtful nod. "I'll see what I can do about the trader. I'll ask which gate you came through last night, and then have the guards ask whoever leaves the city in that direction to keep a look out for him."

He started walking back and she reached out and caught hold of his arm.

"Can you tell me where I am? What they plan for me?"

He hesitated. "You're in the guard barracks. In the cells set aside for guards who've broken the law." He looked past her, down the corridor toward the staircase, and shook his head. "I don't know what they're planning to do to you."

His expression suddenly changed to one of wariness, and she turned, saw the door at the top of the stairs swing open. Gern gave a fierce jerk of his head and she scurried toward her cell, her heart leaping and slamming against her rib cage.

Gern had left the door open when he'd let her out, and as she stepped back inside he closed it and locked it in one smooth movement.

He'd taken the key to her door off the keyring, she noticed, and he slid it into his pocket, rather than back with the others.

She lifted her head and exchanged a quick look with him before he turned to face whoever was coming toward them.

It was the four guards from the night before. Some of them moved stiffly, and while one had a split lip and the other a cut on his cheekbone, quite a few of their bruises looked a few days old.

"You're cleared," the woman said to Fek. "Apologies for the rough treatment, but we had to be sure of you."

Gaffri must have woken while she was washing up, and he was on his feet.

"I told you," he hissed to Fek.

Fek leaned against the bars. "How were we cleared?"

"An assistant to the Harven ambassador to Garamundo just arrived in the city last night. He vouched for you."

Fek relaxed a little. "What did he have to say?"

"Apparently the town master and town guard of Garamundo have been arrested. The ambassador sent a messenger to our liege as fast as he could to let him know the news."

Gaffri made an involuntary sound. "Arrested?"

Fek looked over at him, his expression forbidding. "So it's just luck we're out today. We could have been in here longer if the messenger hadn't arrived last night."

The woman nodded and lifted her hands up in a placating gesture. "You know how it works."

"It was thanks to me we never went back to Gara. I told you this was the better course." Gaffri was scowling at Fek.

"Maybe." Fek agreed easily. "Well then, let us out."

Gern looked over at the woman, and at her nod, moved forward to unlock the door.

He stepped back and Fek and Gaffri shuffled out.

Gaffri stretched, yawning widely, and took a step toward his pack.

Taya's gaze went to it and then she flicked a desperate look at Gern, but he wasn't looking her way. She opened her mouth to speak when all four guards struck out at Fek and Gaffri in a coordinated attack.

As he fell, Fek ducked a blow by a guard holding what looked like a cosh, and it only glanced off his head. He landed, dazed but still conscious, on the floor. The guard stepped in and hit him again.

Taya stared, mouth open.

"I'm assuming you had a good reason for that?" Gern asked, voice tight.

"Orders," the woman said. The look she sent Gern was earnest, and fake. "They were probably spies. Had some big story about how they were doing our liege's bidding, but it turns out that West Lathorian, the big one who flies that sky craft, was expecting them. Asking after them at the gate. Waiting to give them instructions, most likely."

The laugh that rose up out of Taya's throat was unstoppable. She put a hand over her mouth and tried to turn it into a cough.

Habred would know why Garek was looking for Fek and Gaffri. That it was in order to get her back.

Now he was planting a story to tidy up his loose ends.

"You got something to say?" one of the men asked her.

If they were going to spread a story like that, maybe she could benefit from it. "Am I free, then?" She stepped closer to the door.

All four guards seemed suddenly uncertain.

"Maybe," the woman shrugged. "But that's not our decision."

"When will I hear?"

They ignored her, lifting up Fek and Gaffri and walking away.

"What's going to happen to them?" she asked Gern as they disappeared into the darkness of the passage on the left.

He forced his attention back to her. "I don't know." He shook his head. "Nothing good."

"What's going to happen to me?"

He put his hand on the bars, his face tight with unhappiness and worry. "There have been things going on. Disturbing things. At least for the last six months, but maybe longer. I'm afraid you're going to get caught up in them."

He looked down the passageway in the direction of the staircase again and shook his head. "I don't think we'll see those two ever again."

That had been her conclusion, too.

"We have rules." He seemed to be trying to convince himself. "You're West Lathorian, a fellow citizen of Illy. They need to have due cause to charge you with something. Need to allow you to see your ambassador."

"But no one knows I'm here. And until he can be sure I'll cooperate, I'm sure Habred will want to keep it that way."

Gern rubbed the side of his nose in agitation. "I have to think. I don't know what to do about this." He turned to the door. "I'll get you some breakfast."

She watched him go, then stood against the bars of the door for a few minutes, enjoying the Star light filtering through the high windows on her face, and then reached out to the knife in Gaffri's pack.

It fell over, and she *pulled* on the shadow ore, crouching down and straining as the other items inside weighed the pack down.

When it was halfway to her, the knife burst from the top of the pack, slicing through the leather flap and shooting toward her.

She let out a squeak of surprise and stopped it just short of her nose, then reached out a trembling hand to grab the hilt and pull it through the bars.

The sheath Quardi had made for her had never left her boot, and she pulled it out, slid the blade home and pushed it all back into her boot again.

Gern stopped dead when he stepped back in with a tray of food and a mug of something hot and fragrant, his eyes on the pack.

"Fell over," Taya said.

He relaxed, gave a nod. There was a slot built into the cell door, and he lifted the flap, slid the tray through, and turned to leave again.

"What can you tell me?" Taya asked, before he could leave. "Is there any news?"

He paused, shook his head. "I promised you you wouldn't be hurt, and I'll keep that promise. But give me some time to work out what needs to be done."

She nodded. What else could she do?

She would like to believe Gern, and she was sure he was sincere, but she knew, as did he, that if he helped her, he'd most likely suffer the same fate as Gaffri and Fek.

There were things going on here neither of them understood, and maybe it would be better if she escaped on her own.

TWENTY-FOUR

TAYA HAD JUST STARTED CUTTING through the second hinge in the cell door when Gern returned.

She froze, as surprised as he was, and then crouched down, sliding the knife back into her boot.

Gern raised his brows. "Can't see how a knife'd cut through the hinges. They're steel."

Still crouched low, she grabbed hold of the bars at the bottom of the door and shook them, and the fact that the bottom of the door was now hinge-free became apparent.

Gern whistled. "What's that knife made of?"

"Shadow ore." There were probably reasons to keep that to herself, but she decided he hadn't looked too upset at catching her trying to break out.

He whistled again. "Can I see it?"

She straightened, pulling the knife out of her boot as she rose up, and offered it to him on her palm.

He took it carefully, touched the blade and then stuck his bleeding finger in his mouth, eyes wide.

"It's sharp," she told him, with a grin.

"You didn't have it before, or you'd have found a way to escape those two," he said, handing it back to her.

She nodded to the pack that Gern had replaced neatly against the wall. "It was in the bottom of Gaffri's bag. And I was a little out of things for a while. I needed time to recover." She gingerly touched the side of her head, but the graze was scabbed over now and it wasn't as sensitive as it had been. The headache was almost entirely gone.

Gern sucked in a breath, looking from the pack to her. "How did you get it out, then?"

She stepped back, tossed the knife into the air, and held it there. "I call it. I call the shadow ore Change."

"Bargat told me you did, but I couldn't see it in my head. It's different to calling the air or the water Change."

Taya shook her head. "I don't think it's different, it's just that when those things are called, the caller has so much more volume to work with. My calling seems to be specifically this one type of metal. My brother calls the earth Change. I think I call an earth Change too, but there's a lot more of whatever it is he calls in the earth than I do."

Gern's focus was still on the knife, so Taya let it drop into her hand, and went back to work on the hinge.

"Thought it would be better if I escaped on my own," she said. "That way, you can't be blamed."

He grunted in agreement. "You'll need to hurry, though. I don't know their plans, but if Xinta and her crew come back to take you, there's nothing I can do." He took her breakfast tray away, came back with a sandwich and some cold water, and took the knife from her, working the second hinge while she ate.

He broke through before she'd finished, and started on the top one. When she was done, she brought the tray over and put her hand out to take over, but he shook his head.

"Save your strength."

"Can you tell me about Garek? What he did while he was here?"

Gern grunted, his concentration on the blade he was using.

"Rumor was that our liege had invited him. That's not likely, though, given what someone I trust has told me about Habred's plans."

"Invading West Lathor, you mean?" Taya asked, and Gern froze and lifted his head.

"You know about that, do you?"

She nodded.

"Well." He shook his head again, went back to sawing through the metal. "Habred went along with Garek's story. Probably didn't have a choice with Luf being so pro-West Lathor at the moment."

"So they met?"

Gern tilted his head from side to side. "Could have met a couple of times, for all I know. I saw him hanging around the palace enough. What I didn't know, but learned last night, was he also spent a lot of time down at the gates, talking to the guards. Xinta was right when she said he spread the word some fellow guards from Garamundo were due in, and if they could let him know when they arrived, he'd be grateful."

"He was waiting for me." She leaned against the wall. "I wonder why he left before we got here?"

There had to be a good reason. And she had to believe he'd be back.

"Heard a rumor." Gern wiped some perspiration from his forehead with his forearm. "A story about some Dartalians being attacked, one so badly, your intended took him back to Valian."

Taya frowned, trying to work it out. There were surely good doctors in Luf, so why had Garek taken the Dartalian back to his home capital, unless there was something more to the story?

Eventually, she shrugged. She would have to find out when they found each other again.

"Looks like you're almost there—"

The door to the cells slammed open and a man stepped in. Gern turned, tension in every line of him.

Taya took a step back, heart hammering.

The man wasn't in uniform, but he held himself ready, like a guard, and his expression, when he caught sight of her, was one of disappointment.

"What are you trying to do? Bring the ax down on us all?" Gern's voice was fierce, his shoulders stiff, but now he seemed more furious than afraid.

The door swung closed, and the man stood silently for a moment, taking in the scene.

"What's going on, Gern?" He was breathing hard, as if he'd run to get here.

Gern shook his head. "Taya, this is . . . Mu."

Mu—the name of a character from the legends, the guard who'd outwitted a monster from the shadow pits, only to be outwitted in turn by an old lady.

She understood. Better that she didn't know his real name.

Gern turned back to working the hinge. "Mu's cousin was once held here, in this very cell, even though he wasn't a guard. He'd fallen on hard times, due to his fondness for firebrand, and he preferred to sleep on the streets rather than at home, because those he loved tried to get him to change his ways."

"They arrested him for being a street sleeper?" Taya asked. Street sleepers were unknown in a place like Pan Nuk, but in cities like Juli and Gara, there were people who looked as if they had no roof over their head.

"The guards rounded them up, but they didn't arrest them. They brought them here." Mu looked at her curiously.

"I recognized Mu's cousin amongst the others," Gern said. "Mu had pointed him out to me once when we'd gone out to the tavern. So I told Mu he was here." Gern sighed, and he seemed to cut more vigorously at the hinge than before.

Mu watched him with a frown. "Why are you telling her this story? Who is she?"

"An ally, one of the prisoners from Shadow."

Mu gaped at her, then turned to Gern.

He held Mu's gaze. "Someone has to get the message out to the other states, and she has the trust of enough people that she'd be believed," Gern closed his eyes for a moment, at if his words caused him physical pain. "You can take her down the same way as the others, but this time it'll be on our terms, and for the good of Harven."

Mu rubbed a hand over the back of his head, moved his shoulders to loosen them, and then gave a nod. "I came when Gern told me Rinwal was here, and we spoke, just a short conversation, but he wasn't reasonable. He hadn't had any firebrand for a few hours, and he was belligerent—most of the street sleepers were." Mu was watching Gern saw at the hinge, as if he'd only just noticed what he was doing and was confused. "And then, the next morning, guards herded them out."

Taya waited, sure the story must be going somewhere important, but unsure where.

"It wasn't the first time it'd happened. The first couple of times, the people in here really were guards who'd committed a crime. Xinta told me they were being transferred to the main prison because they'd been found guilty. But the street sleepers weren't guards. They were citizens who hadn't done anything wrong that I could work out. Xinta and her friends took them down a secret passage, one I'll get Mu to take you down when you're free. It goes right out of the city—must have been built as an escape hatch in case Luf was ever besieged." Gern gave a crow of triumph as the hinge gave. He handed her back her knife, and she slipped it into her boot.

He stood back, and Taya pulled the door inward with a scrape of metal on stone. There was just enough space for her to fit through. She reached back for her sleeping bag and sidled out.

"Give me a few minutes to get you some food and water." Gern stopped beside the door and looked over his shoulder at Mu. "Tell her the rest of it. It's your story to tell."

Taya crouched beside her pack and started going through it, neatly setting each item aside to repack. Mu was silent, and she looked up at him to encourage him to speak.

He blew out a breath. "As Gern said, Xinta and her team took

Rinwal and the other street sleepers down the tunnel. She wouldn't tell Gern where she was taking them, so he called me and the two of us followed."

Taya watched him carefully, saw that his hands were shaking, and he grabbed hold of the fabric of his trousers to keep them still. Noticing that her gaze on him made it more difficult for him to speak, she went back to repacking her bag.

"Once we were out of the tunnel, which came out in the forest about half an hour from the city wall, a trader met Xinta on a relatively disused track. I heard Xinta promising the street sleepers they'd be given firebrand if they got into the trader's cart, and so they did. And they did get firebrand. Bottles of it. Xinta and her friends headed back, and we decided Gern better go back as well, in case someone came looking for him. I followed the trader."

He said nothing for a while and Taya paused as she was rolling her sleeping bag into a tight roll, and looked up. "What happened?"

Something terrible.

She'd seen that look in people's eyes in the sky raider camp on Shadow. The haunting look of seeing tragedy first hand.

"They didn't go that far. Maybe two hours on the road—long enough to get out of the woods and down into a valley that had low bushes and a lot of open fields. And then a sky raider craft came screaming overhead." He rubbed the back of his head again. "I threw myself down in the bushes, and I was thinking, at least there's nothing to steal here. They'll pass over."

Taya stood mute, unsure if the path he seemed to be leading her down could possibly be correct.

"They didn't pass over, though. They landed, and even those who were far gone on firebrand realized they were in trouble. They tried to get out the cart, but they were all hit by a white light. The screams . . ." His gaze met hers.

"I've been hit by white lightning. I know." She closed her eyes for a moment and tried to shake off the memory.

"You were hit by the white lightning and lived. Rinwal and the others didn't live." He sucked in a breath, and then fisted his hands. "When the white lightning shut off, something got out of the craft. It was in a dark blue suit that covered its whole body. It walked to the cart. That's when I realized the trader hadn't been hit. That he'd run back, and was close to where I was hiding. He'd even loosened his zanir's harness, and it had run away from the cart. He watched the sky raider from a distance, and when the sky raider turned and went back into the craft, and it flew away, he stood looking at the cart full of bodies for a long time."

"When was this?" Taya asked, her voice hushed.

"Six or seven months ago, now."

"They hadn't got the strength of the white lightning right." She, Kas, and the others had speculated when they were on Shadow about that. About how they were the only ones there, yet the sky raiders had been taking people for a few months before they'd been taken themselves. They'd also wondered at the delay between being abducted and arriving at the camp.

They'd wondered if the sky raiders were waiting to see if they recovered first, before they took them all the way to Shadow.

Mu was staring at her. "What do you mean?"

"I mean, people were taken by the sky raiders for months before my village was taken. But everyone else there was abducted around the same time as we were. No one had been in the camp before us. We set it up ourselves with what the sky raiders gave us. So where were the others?"

His mouth opened. Closed. "What are you saying?"

"I'm saying when we were up there, we wondered what had happened to those people who were taken before us, and one of the answers we came up with was that in the beginning, they didn't know how strong to make the white lightning. That it might have taken a little time to work out how to knock us out but not kill us."

"They didn't need to be provided with victims to test it, though." Mu crouched down beside her, face to face. "They could test it by hovering over any village they wanted."

She thought about it. "Maybe they started out doing it that way, hovering over villages. But were there any children in the group Xinta put together, any old people? Because the sky raiders aren't interested in anyone in those groups, just adults in their prime. If they were trying to set the right strength for a very specific group, in a safe environment where they could check on their victims without worry of attack, then providing them with a cart full of people the right age would have been perfect for them."

She'd been speaking matter-of-factly, but suddenly her legs collapsed under her and she sat down hard on the cold stone floor, because she realized that Luca, that the children and the elderly in Pan Nuk, hadn't been expected to survive. The white lightning had been set to incapacitate those in her age group, but administered to the whole village. The sky raiders hadn't cared one way or the other if anyone they left behind lived or died.

It was luck, pure luck, that the strength level they'd chosen hadn't killed anyone. Either that, or Pan Nukkers were extremely tough.

"They were all Rinwal's age. From twenty to about forty." Mu stood again, and began to pace.

"Xinta cheated the sky raiders, because I'm sure if the men she supplied were all firebrand addicts, they would not have been as physically able to deal with the white lightning as a healthy person." That might have been what saved the children and the elderly. They'd lowered the strength of their weapon because they'd practiced on firebrand addicts without knowing it. Not that helping had been Habred or Xinta's intention. Those street sleepers had simply been easy targets because few would notice their disappearance.

"What did the trader do with the bodies?"

Mu sucked in a breath. "I got up slowly after the sky raiders flew away. I didn't worry about showing the trader I was there, I simply walked out onto the path and passed him on my way to the cart. He started after me, and his face . . . It was sullen, and it was fearful. He saw my guard uniform and thought I was checking on him, making sure he'd done his part. We walked to the cart, and they were all lying still, eyes open, faces twisted in agony. He walked past, heading toward his zanir, who'd stopped a little way away, and was eating grass. Then he turned and he said I could tell Habred that was the last time he was doing this. He couldn't take it any more. It was all right when it was vicious criminals, but now they were sending him drunks and street sleepers, it was too much. He was done with it all." He paused.

"He said something about a wreck, too, about how finding it was the worst thing to happen to him."

"He mentioned a wreck?" Taya glanced at Fek and Gaffri's packs, lying against the wall, and wondered how much of their strange treatment by Habred was due to their enthusiastic mention of a sky craft wreck, and producing evidence of their find.

"You know of it?" Mu stopped pacing and looked down on her.

She straightened, still shorter than him, but he wasn't looming over her any more. "I've seen it. Coming through the mountains. I wonder . . . what you've told me, what it seems like, is that the sky raiders have some kind of agreement with Habred—he provided them with people to experiment on, but what did he get out of it? And how did they make contact with him in the first place? Through the trader? Maybe he encountered sky raiders at the wreck, and they asked to speak to the liege."

Mu shrugged. "Maybe. I think I know what Habred gained, though. Luf has never been directly attacked by the sky raiders since the first few months after their arrival. And when I saw Rinwal and the others killed, I started asking around. Only traders leaving the city are targeted, no one coming in has been attacked, and even then, those who are attacked are few and far between, almost as if it's a cover so no one starts wondering why we're exempt."

Mu turned suddenly, settling into a battle-ready stance as the door opened, but it was only Gern, a large bag in one hand.

"Food and water for the road," he said.

"Thank you." Taya put it into the top of her bag, buckled the straps and lifted it onto her back. "Tell me, who else have you told about this?"

They exchanged looks.

"No one."

"Why not your cousin Bargat? He's suffered the full force of sky raider invasion."

Gern sighed. "Because he was so relieved to be free. So happy the liege was giving them a new herd of leviks. I tried a few times to tell him, but I couldn't do it. I was afraid he wouldn't believe me and would mention it where the wrong person could overhear."

She could understand that. She knew how hard it had been for West Lathor to accept their liege was no longer the man he'd been, and that had happened over a few years.

"Where will you go?" Gern asked.

"Back to West Lathor. I don't have any other option. I'm sure there's a West Lathorian embassy here, but I don't know if I can trust the ambassador, given the deal between Habred and the Garamundo town master, so I'll have to get to Juli with this information myself."

Gern gave a nod. "Good luck."

She leaned forward and gripped his forearm. "Thank you."

"We need to move. Now." Mu was staring down the passage, toward the stairs, and Taya sucked in a breath as she heard the sound of voices.

Gern opened the door behind him, and they hustled through it.

Beyond was a small office space, which she assumed was Gern's, and then another passageway.

They went through the office, closing the door behind them, and Gern went one way while Mu led her in the opposite direction.

The door he opened led down a staircase, steep and unlit, and he didn't light a torch or lantern, so she was forced to go as fast as she could in the dark.

When they reached the bottom, she got the impression of a large space that smelled of ale and wine, and the tart fruitiness of cider.

"Here." Mu's voice came from the right and she turned and

bumped into him. She heard a lock turn, and then felt the flow of cool, musty air.

Mu pulled her in, closed the door and locked it, and started walking.

"They'll wonder where the key is," she said.

"No. I had a key made. They never leave one in the door. They'll have their own."

The tunnel he was leading her down was wide enough to move easily, and high enough she could walk upright.

She had to jog to keep up.

The guards would be looking for her. And while they would hopefully not expect her to have come this way, most likely one or two of them would check.

She'd like to be long gone before that happened.

TWENTY-FIVE

A LIGHT SHONE in Deva's garden.

The relief that flooded him was so intense, Garek's fingers trembled as he ran them down the arm rest that was also the control panel of the craft, and landed lightly on the grass.

For two nights it had been dark, and he had begun to worry Janu had lied, or that, worse, he hadn't, and somehow they were all dead, lying in the mountains under a pile of rock.

He had the door open, and was swinging down, before the engines had finished powering down.

Falk was right behind him, but his gaze was focused up, looking for sky craft, leaving Garek free to walk forward toward Deva, who stepped out of the shadows.

"You have news?"

"Two pieces. Earlier today, a guard from the gate asked one of my staff if Garek's friends had been in touch, because they'd come through as expected the other night, and he'd passed on your message to them."

"That must have been a nasty surprise." Garek had known that was a potential consequence of his enquiries. That Fek and Gaffri would be forewarned, but he couldn't think of a more efficient way to learn when they arrived.

"They played along, it sounds like. And your mentioning them in advance appears to have gotten them through the gates. The guards were suspicious of the cart full of huncree they were driving."

That, he couldn't have predicted. "Taya was in that cart."

Deva nodded. "I think so. But there's more. They got here two days ago. Today, one of my spies heard there was a big fuss at the guard house yesterday. Someone escaped from the jail in the barracks. There's no description of the prisoner, no official confirmation the escape even occurred. The gossips think they're keeping quiet because they're embarrassed someone escaped. But it could be they had someone they shouldn't have had."

"Taya," Garek agreed.

"Could she do something like that? Escape?"

He nodded, distracted. Thinking through his options. If she was on the streets of Luf, she'd been there for over a day. Her places to hide would be few, and she had no allies.

Habred, and anyone he sent after her, would have the advantage.

"I'll start at the barracks. Try to speak to whoever is in charge of the jail. If it wasn't Taya who escaped, we need to know that before anything else."

"Have you slept?" Deva asked, peering at his face in the darkness.

"Falk and I took turns at flying. I'm rested enough. But we could both use some food and drink. We ran out a day ago."

"Follow Arne." Deva turned slightly, and Garek saw her aide standing a little way back. "She'll take you to the kitchens."

When Garek returned, he felt much better. He'd eaten and drank while Deva's cook put together a big basket of food to go in the sky craft, and then made up a tray for Falk.

Falk took it with hands that shook, and sat down on the grass, mug already half-drained.

"So, you've taught Falk to fly the craft?" Deva was no fool, she would wonder why he'd give up such a huge advantage.

Garek shrugged. "I need to be alive to find Taya, and I have to sleep sometime. We had to evade the sky raiders three times in the last two days."

Falk swallowed a huge bite of meat pie. "He taught me, but there's something we're missing. Something we're not doing right. When the craft is in the air and going straight and fast, it's relatively simple to fly, actually. But the moment you need to maneuver, slow down to land, or lift off, the controls are lacking. There is something we haven't worked out yet."

"But . . ." Deva frowned. "I've seen Garek do it."

Falk barked out a laugh. "Yes. Because Garek lifts the sky craft up, and lowers it down, and jinks and twists it in the air by calling his Change." He looked at the sky craft and shook his head. "I tried to land and take off three times. I nearly killed us each time."

Garek shrugged his shoulders. He hadn't realized how much he was drawing from his Change to fly the craft until Falk had shown him how poorly the craft handled when Garek wasn't flying it.

That was notable in itself.

He should have felt it. Lifting a craft of this size should have strained him.

In the last few months he'd sensed he was getting stronger, but he hadn't had time to stretch his boundaries, work out how much stronger.

And he didn't have time now, either.

"Can you spare someone to come with me into the city?" Garek asked Deva. "I'd like someone who knows Luf well, can help me decide where to ask my questions."

Deva nodded, and Arne stepped forward again.

Garek really looked at her for the first time. Her hair was short and straight, her skin a few shades lighter than Deva's. He'd had the sense before that she was a former guard, and now he could see it for sure.

"What Change do you call?"

"Earth," she said.

He nodded. "Lead the way."

TAYA APPROACHED the raucous campsite cautiously. It seemed to be spread among the ruins of the old fort, as if there were too many people for one clearing, and she was torn between approaching the group or potentially exposing herself to harm.

At least she knew she was on the right path.

When she and Mu had emerged from the tunnels, they were in a thick forest. When she'd questioned him about where it lay in relation to the city, she thought it might be the long, wide swathe of dark green she'd seen from the air when they'd first flown to Luf.

Luci, the town master of Cassinya, had pointed out the route from her village to Luf, and she and Zek, the trader who'd been abducted near Luci's village, had exclaimed over a shortcut that neither had known about. The rare bird's eye view had excited them both, as well as the old fortified castle they'd caught a glimpse of.

There could be no doubt that the crumbling building before her was the same one she'd seen from the sky craft, but someone most definitely did know about it.

Ahead, flames from campfires danced and flickered between what remained of the walls, and then she heard a sound she hadn't heard for too long. The bleat of a levik.

Shepherds. Probably.

She moved closer, taking a route that brought her close enough to listen to what was being said before she stepped out and revealed herself.

A laugh rang out, a joyful sound she knew well.

She walked forward, almost tripping in her haste to leave the security of the trees, and stepped through an archway into the ring of light thrown out by the fire.

"Gera?"

The conversation around the fire cut off, and a dozen faces looked up. With a shriek of delight, Gera detached herself from the crowd and threw herself at Taya.

"What? How in the Star?" She crushed Taya to her, and then turned to look through a gap in the stone wall to another fire. "Luci!"

A few people came running, all familiar, and Taya realized there were tears on her cheeks.

"Taya?" Luci pushed the others aside.

Taya looked around more carefully, saw she truly was among people she would consider a second family. "I can't believe you're here, I thought you'd be home by now."

The bleat of a levik came again, and she turned to look in its direction. There were hundreds of leviks, she realized, corralled in what was most likely the original central courtyard. Some were watching the excitement, most were grazing placidly on the thin grass growing up between the flagstones.

"You were getting together a new herd." That explained why they were still so close to Luf.

"The liege provided them from his own stocks," Luci said. "But it took us time to finish up in Luf, negotiate how many leviks we'd get, and then we had to collect them from the liege's estate, a few days from the city, and herd them home."

"Well, I'm very glad of the delay." She gave a weak smile, suddenly not sure if she should tell anyone here the truth of her story. They owed Habred for his donation of the leviks, and he was their liege.

What she had to say would shake their faith in everything they thought they could trust.

"What is it?" Gera was watching her.

She bit her lip, shook her head. "I don't know if you want to hear it."

"Well." Luci put out a hand, and Taya grasped it. "While you decide whether you'll share your story with us or not, come sit and eat."

TWENTY-SIX

GAREK STOOD next to Arne in the shadows, watching the guards rotate through their watch duty outside the barracks.

They were bored and sloppy, but Garek assumed the duty itself was more for the look of things than from a serious belief that anyone would try to break in to the guard barracks.

"It's after dinner, so most of them not on duty will be at the tavern," Arne said, and just then, a side door opened and three guards strolled out, one complaining about the food and his shift roster.

They stopped the guard who was patrolling this side of the building, talking with him and laughing, and just like that, the way was completely clear.

Arne moved immediately, and Garek appreciated the way she seemed to float across the ground, with barely a scuff of her soles on the stone pavings.

The door wasn't locked, and even Arne seemed shocked at that, but shouldered her way in without a pause. He stepped in after her, found they were in a small hallway, connected to a long passage running from right to left.

From the left, someone shouted out in laughter, someone else banged a door shut.

He stepped around Arne, and turned right, away from the noise of what was probably the dormitories, passing heavily locked doors he guessed were the armory and the uniform store.

Arne drifted behind him, and he was happy to have her at his back.

A clatter of pots and the smell of overcooked meat came from a side corridor and a little further down, the way seemed to open up into a foyer.

Large double doors marked the front entrance to the building and on the other side of the big space the corridor continued. He crossed to it over a smooth stone floor dappled with the light of the outside lanterns.

A short way down the passage an open door led to a small office, shrouded in darkness, but before he could turn back for a light, he heard Arne strike a match and then light a lantern hanging on the wall.

There was paperwork on the desk in the office, but it was schedules and rosters, nothing of interest.

To the left of the desk was a door, and Garek carefully tried the handle. It opened easily, the area behind it also in total darkness.

Arne lifted the lantern behind him, and it illuminated two cells sitting side by side, and a long passage, stretching away into the darkness.

"The jail." Arne slipped around him to explore.

Both cells were empty and the door of one had been completely removed and set against its inside wall.

Garek stepped closer and tried to see why it had been taken off its hinges. He frowned, crouching down, and Arne brought the lantern closer. The hinges looked like they'd been sheered off. Taya couldn't have done that, she wasn't strong enough, but he didn't want to believe she wasn't the person who escaped.

"Have you seen these?" Arne asked, her voice echoing a little in the empty space.

Garek lifted his head, saw the two packs she was standing next to.

"They look like Gara guard packs."

"Yes. I served in the Juli guard, but you could tell if they're from Gara." Arne crouched down and set the lantern on the floor so she could use both hands. "This one looks like someone slashed it with a knife."

Garek joined her, examining the cut leather flap with a frown. He pulled out a few things, then rocked back on his heels.

"These are Fek and Gaffri's packs, no doubt about it. So they were here."

"Could one of them have been the person who escaped?"

Garek was afraid the answer was yes, which still left the question, where was Taya? What if she wasn't with them?

He drew in a sharp breath, refusing to contemplate it. "How do we find out who the escapee was?"

He wanted his hands on Fek and Gaffri, wanted to choke the information on where to find Taya out of them.

Arne gave him a strange look and then pointed behind him.

He turned, then registered the sound of someone walking toward them down the passage. Whoever it was carried a lantern, and the light bobbed up and down. Arne blew their lantern out.

Now that he was concentrating on it, Garek could hear it was more than one person. They were talking in low, angry tones, and coming closer fast. Garek propped the packs against the wall and followed Arne back into the little office.

They moved quickly as they made their way out of the building, even passing a guard, to whom they both gave a quick nod.

He seemed puzzled, but not worried enough to ask them who they were.

Once they were out on the street, Garek waited until they were out of sight of the barracks before he put a hand out to stop Arne going any further.

"We need to find out who escaped."

She gave a nod. "The tavern is the best place, but you'll be recognized. Even if you weren't, they'll be less inclined to talk in the presence of a guard from another state. I, on the other hand, go there at least once a week and mingle."

"You're saying I should wait outside."

She looked at him without saying anything, and eventually he gave a nod. "One hour only. If you don't have anything by then, I'll go in and make someone talk."

She gaped at him. "That would be . . . unwise."

It was his turn to stare at her. Eventually she closed her mouth. "Just pretend you don't know me, if it gets that far. I still have to live here."

He gave a curt nod and she turned on her heel, her back stiff, clearly angry at his threat to cause a scene.

When they were in sight of the tavern, Garek eased into the shadows to wait. "One hour," he reminded her softly.

He thought she muttered something under her breath, and then she was pushing at the doors and stepping in to the warmth and laughter.

Somewhere in the distance, a clock tower rang the hour. It was eleven. That made it easy enough. When it rang again, he'd be showing Luf just how dangerous he truly was.

"WHAT HAPPENED TO YOUR HEAD?" Gera had settled down next to her by the fire, and now she leaned closer, frowning.

The external injury was more a nasty graze than anything else now, but because her hair was so light, it was easy to see.

"I was caught in a rockfall going through the Dartalian Range."

She still wasn't sure if she should say anything about Gaffri and his deal with Habred. She leaned forward, elbows on knees, just happy to be warm and sitting down for a little while.

"What were you doing going through the Dartalian Range?" Vanu sat on her other side, the big levik farmer one of her favorite people from the camp on Shadow. "And where's Garek?"

She sighed. These people knew too much about her life for her to do anything but insult them by refusing to talk.

"When we took the Kardai to Juli, the sky raiders were waiting, and they took back Dom's sky craft."

"While the Kardanx were inside?" Gera's voice was weak with shock.

Taya shook her head. "No. They were already out, and Garek was walking toward it to turn the engine off. They shot him with white lightning."

There was silence as everyone shivered at the thought of it.

"So they stole it back. But not the other one?" Luci handed her a bowl.

She shook her head. "But we realized we'd have to be very careful if we wanted to keep the other craft. We went back to Pan Nuk, to help everyone move back to the village, but the sky raiders found us there, too. Garek took off without me, to draw them away from the village."

She realized she needed air, and took a deep breath.

"He's all right?" Vanu asked.

She shook her head. "I haven't seen him since. I heard he was in Luf two days ago. I'm sure he was there looking for me, so I think he's fine."

"Why aren't you waiting for him back home?" Luci crouched in front of her and handed over a spoon to eat her stew with.

"Because the day after Garek left, I was abducted by some guards from Garamundo." She paused, shook her head. "They were acting for your liege—for Habred. And they took me straight to Luf, through the mountains."

There was absolute silence.

"Our liege?" Gera tipped her head to the side. "But why?"

Taya said nothing, looking down at her bowl of food.

"Because of us." Luci slapped her forehead with her palm.

"What . . .?" Vanu looked between them.

"Habred wants her for her Change. And he knows about it because of us." Luci said each word distinctly. "Oh, Taya, I'm so sorry."

"This isn't your fault." She took a bite of stew, her stomach growling in anticipation. "This is on Habred. And the guards who brought me to him."

"Hold on." Vanu shook his head. "If they brought you to Habred, how did you get away?"

"Because . . . and I won't name names for obvious reasons, one of the guards I was handed to is the cousin of someone in this group."

Everyone mulled that over.

A man walked up behind her. "I can understand a Harven guard thinking they owed you for helping with our rescue. What I can't understand is the other guards thinking Habred abducting an Illian citizen in order to use her for her Change is all right." He stepped around her, into the ring of firelight, but Taya already knew it was Bargat, Gern's cousin.

They shared a look.

He must know the position his cousin held. Must have a good idea which guard had helped her.

"Habred didn't parade me through the streets. He hid me in a small cell in the guard barracks."

"If someone in the guard barracks had spread the word on who you are and what Habred had done to you, surely that would have been better for you?" Gera asked. "Then Habred would have been forced to release you and probably treat you like visiting royalty."

That was true. The pro-West Lathor sentiment must still be high in Luf. And the very stories that had focused Habred's attention on her would have made her a hero in the city.

"There's more." She took a bite of stew, so she didn't have to speak straight away.

"You want to say this even less than you wanted to tell us Habred was behind your abduction." Luci's face was grim in the fire's glow.

"Let me give you the information I was given, and you can decide what to make of it." She laid out the story Gern and Mu had told her, and when she was done, there was silence except for the shuffle and bleat of the leviks.

"Why didn't he tell me?" Bargat spoke first. Everyone looked at him, confused, but Taya knew he was talking about Gern.

"I asked him that." Taya tilted her head so she could look him in the eye. "He said he tried, but you were so happy to be free, so happy about the leviks Habred had pledged to Cassinya, he was afraid you wouldn't want to hear it."

"What do you plan to do with this information, Taya?" Luci was watching her with sad eyes.

"Take it to Juli. And my liege, or most likely Aidan, will take it to the Illian Council."

Luci nodded, her face stoic.

No one else said anything, and Taya looked down miserably into her empty bowl. Of everyone in Harven—aside from the victims the liege had provided to the sky raiders—the people sitting around her were the people Habred had betrayed the most.

"Habred will come after you. You must know that," Vanu said.

Taya nodded. "When they can't find me in the city, they'll start searching the roads to West Lathor. I've got no doubt about that."

"Then eat, and get a good night's sleep." Gera's face was solemn. "Tonight, you have a hundred guards on watch."

TWENTY-SEVEN

THE BELL STRUCK THE HOUR, and Garek stepped into the street, heading for the tavern door.

He had almost reached it when the door opened, and Arne stepped out.

"Anything?"

He didn't think she had, or she wouldn't have waited until the very last moment.

She shook her head. "No one knows, I don't think."

"Someone must know." And he would make sure they talked.

"Garek." Arne put a hand on his arm. "Right now, you're a hero, and West Lathor is considered Harven's friend. If you do this, that will change, and it'll make Deva's job that much harder."

He knew that. He simply didn't care enough. He was about to move his arm away when two men stepped out from the door into the night, one older than the other, both obviously guards.

The older man stopped dead at the sight of him, shocked recognition in his eyes.

His companion looked nervously over his shoulder, back toward the tavern door, and pulled the older guard away, walking with a quick, nervous step. The older man kept pace, saying nothing, but he looked over his shoulder more than once.

Garek hesitated. If he was going to question the people in the tavern, he could start with those two, but before he could take a step in their direction, the door opened again, and two guards stepped out. Garek recognized them immediately.

They were both from the attack that had injured Zek.

Their gaze was fixed on the retreating backs of the older guard and his friend, and they didn't notice Garek until he stepped right in front of them.

"You." The first guard pulled up short.

"Me." If anyone knew where Taya, Gaffri and Fek were, it would be Habred's trusted henchmen.

One guard reacted faster than the other. He put on a burst of speed, heading for a dark alleyway, and Garek called his Change and smacked him down.

When he turned back to the other man, it was to find Arne had him in a head lock, with a viciously curved knife to his throat.

"Let's go find a private place to chat, shall we?" Garek asked.

Arne nodded, and Garek couldn't help the quick grin he shot her at her obvious relief his plan to wreck the tavern in a mass interrogation hadn't been necessary.

He strode to the guard he'd incapacitated. He was struggling against the air pounding him down, and Garek let go of his Change as he grabbed him, lifted him up, and walked him into the alley he'd been running toward. He pushed him up against the wall, and Arne did the same with the man she'd subdued.

He could call his Change again, use it on them. But he wanted to use his hands.

"Where is Taya?"

They both looked shocked.

"Where. Is. Taya?" He kept his voice pleasant and clear.

Very little of the light from the street lamps filtered into the dark space, but there was enough light to see the glint of Arne's knife blade as she lifted it up, and the flick of an exchange of glances between the two guards.

"We don't know. She escaped." The guard Arne was holding lifted his chin as far away from her blade as he could.

"So it was her who escaped." Garek said it matter-of-factly, but the relief he felt made his knees weak. He narrowed his eyes. "Where are Gaffri and Fek?"

He put a hand on the guard's shoulder, tightened his grip.

The man shared another look with his companion. "I don't kno —" He squeaked as Garek applied some pressure.

"Where are Gaffri and Fek?"

"Dead," the other one said, his voice harsh.

Garek hadn't expected that. He lifted his brows. "Now, why would Habred kill two men who'd done him such a big favor?"

"Favor?" The guard gave a scornful laugh. "They were bumbling idiots who didn't understand half of what they'd gotten in to."

Now that, Garek believed.

"What do you want to do with them?" Arne tilted her blade and it gleamed bright.

"Perhaps we can let the Dartalians know we've found two of the thugs who attacked Zek," Garek said. It was time to start exposing Habred to the consequences of his actions. Time to lose him some friends.

He cut the guards' air off as he held their gaze, so they could see just how much he'd like to do more, and then stepped back as they both went down.

Arne crouched beside them and pulled out rope to tie them with from the small pack on her back. He gave a grunt of appreciation for her preparedness.

"Let Deva send the note to the Dartalians that we have these two. Let's make this official. West Lathor doing a favor for Dartalia."

Arne gave a nod of agreement and stood, and he followed her out of the alley.

He nearly walked into the back of her.

She was stopped in her tracks, staring down the two men who had come out of the tavern just ahead of the two guards he'd interrogated.

"Are they gone?" the older man asked.

Garek stepped aside, allowing them a view of the two guards lying, trussed up, in an unconscious heap. "You mean those two?"

"Yes." The old man's voice was bright with glee.

"And who are you?"

Something on his face must have alarmed them.

"I'm a friend. A friend!" The older man gasped, and Garek realized he'd been stealing the man's air.

He pulled back.

"You recognize me?" Garek watched the man put his hands on his knees and get his breath back.

"You're Taya's intended." The man lifted his head, and then straightened. His companion shifted nervously beside him. "I saw you around Luf when you were here a few days ago. Have to admit, I didn't know you'd be back, or I'd have got Taya to wait for you."

For a moment, he felt lightheaded. "You've seen Taya?" His voice was so low, it hurt his throat to speak.

The man gave a nod. "Name's Gern. They put her in my jail." His voice quivered a little. "Mu here and I helped her escape."

———

A SKY CRAFT SCREAMED OVERHEAD.

Taya looked up, but once again, the thick branches above obscured any sight of it.

She'd left Luci's camp just before dawn, loaded down with food and water, safe in the knowledge Luci would lie for her if the Luf guards came looking for her along this path.

The herd of leviks meant the villagers couldn't go as fast as she needed to, and it was less trouble for everyone if she wasn't caught amongst them.

She'd been walking for seven hours almost without a break, and from what little she could see of the sky through the branches overhead, the Star was almost directly above her.

The path narrowed and became more overgrown, and just when it seemed to disappear entirely, Taya shoved through, sweaty and scratched, onto the main road.

She moved to the middle of the road, looking right and then left down the open track, then staggered to the side and sat, pulling out her canteen and taking deep gulps of lukewarm water.

When she'd eaten something and almost finished her water, she forced herself to stand. She was on one of the main routes, now, and she needed to move as fast as possible. Whatever time she'd saved taking the shortcut, she needed to preserve her lead and push for the mountains as fast as she could go.

The road ran alongside the forest, so there was a deep, cool green shadow to her left, with rolling hills and the occasional cultivated field to her right.

Up ahead she could see the gray of the mountains, not close enough to loom over her, but a solid presence in front, as if they were blocking the way.

The pain in her head, which had seemed so much better, began to ache in the bright light of midday. She shouldered her pack, and started walking.

She'd been going for an hour when she first understood the pounding she could hear was zanir hooves on the hard-packed earth, not an increase in the thump of her headache.

She turned to look behind her, but the way was curved and twisty, and there was nothing to see.

She moved to the forest side of the road, looking for a gap in the foliage to slip back among the trees, but there was no getting in. The bushes were so thick and matted together, it was more solid than a hedge.

The road trembled beneath her feet and she turned again and saw two riders, bent low over the necks of their mounts, turning the corner.

She ran, eyes on the wall of greenery, looking for a gap, for any way in.

Overhead, the scream of a sky raider craft drowned out the thunder of the hooves, and she risked looking up, saw the sleek silver of the sky craft swoop low and then land in front of her, blocking the way and blowing up dust.

She stopped, lifting an arm to shield her face, and then darted a quick look at the guards.

They had stopped, too, dancing their panicky zanir in place.

She looked back at the sky craft and the first dart of hope pierced her chest, a painful, stabbing joy that made her want to cry out.

Garek?

The guards made no effort to come closer, struggling to keep their zanir from running, but not urging them forward, either.

"I must admit, this is a surprise." It was Xinta, the guard who had tricked Gaffri and Fek, and then killed them.

The guard with her was edging back, but she forced her zanir forward a few paces.

They weren't looking for her.

The thought held Taya still for a moment. The look of shock and interest on Xinta's face had been real.

So who were they looking for, especially in conjunction with a sky craft?

Her breath caught in her throat, and her eyes widened.

Luci.

Everyone from Cassinya, headed back home on a long, lonely road, slowed down by leviks and delayed on their journey by the liege himself.

The depth of the betrayal made her knees weak. If they hadn't chosen to use the short cut, the path that had been lost through the years and only seen from above, they might already be in the sky craft, on their way back to Shadow.

"We might not have been expecting you, but you're definitely of interest to them, too. There's nowhere for you to go, so I would suggest giving in gracefully." Xinta's zanir danced in place, wanting to retreat in the face of the noisy sky craft, but too well-trained to disobey its rider.

Taya took a deep breath.

Knowing what Xinta had done to Fek and Gaffri, the sky craft was the better bet. And there was a chance Garek was inside.

Taya moved toward it, not hurrying, but putting distance between herself and the two guards.

The longer the sky craft sat there, though, the faster her heart sank.

Garek would at the very least have opened the door for her by now, if not jumped down and helped her any way he could against the guards.

Her steps slowed.

She swung her gaze back to Xinta, but she and her fellow guard were still hanging back, no closer to her than they had been before.

It seemed even though Habred had done a deal with the sky raiders, his people were still afraid of them.

She made her choice, and started walking toward the craft again, but she kept glancing at the wall of green, looking for a small gap to squeeze through.

The door of the sky craft opened, and she stumbled to a stop.

The tall figure in the doorway was in a dark blue suit and wore a helmet. There was something clutched in his hand.

She looked back at the guards, but instead of running, they were now, at last, moving forward. Forcing her ahead of them, like a levik to its slaughter pen.

Taya looked down at her boots, her vision narrowed for a moment on their shape and color, the way the dust of the road coated them, the way they molded her legs.

She was trapped.

She could sit down, refuse to move, but the device she'd seen in the sky raider's hand was a familiar one. The little boxes that shot white lightning.

She did not want to be shot again, even with the smaller, portable version of the weapon.

She let her shoulders droop, and began walking again, head down, toward the sky craft.

When she reached the ladder, she grasped it and pulled herself up a few steps, and looked back at the two guards.

"Aren't you even a little ashamed?"

They'd moved back when it was clear she would allow herself to be taken without a fight, and neither of them answered.

They turned and began galloping away, back toward Luf.

She watched them go with a sense of satisfaction. Only one front to fight on, now.

She reached the top of the stairs, and the sky raider, who'd climbed back into the craft when she'd started up the ladder, leaned out and handed her a helmet.

She looked at her reflection in the glass of his visor and then at the same reflection in the helmet she was holding. Of course they'd have the air mixed to suit themselves inside the sky craft, not her.

She put the helmet on and suppressed a moment of panic when the sky raider leaned out again to twist a clamp at the back of it to create a seal, then pulled her pack off her shoulders and threw it down onto the ground below.

She turned, a protest on her lips, and saw the sky raider had his white lightning device pointed at her, the inference being she should shut up and get inside the craft.

She complied, unsurprised to find there were two of them, one sitting in the pilot's chair.

The door closed behind her, and both sky raiders took their helmets off.

She'd seen a sky raider before, but never without a helmet unless they were dead. There was the same detached, frightening interest in their eyes when they looked her over as she'd encountered before.

The shock of being studied so intently meant it took her a moment to register the noise, a kind of high pitched shriek, which had started up the moment she stepped into the cabin.

The sound forced the sky raiders' attention away from her as they registered it, too.

The engines had never been switched off, and the craft had lifted off the moment the door had closed behind her.

Over the noise, the two sky raiders were barking at each other in their own language, and they seemed panicked.

She used their distraction, pulling on the shadow ore knife in her boot so it slid up her leg into her waiting hand.

Then she lunged forward, running the flat blade of the knife along the console on the arm rest of the pilot's chair.

The craft dropped, skipping along the road like a stone on a rough sea.

The engine failure threw her against one of the walls of the craft, the helmet cushioning the blow. She held on tight to the knife, dragging it against everything in reach, above her head, on the ground, against the wall.

The piercing shriek did not let up, and as she was flung across the floor again, she saw the look of horror on the pilot's face as he realized what was in her hand.

It took her a moment to understand the air burning her throat was because her helmet wasn't working anymore, and as she reached back to twist the clamp and pull it off, she recalled the hiss of sound when she'd brushed her knife against it when she was flung across the craft.

She finally got the helmet off, but the air was no better inside the cabin.

As she struggled up onto her elbows, head bowed, to cough, the sky craft spun around and she caught a glimpse of the sky raider not in the pilot's seat kneeling over a depression in the floor.

The sky craft door opened as he reached in and turned a dial and she gasped and tried to take a deep breath as air from outside began to flow in.

The craft tilted downward at her end, sliding down a hill with a screech of metal on rock, and the sky raider who'd opened the door was screaming something at the pilot.

Another crazy turn flipped her over, and the next time she looked up, the pilot was staring at her again, helmet poised above his head, the cruel interest in his eyes gone now, replaced by wild terror.

He slammed the helmet down and jumped out after his co-pilot, and Taya slid her knife back into her boot and started crawling across the floor to the door herself.

With a shudder, the craft came to a halt.

She was thrown flat on her back, but when nothing more happened, she managed to get to the door on her hands and knees and stick her head out.

The sky craft lay half on its side, one end in a shallow stream, the rest leaning at an angle against the steep bank.

She scrambled out the door, which was facing straight up at the sky and leaned over the side to find the ground wasn't too far away.

A movement caught her eye, and she looked up the hill.

The two sky raiders were struggling to their feet in a sloping field whose ground had been torn up by the sky craft's passage.

One of them started fumbling at his belt, and she saw he was going for the white lightning device clipped to it.

Taya called her Change, the shadow ore knife sliding into her hand with a sweet inevitability.

She threw it, aimed it in mid-flight, and the tip struck the sky raider's helmet with a satisfying crack.

She called it back, needing the feel of the smooth metal on her skin before she threw it again.

The second sky raider was staring at his friend.

It was possible he didn't understand what had just happened.

Taya threw the knife again.

The sky raider saw it coming and staggered back, stepping out of the way.

She changed the knife's course.

It didn't hit with the same velocity, but it did hit.

This time, the crack of metal on glass was softer, and she was able to hear the fizz as the helmet's systems died.

She called the knife back, crouched on the edge of the sky craft, and watched them run out of air.

She was breathing hard by the time they died, in sympathy with them, even though she did nothing to help them.

Both of them took off their helmets toward the end. The one with the little white lightning shooter tried to shoot at her when he realized there was going to be no help, but the shot went wild and he hit the ground instead.

After they fell down, she stayed where she was, lightly balanced on the lip of the sky craft, until she was sure there was no way they were getting back up.

She jumped down, shook out the ache in her legs, and went to collect the little black device.

Garek had taken four of them on Shadow and given two to Kas. She didn't want Habred to get hold of one.

She had to look for it, because he'd dropped it, and then spun away from it toward the end, but eventually she found it trodden into the dark, churned earth of the field.

She put it into her coat pocket and then headed up the deep groove the sky craft had carved out of the field, to go get her pack.

The scream of another sky craft stopped her in her tracks.

She looked up and found it hovering overhead.

If the sky raiders had gotten in a call for help, this could be it.

The shadow ore knife slid back into her hand and she grasped the black device with the other.

The craft settled down in front of her, throwing up so much dust she had to turn away, in an exact repeat of what happened earlier.

Only this time, as the craft settled onto the ground, the door opened immediately, and the person who flung himself out of it was exactly the person she wanted to see.

TWENTY-EIGHT

GAREK DIDN'T KNOW how long they stood in each others arms in the field.

He didn't really care, other than to worry a little about the sky raiders who might come looking for their people and their craft.

His face was buried against Taya's neck, his lips pressed against her skin, his arms tight around her.

She was thin. Even thinner than she'd been when they'd gotten back from Shadow. She seemed more delicate, more breakable than before.

He inhaled a breath, drawing her scent into his lungs.

She pressed a kiss against his collarbone and then leaned back a little to cup his face between her hands.

He saw the scrape on the side of her head, and brushed back her hair for a better look.

"Who?"

"Rock fall, created by Fek and Gaffri fighting each other." She was threading her fingers in his hair, and he tipped his head to give her better access.

"They're dead." He heard the regret in his voice, and didn't know whether to tell her it was because he wouldn't have the opportunity to kill them himself, or not.

She nodded. Pulled his head down closer for a kiss, and then he was lost for long moments, exploring her mouth.

He didn't know how long Falk stood waiting behind him, but the scientist eventually cleared his throat.

Taya went still and tried to pull away.

"It's just Falk," he said against the smooth skin of her cheek.

"Who's Falk?"

"No one." He drew her closer again, but she ducked her head to look around him and with a sigh, he stepped to the side so she could see, sliding his arm around her shoulders.

"Sorry to interrupt, but how did that happen?" Falk pointed to the sky craft, tilted at a drunken angle, and the two bodies lying in the field.

Taya didn't answer right away. Then she drew in a deep breath. "I happened."

Falk jerked his gaze to Garek, disbelief in his eyes, and Garek gave him a shrug. He was more interested in the two guards they'd seen riding away. "What were those two Luf guards doing, heading back to Luf? Did you see them?"

She nodded, leaning against him in a way that made his heart full. "I took a shortcut through the forest, and came out a little way from here." She waved her hand in the direction of the road. "I hadn't been on the main road for long when Xinta and her friend came galloping along, and I was caught between them and the sky raiders."

"They were working together?" This is what Gern had told him, that Habred had some deal with the sky raiders, but he'd been reluctant to consider it.

She nodded. "They weren't looking for me, though. I was just a bonus. Xinta blocked my way and waited until I was climbing up into the sky craft before she left."

"Who were they looking for?" He could feel her trembling

against him, and looked down. It was a shock to see the expression on her face was of rage, not fear.

"They were looking for Luci. For everyone from Cassinya."

Garek was so shocked, he couldn't speak.

"Never mind that." Falk was shaking his head. "How did you bring them down?" He started walking toward the sky raiders.

Garek sensed Taya hesitate as she watched him pick his way over the furrows. "I used my knife."

Falk looked over at her, startled. "How big is your knife?"

She put her hand to her side, and suddenly the knife was there. She lifted it up to show Falk.

"That's it?"

"It's not a normal knife."

"Shadow ore?" Falk looked over at Garek, as if he could confirm it, rather than Taya herself. "It's made of shadow ore?"

"They made the mistake of allowing me on board," Taya told him with a shrug. "I don't think I could have done much from the outside."

"Did you know this would happen?" Falk was standing over a sky raider's body, his gaze riveted by what he saw.

"I had a good idea." She lowered her hand, and slid the knife back into her boot. "It was either climb into the sky craft and hope the shadow ore affected it, or be knocked out. So I chose to do things under my own terms."

"How could they have knocked you out?" Falk asked, but he had turned away, and was walking toward the sky craft.

Taya flicked a glance up at Garek, and tapped her pocket.

He ran his hand down her side and felt the hard square lump of a device he knew well. He'd given two of the four he'd stolen to Kas, but he still had two at the bottom of his pack.

They had threatened her with it.

He forced himself to give her a tiny shake of his head, to let her know not to say anything to Falk about it, but it was hard to remain calm, to act normally.

He remembered how it felt to be shot with one.

He looked up, and for the first time in a while, hoped he *did* see a sky craft coming to help the downed sky raiders.

Falk was standing in front of the sky craft now, looking for a way up, and then he disappeared around the back of it.

"Who is he?" Taya asked as they walked toward the sky craft after him.

"He's a scientist. He used to work for the Gara town master. He was studying the sky craft I brought down. I used him to get it back when I found out you'd been taken."

"Ah." She said nothing more, and he was content not to speak as well. There would be time for that. For them to fill each other in on what had happened. Right now, he just liked the feel of her against his side, the way she fitted under his arm and matched her steps to his as they navigated the thick clods of earth ripped up by the sky craft as it had slid across the field.

Her touch, the feel of her, was as vital as the connection he felt when he called his Change. When he became one with the air.

Falk reappeared, scrabbling for purchase on the roof, and then disappeared from sight.

The ladder to the door stuck out horizontal to the ground, and Garek put his hands on Taya's hips, kissed her neck again, just because he could, and threw her up, calling his Change so she landed lightly on the ladder.

He waited for her to walk along it to the door, then launched himself up.

"Hey." Falk's head popped out of the door as the craft groaned a little under the weight of his landing. "What are you . . .? Oh."

He disappeared back in, and Taya swung in after him. She was sitting on the floor, legs braced to keep her in place because of the steep angle, when Garek joined her.

She pointed to a small open panel. "Emergency door opener," she said.

He knelt beside it, trying to picture where it would be on his sky craft for future reference. Which reminded him, they couldn't leave his craft in the field unprotected for long.

"We need to go, Falk."

"I know, I know. But this thing is dead. Totally dead." Falk was fiddling with the console and shaking his head. "I was hoping we could revive it. Another one would be good but . . . what did you *do*?"

Taya pulled out her knife, slid a little closer to the pilot's chair, and ran the flat blade of the knife along the arm.

"That's it?" Falk held out his hand for the knife, and after a moment's hesitation, Taya handed it to him.

"Where were the sky raiders when you did that?" Garek asked her.

"One was piloting, the other was standing next to me. But they were distracted by the screeching."

"The craft was flying when you did it?" He should have understood that. How else had it dug a groove in the road, spun across a field and ended up in a stream?

"They took off the moment the door closed." She was watching him with steady eyes, and then she smiled, and his breath caught. "They weren't actually looking for me, I was a surprise catch, so I don't think they understood much about me. If they had, they'd have been more concerned at first when that warning alarm sounded."

"Well, this obviously can't come with us." Falk stared at the knife, then touched the tip and jerked his blood-smeared finger back.

"I'm not leaving it. I'll walk back to the road and get the water pouch from my pack. It should fit in there."

Falk looked up at her and waved the knife in her direction. "Are you crazy? This brought down a sky craft. We can't risk it."

"We risked taking it, and a whole lot more, from Shadow." She turned to go, and Garek offered a hand to her, pulling her up and boosting her out of the door.

He wanted every excuse he could find to touch her. And she was letting him, no matter that she didn't need his help.

When they both stood side by side on the top of the sky craft, she turned back. "I'll take my knife back now," she called down to Falk, and he heard the scientist yelp.

The knife flew up out of the door and hovered in front of her before she slid it back into her boot. Then she took Garek's hand and they both jumped to the ground together.

TWENTY-NINE

GAREK SHADOWED HER.

He went with her to fetch her pack, and then back down to the stream to fill her empty leather water pouch with water.

Taya felt the tightly-wound spring inside her slowly loosen.

She'd made peace earlier today with the possibility that she might die or fail. That she could be taken back to Shadow, or that the crash she hoped she could engineer might kill her.

But instead, she'd won.

And now she had Garek back. She smiled at him for what was surely the hundredth time, and he reached out to touch her again in response.

Falk watched them from the bank of the stream, still scowling.

When the pouch was full, she let Garek help her up the bank and then pulled out her knife to make sure it would fit inside.

It did.

She grinned. "All set."

"No." Falk shook his head. "It's just a knife. Bury it somewhere and come back for it."

Garek turned to him. "Luf's not that far of a walk," he said. "You could be there by tomorrow if you start now. Deva will put you up."

He turned back and held out his hand, and Taya took it, let him pull her up the slope until they were level with the scientist.

Falk's mouth hung open. "You're taking her side? It's just a knife."

Garek laughed. "I will always take her side. What about the last few days made you think otherwise?"

Falk pointed at the pouch. "It's dangerous."

"It's safe in the water pouch," Garek told him. "Choose. But choose quickly. We've been here too long already."

"Because we were wasting time fetching a pouch and filling it with water!"

"To me, this isn't a waste of time. I only have a few things made of shadow ore. I can't afford to lose any of them." Taya started walking, and Garek kept pace at her side, still holding her hand.

Behind her, she heard Falk kick something.

"He's been a real help these last few days, flying the sky craft so I could sleep. Watching it while I looked for you in Luf." Garek shrugged apologetically. "I didn't realize he'd be so difficult."

Taya looked over her shoulder. Falk was glaring at her.

"To be fair, I did a lot of damage to that sky craft." She turned back. "Maybe we can take off and land again. That'll convince—"

She jerked her head up, eyes narrowed, and saw Garek had done the same.

The scream of a sky craft coming toward them was unmistakeable.

She opened the pouch and pulled out the knife.

The craft came over the forest, one of the smaller, fighting craft, not a larger one like Garek's or the one she'd just brought down. It shot out from behind the wall of green and then halted in place.

She wondered whether it was shock that made them do that.

The bodies of their fellow raiders lay on the field, their craft destroyed.

The sky raiders weren't used to being the ones mourning the dead and losing property.

Taya stepped away from Garek and drew back her arm.

"No!" Falk had somehow gotten level with her, and he ran in front of them both. "Don't destroy this one, too. I need—"

The white lightning flashed out. She braced herself, but suddenly she was in the air, held tight in Garek's arms, above where the white lightning danced over Falk.

"Now," he said softly as they reached the top of their trajectory and started to fall again, and she threw the knife as hard as she could, sensed the moment when Garek's own Change caught it, sped it up, so even as they fell back to the ground, it hit the window of the sky craft like a stone from a catapult—burying itself to the hilt with a satisfying crack.

They landed and Garek set her down, and she pulled, trying to get the knife back.

It wouldn't come.

She braced her legs, concentrated. She was panting with exertion by the time it flew back to her.

"Again," she said to Garek, and flung it back at a sky craft that was no longer steady but dipping from side to side under the onslaught of Garek's air attack.

This time it hit harder, slamming in up to the hilt again, and she realized Garek had stopped buffeting the craft and had used all his power on it.

She flicked a quick glance at Falk, but he was down, and she forced her gaze back to the window of the sky craft. Nothing she could do to help him now.

Or even later.

You either got over being hit by white lightning or you didn't.

The knife was easier to get out this time. It had created a crack in the screen, and she made a sound of satisfaction when it landed back in her hand.

There would be outside air leaking into the craft now. The sky raiders would need to get their helmets on.

She threw the knife again, and Garek must have really pushed, because the screen shattered as it stuck, and then the glass blew inward.

Garek had done that. He'd forced the air inside the craft, making it impossible for the sky raiders to breathe.

She let the knife follow the shards of glass in.

She couldn't see the pilot's chair, so she let the knife drop to the floor of the craft, and then pulled it from left to right, felt it slam against objects.

The craft dropped to the ground.

A sky raider tried to climb out the smashed front screen. He had no helmet on. He collapsed over the jagged edges, and after a moment was still.

They waited, but no one else came out.

"There are sometimes only one of them in the smaller ones," Garek said after a long beat.

They moved closer.

He was right. There was no one else inside.

"Time to go," he said, looking up at the sky.

She nodded, calling back her knife. When she had it back in her hand, she looked for her water pouch, which she'd dropped on the ground. "I'll need to refill my pouch."

"I'll get Falk in the sky craft."

She glanced at him, and then they both stepped closer, looping their arms around each other.

He looked like he was going to speak, but in the end, neither of them said a word. He bent and kissed her, then let her go, looking upward again, alert and calm.

She jogged back to the stream, the weariness and fear she'd felt ever since she'd heard Xinta coming up behind her gone, replaced by determination and elation. She wasn't alone anymore—Garek had never stopped looking, had never let her down. And his presence was the sweetest comfort of all.

THIRTY

TAYA PACED the pilot's cabin.

Garek watched her walk out her agitation.

"What if Luci doesn't see the letter?" she asked suddenly, turning back to face him.

"She may not even reach the road before we can go back for her," Garek reminded her.

She nodded, leaned against the wall as if all the energy that kept her moving, kept her going, had drained away.

"At least Falk had pen and paper in his pack," she conceded. "And she should see the letter nailed to the tree when she gets to the end of the path." She closed her eyes, and when she opened them again, he patted his lap in invitation.

She smiled, a quick gleam lighting her eyes. "Don't you need to concentrate?"

"I can hold you and fly."

Her grin widened, and she walked over and slid across his thighs, curled in close. "Have you spoken to Kas?" she asked, and he felt her whole body tense again at the thought of her brother, and how he would be worrying.

"Yes." He ran a hand down her back. "He came with me to Garamundo. I dropped him back in Pan Nuk when I flew to Luf, though. He wanted to come with, but they needed him at home."

"He's tired," she said. "He'd been holding everything together for everyone for too long. I saw true despair in his eyes when Gaffri took me. I've worried about him ever since."

He rubbed a thumb gently back and forth across the back of her hand. Trust Taya to be worried about how her brother was coping with her abduction while she was being abducted.

A low moan from the corner broke the moment, and she lifted her head and then hopped off his lap.

Falk was on the pallet Deva had given them to take turns to sleep on while they flew.

Taya crouched beside him, and he opened his eyes. Closed them again. "Hurts."

"All I can tell you is that it will take time, but you'll feel better and better from now on. In a couple of hours, you'll be okay." Taya dipped into the pack beside him and took out a water pouch, lifted it to his lips.

He drank greedily, and then looked at the pouch in horror. "Not the one with the knife—?"

She chuckled. "No. That one is stored in the back, as far away from the console as possible."

"Did you destroy that sky craft?" he asked.

She nodded. "It would have taken us, otherwise."

He nodded morosely. "Just such a waste." He struggled up on his elbows. "Where are we?"

"Ten minutes outside Garamundo," Garek told him, and Falk flopped back down with a groan.

Garek felt like doing the same.

He was tired.

The adrenalin that had kept him going, kept him pushing until he found Taya, had at last subsided, and there would be no rest when they reached Gara.

They had a lot of information for Aidan and Vent.

He and Falk had spent the days since they'd left Luf flying the borders of Harven, Kadmine and Fabre, and it was clear the three states were cooperating with each other.

They'd spotted two newly established camps on their borders with all three guard uniforms present.

The numbers in the camps weren't that big—yet—but there was no good reason for the camps at all, unless the three states were planning a military action.

And now it seemed certain they were doing exactly that.

Garamundo came into sight in the distance, and Garek took an oblique angle as he approached the city walls, banking the sky craft as he circled around.

Taya rose up from beside Falk and leaned against the window, looking out.

"One of the buildings seems to have burned," she said, and Garek tipped the sky craft a little more so he could see.

"The guard barracks," he said, suddenly feeling the full weight of long nights and bone-chilling fear. This could not be good.

He headed to the Four Towers and landed in front of it, but this time he kept the engines on and waited to be approached.

Eventually, Vent appeared, a small cohort of guards with him, all of them with packs slung over their shoulders, and Garek opened up the back for them.

It seemed like Vent wanted a lift.

He didn't take off immediately, though. He waited for Vent to come through from the back.

The big barrel-chested guard master looked around the pilot's cabin, taking in Taya, Falk lying on the floor, and Garek at the controls, and gave a grunt of satisfaction. "Looks like you tracked your girl down."

Garek flicked a quick glance at Taya, and saw she had decided to be amused by the comment, rather than insulted.

"I need you to take us to Juli." Vent unhooked his pack. "Aidan already left a few days ago but if we go now, we probably won't be far behind him."

"There was trouble here?" Garek tipped his head in the direction of the guard barracks.

"A couple of idiots who were loyal to Utrel and the town master. They attacked the guard barracks, screaming about being promised trade favors, and unfortunately no one took them seriously until they set the place alight."

"Is it safe for you to leave with so much unrest?"

Vent sent him a hot look for questioning his decisions, and then shrugged. "Aidan made Nostra the new guard master of Gara. She'll keep things calm."

Taya turned away from them and looked back out the window.

She hadn't asked Garek, but he knew she would be desperate to get to Pan Nuk. To let her brother know she was safe.

So they would drop Vent off, and then go on to Pan Nuk. Maybe he could dust out his small room at the back of his father's forge and spend some time with Taya, just the two of them.

He realized he was pushing the craft faster than usual, and didn't let up.

The faster they reached Juli, the faster they could leave.

VENT HAD GOTTEN QUIETER, and more serious, as Garek and then Falk, had told him what they'd seen, and the information both Gern and Mu had given them, as well as Taya's own experience with Xinta and the sky raiders.

Taya watched him absorb the information, but she couldn't tell what he felt about it.

"What do you think Habred is getting out of the deal with the sky raiders?" he asked when Garek was done.

"Protection, Gern said." Falk spoke from his pallet. "Less attacks and fewer losses."

"Hmm." Vent nodded. "How do they communicate? If there were regular sightings of sky craft over Luf, I'd know about it."

Taya shifted against the window. "I know it started with a merchant who discovered a downed sky craft. I saw the wreck myself and it could be as much as a year old, maybe a little less than that. Maybe the merchant was drawn to it because he saw it fall, so he was on the scene when it came down. It's possible he came into contact with the sky raiders then, and they gave him something to communicate with."

Vent stared, his dark brown gaze boring into her. "This is just guesswork?"

She shrugged. "A good guess, though."

He shook his head, whether to clear it, or to reject her opinion, she didn't know.

"Maybe we can go back to those two craft you brought down, Taya, and pull them apart. See if there's a communication device to be found." Falk's voice lifted in enthusiastic excitement.

"You brought down two sky craft?" Vent was standing on the other side of the window to her, and he rounded on her, face hard.

His change of tack took her by surprise and she frowned at him. "Why the hostile tone?"

"You expect me to believe you brought down two sky craft?" Vent was incredulous.

"I don't expect you to believe anything, and I don't answer to you. Right now, Garek and I are doing you a favor."

"A favor?" He looked over at Garek. "This isn't your sky craft."

Garek flicked the guard master a glance. "Yes, Vent. It is."

Vent narrowed his eyes. "Falk, could you fly it?"

Falk laughed. "Right now? No. Not even if I hadn't been hit by white lightning, unless it was in the air, going forward. Garek's shown me how to keep it steady, and turn, and go up and down. In a few months, when I've had the chance to work out everything it does? Maybe I could take off and land. Maybe. But I'll never be better than Garek. Because half the time, he's calling his Change while he's flying it. I bet he ends up getting it to do things even the sky raiders don't know it can do."

Vent's face told Taya that wasn't the answer he'd been hoping for. He took a breath. "All right, then. Please could you tell me how you brought down two sky craft?" His smile was forced, his teeth showing, and his words were only just over the line into polite.

She sighed. "I couldn't have brought down the second one without Garek. I was inside the first one, so it was easier."

"Easier how?"

"I had a shadow ore knife on me, and shadow ore disrupts their systems."

He blinked. "Shadow ore?"

"The mineral they had us mining up on Shadow. We called it shadow ore." It was a shock that he didn't know about shadow ore. She thought Aidan would have told him, but perhaps he hadn't had time.

"Why would they want something that disrupts their systems?" Vent asked.

She shrugged. "Maybe they're fighting each other, back on their home planet. As I've shown, it makes a good weapon."

He digested that in silence for a while. "How did you use the shadow ore to bring them down?"

"Ran the blade along the console."

He mulled that. "So anyone with a shadow ore knife could have done it?"

She nodded.

Garek was looking at her, head cocked to the side, as if he was surprised she wasn't mentioning her Change. She met his gaze and his lips twitched.

"And Garek helped with the second one?" The way Vent asked, she could tell by 'help' he assumed Garek had mostly done it himself. She looked over at Garek again and saw the amusement in his eyes.

He'd heard the innuendo, too.

"Yes."

"And was it absolutely necessary to destroy both of them? We could have had another sky craft." Now he spoke directly to Garek.

"It was necessary, unless we wanted to be dragged back to Shadow." Garek didn't even look his way, his gaze focused on flying.

"I wanted to save one of them," Falk said. "Which is how I came to be shot. If Taya and Garek hadn't been there, I'd have been on my way to Shadow right now."

Vent gave a grunt at that. "And you're sure about the cooperation between Harven, Kadmine and Fabre?"

"Unless someone is running around in border camps in uniforms they have no right to wear." Garek dipped the sky craft, and Taya realized they had already reached Juli.

"I'd hoped it was just Harven," Vent said. He rubbed a hand over his leather chest plate. "I know Vaar said Kadmine and Fabre were involved, but I hoped he was lying. It looks like we're in big trouble."

It sounded like he thought they wouldn't be able to survive an attack from all three. Which she supposed made sense. West Lathor was no bigger than any of the other states, and it had been neglected for the last two years.

"What's the chance we can get the Illian Council to intervene?" Falk asked.

Vent shook his head. "For it to have gotten this far, my guess is the Council have watched Valtor slowly abdicate all responsibility while refusing to let his children take over. They probably think it'll be a good thing for West Lathor to be taken over by lieges who are more involved."

"And what will they think of Habred betraying us all by doing a deal with the sky raiders?" Taya asked.

Vent lifted his shoulders. "Hard to prove that, and it's a massive accusation. No one will want to believe it."

"It's the truth, though," Falk pointed out. "So there is proof of it, somewhere."

"Good luck getting the council to even hear the charge." Vent dismissed that as an option. "What we need is to get the Iron Guard back."

"What are the chances of that?" Garek asked. He sounded as if he thought chances were slim, and Taya wondered what he knew about the Iron Guard.

While they were on Shadow, she, Quardi and Kas had worked out that West Lathor's famous Iron Guard had to be made up of people who could call a similar Change to her. The only difference being their element was iron.

The legends and stories that always accompanied the Iron Guard suddenly made sense when seen in relation to her own newfound abilities.

She suddenly realized she'd never told Garek about that, about what she had discovered. She would have to find time.

Vent made a face at Garek's question. "I don't know what the chances of getting them back are. After Olla, the liege's wife, died, General Hanson presented Voltar with an ultimatum—he either met certain demands, or she was going to disband the unit. She didn't like his answer and they were gone the next day. Just . . . gone."

"Do you have a way to get in touch with her?" Falk stood, wobbly on his legs, but looking stronger all the time.

Vent lifted a single shoulder. "Aidan might."

As Garek swooped down to land on the palace wall, the look on his face told Taya he didn't think that was true.

THIRTY-ONE

DARTAN WAS WAITING for them when they landed. The liege's advisor looked grim, dressed all in black, face frowning.

Garek lowered the back of the sky craft and walked down with Taya behind Vent and his small team of guards, to meet him.

They waited for the guards to disperse, and Taya urged Falk to go in search of a doctor to look him over.

When the only ones left were himself, Taya, Dartan and Vent, there was a moment of silence.

"Where's Aidan?" Aidan, of anyone in this place, would care if he'd found Taya and that she was safe. It bothered Garek that he was nowhere in sight.

"He's with the liege." There was something there, just under what Dartan was saying, but Garek couldn't quite grasp it and Vent had already launched into his report.

Dartan's face turned grimmer still as Vent finished his news on the troubles brewing in Gara, and gestured to Garek.

"These two have their own bad news."

Dartan turned his scowl on them both.

"The most important is that Habred has a deal with the sky raiders," Taya said.

Dartan staggered back, as if she'd punched him.

"A deal?" His voice dipped, and he was forced to clear his throat.

"He provided some of his own people to the sky raiders for them to test their weapons on so they could calibrate them to knock us out but not kill us, and then he gave up the position of the Harven villagers we rescued from Shadow so the sky raiders could take them back."

Dartan's gaze darted around, as if he needed an anchor to keep his balance. "Why? What is he getting out it?"

"We don't know, but at a guess, minimal raids on Luf, and some promise of help in taking over West Lathor. Because it's confirmed he's planning on doing that."

"This is . . ." Dartan ran a shaking hand over his head. "Treachery." He spun on his heel, then looked back over his shoulder. "I need to think on this. I'll need you to put down all your proof for me when you can." He walked away, but no longer with the ground-eating, arrogant stride he'd had before. He was like a man lost.

"I never thought he'd take that so hard." Vent looked after him thoughtfully. "I'll need to go in, see what's happened in my absence. You staying here?"

Garek shook his head. "We want to talk to Aidan, so tell him to come up as soon as he can, and then we'll go on to Pan Nuk."

Vent nodded and disappeared down the stairs to the palace below.

He and Taya moved back into the pilot's chamber, closing up the back and settling in to wait.

Minutes ticked by, turning into half an hour, and then an hour.

Taya shifted restlessly from her position by the window, scanning the skies for any hint of sky raiders. "What could be keeping him?"

"Maybe he's letting the liege know he's taking over. That would be a delicate conversation, not easily rushed." Garek wondered why Vent hadn't come to let him know it would be a long wait, though.

Taya stiffened, gaze focused upward. "Sky raiders."

Garek didn't question it, he simply shot them straight into the air, then tipped the craft to one side and spiraled upward, searching for the enemy.

He saw them, flying low to the right of the city, over the big open road to the south west, and was momentarily shocked. He knew that approach, that style. He'd seen it on the walls of Gara often enough.

"They're attacking someone on the road. Do you think they don't realize we're here?"

"What can we do to them?" Taya asked. "We don't know how to activate the white lightning, and we couldn't anyway, because we'd only hurt the people on the ground. I don't think the white lightning affects the sky craft, does it?"

She was right, but the brazen nature of the attack shocked him.

From the sky, they watched the sky craft shoot out white lightning at a big group of people walking along the road. Just as Taya said, they were powerless to stop it.

"Is that . . .?" Taya pressed up against the glass. "The Kardanx? Going back home?"

Something dark and icy gripped Garek by the throat. They were stealing the Kardanx back, just like they'd planned to steal Luci and her villagers. Pan Nuk had to be next, if it wasn't too late already.

"We have to land," he said, and it was only at her definitive nod that he realized he felt sick at the thought of doing what was right. Because it would put Taya directly in harm's way.

They would be exposed on the ground. They could be taken.

He did it anyway, landing behind a stand of trees beside the road. The sky raiders would have to be blind not to have seen them, but they wouldn't have easy access to the sky craft, either. It would take time to find it and steal it back, if he and Taya lost this gamble.

They scrambled out, the engines still running, and she fell into step with him as they jogged toward the road.

They could hear screaming, and then the terrible silence as it was cut off.

The first shot of white lightning hadn't brought everyone down, was his guess, and now they were out of the sky craft and were picking off people individually with the small, hand-held devices.

Three men appeared through the trees, running from the road, eyes wide with fear.

They reared back at the first sight of Taya and Garek, shocked, and then stumbled forward, relieved.

Garek didn't recognize them from Shadow, but Taya nodded to them as if she did.

"Keep to the trees."

They nodded, their breathing harsh and stuttering, and they disappeared down the tree line, moving in the direction of Juli.

Garek slowed when the road became visible between the trees. There was a glint of metal as the Star light reflected off the sky craft and someone was sobbing, somewhere close by.

Taya drew out her knife and tried to hand him the device she had in her jacket pocket, but he shook his head. He wanted her to keep it.

They stepped into the open.

Up ahead of them, the back of the sky craft faced them, ramp lowered, taking up the whole road.

Like there had been on the road out of Luf, there were two sky raiders, dressed in thick blue suits with helmets. One stood guard, white lightning device ready, while the other dragged Kardanx two at a time up the ramp and into the back.

There were very few Kardanx left lying on the road. They had already loaded most of them.

This close to the city, he guessed they knew they had to move quickly.

Garek turned to Taya, saw her arm was already back. She threw the knife, sending it high into the air.

He frowned, trying to work out where she was aiming, and then the knife came down on the sky raider who was standing guard from above, the knife hitting the top of his helmet. It flew straight up again and curved in a graceful arc back to her.

The guard's reaction was immediate. He started visibly, hands going to his helmet, but then he raised his arm and shot his device at the ground to get his copilot's attention. The second sky raider turned, let go of the two Kardanx he was dragging, and they ran into the craft.

The door started to close, and Garek fought it, calling his Change and driving a wedge of air in to keep the door open.

He ran toward the craft, but it didn't need the back closed up to take off, as he knew very well, and it rose up, turning around to face them as it lifted up.

He hammered down on the craft and it tilted drunkenly, but this was a big transport, not the smaller fighter craft he'd managed to smash out of the sky before, and it didn't go down.

Taya threw her knife again.

It flew past him, and he used his Change to help it along, so it hit the glass at the front of the sky craft with a crack.

The craft lifted even higher, and he buffeted it with winds, putting all his strength into slamming it down.

It dipped again, but as it did, it shot white lightning at them.

No. Not at them.

"Garek. Stop." Taya reached out and grabbed him by the arm, her face a mask of fierce concentration. Her knife came flying back. "They're shooting at the Kardanx they haven't taken. They'll die if the sky raiders keep that up."

It's what the sky raiders had threatened to do to him when they'd stolen back the sky craft on the palace roof the night they'd brought the Kardanx and Aidan to Juli.

He stopped, and Taya stepped out more fully into the center of the road and lifted her arm, knife raised high. The sky craft hovered in place, the faint crack in its windscreen clearly visible.

It was a standoff.

He came and stood behind her, hands curling lightly around her waist, ready to call his Change and lift them up out of the way if the sky raiders tried to shoot again.

Taya waggled the knife at them, and with a scream of engines, the sky craft rose higher, turning east, and then accelerated away.

For a moment, the only sound was the retreating whine of its engine.

Garek stepped back, and Taya turned to him, her face stamped with raw horror.

"They've taken them." She looked around her, and he saw tears on her cheeks.

The bodies of the Kardanx lay all around them, at least twenty men.

There had been around eighty Kardanx on Shadow, but all of the women, what few there had been among them, and some of the men, had chosen to stay in Juli, and there were the three who'd managed to escape. Which meant there might be as many as fifty in the back of the sky craft.

Taya took his hand and squeezed it before dropping to a crouch beside a man. She placed her fingers against his neck.

"He's breathing."

But as they moved through the victims, they found some who weren't. The second hit of white lightning had struck those closest to the sky craft, and there were six who must have caught the brunt of it.

A shout from down the road had Garek rising to his feet, tense and ready.

A group approached, most riding zanir, but there were also guards sitting inside two carts.

Vent was at the front, and Garek saw Dom, the Kardanx man he'd taught to fly the other sky craft so they could escape Shadow, was next to him.

The one person he expected but didn't see, again, was Aidan.

"Where's Aidan?" he asked Vent, but the guard master shook his head in a surreptitious movement, and mouthed: *Later.*

"We saw . . ." Dom looked around at the bodies. "I watched them leaving from the ramparts. We said our goodbyes at the gates and then I climbed the stairs to watch them from the wall, and then we saw . . ."

He slid off his zanir and walked forward on stiff legs. "This is my cousin." Like Taya had done, he put a hand to his neck, and sucked in a breath when he registered the pulse.

"There are six dead." Garek let his gaze move past Vent to the others looking around in shock.

Someone had given the sky raiders the day, even the hour, of the Kardanx departure. This could not possibly be a coincidence. And of everyone here, Vent was the only one off the hook.

He'd been in Gara.

No matter what method of communication there was between the sky raiders and the traitors in their midst, Vent would have had no time to pass the message on.

But someone had.

"How long has their trip been planned?" Garek asked Dom, and he looked up from his place on the ground at his cousin's side.

"Since last week," Dom said. "Why do you—?" He went absolutely still. "You think the sky raiders were *waiting* for them?"

"They were waiting for Luci and all the villagers from Cassinya," Taya said, her gaze meeting Garek's in quick agreement. "It seems a little much to think they simply got very lucky both times."

"That's quite an accusation." Vent scowled at him, and Garek realized the other guards and spectators in the group were staring at him in horror.

"You tell me, then, how were they right here to swoop down on the Kardanx just when they were outside the protection of the city, in a nice, easy-to-scoop-up group?"

"Someone told them? How? Who would do that?" The voice came from among the guards.

"That's for you to find out," Garek told Vent. "Taya and I have to make sure Pan Nuk is safe."

He realized he should have warned her somehow before he

spoke, but it was too late. Taya gasped, eyes wide, as she realized what he was saying, as she worked out what he'd already realized.

The sky raiders had made a plan to take back their old prisoners. And why should Pan Nuk be any different from the rest?

THIRTY-TWO

TAYA COULDN'T SPEAK, her throat so tight she could barely swallow as Garek piloted the sky craft faster than she could remember it ever going before.

They came over the pass and dropped toward Pan Nuk, engines screaming as Garek pulled back, slowed down, and then landed just outside the village.

It looked empty, but then, they would hide at the sound of a sky craft, they couldn't know it was her and Garek.

She held on to that excuse as the door opened and she threw herself out.

"Kas!" Her shout seemed to be swallowed up, weak and faint, and she dropped to the ground and ran down the street.

Behind her, the sky craft shut down and then she heard Garek coming after her.

"Kas! Luca!"

"Taya."

Taya sagged, would have fallen, except Garek was there, grabbing her from behind and lifting her up, holding her against him as Kas, and Luca, and Min, too, stepped out from behind one of the houses and ran toward her.

"We were so afraid . . ." Taya held out her arms as she found her own feet and Luca threw himself at her. Garek caught her again as the weight of her nephew made her stagger back.

She hugged him so tight he made a sound of protest and she eased up a little and raised her head.

Kas was looking at her, and there was such a mixture of emotions on his face she went still. "What is it?"

"The sky raiders attacked."

Behind her, she felt Garek stiffen.

"Did they get anyone?"

Kas gave a nod, and swallowed. It was Min who answered, though, her voice ragged.

"They got Eli, they got Noor. They got everyone who was standing guard duty on the hill. They got a few others who were working in the fields." She kneaded her skirt with restless hands. "We heard them coming. Eli had some of your spears, Taya. He carried them with him whenever he was out.

"He couldn't throw them hard enough, though, and they hit him with white lightning. Kas had the idea a few days ago to make shallow hiding places all over the village, to make it hard for them to find us. He used his Change and dug them, so most of us went to ground, and Quardi and Kas took a few of your spears and waited for the sky raiders at the end of the village, but they didn't try to come in. They left with whoever they could grab in the field." There was a wobbly, unhappy quaver to her voice.

"How many in all?" Garek's hands were still holding Taya up, and now they tightened.

"About twenty."

"When?" It couldn't have been after they'd attacked the Kardanx. She and Garek would have beaten them here.

"Two days ago." Kas rubbed his face, and it looked as if he hadn't slept since it happened.

"They were waiting for Luci and her people on the road to Cassinya. And we just came from Juli, where they grabbed all the Kardanx traveling on their way home."

There was utter silence, but Taya looked past Kas, and saw most of the villagers had stepped out from their hiding places now, too.

"They wanted us all back," Min said. "Because we know how to do the work."

Garek dipped his head. "They didn't get Luci. Taya stopped them. And they only got about fifty of the Kardanx. That means they have a total of seventy prisoners up there."

Taya straightened, her arms dropping from around Luca. "That means we can fit everyone in one sky craft."

Garek met her gaze, nodded.

"You're going to get them back?" Min's mouth opened in astonishment.

Taya felt the cold grip of terror in her gut at the thought, but she nodded her head decisively. "Of course we are."

WHILE GAREK and Kas argued about who would come on the rescue mission, Taya looped an arm around Luca and another around Min, and found her way to Quardi's forge.

He was still in his wheelchair, and his forge was not the same, efficient place it had been, but she could see that he had started cleaning it up, and a fire burned bright. Pilar sat on an upturned bucket. His gaze met hers, and he tried to smile.

"I'm glad you're safe, Taya."

She knelt in front of him and hugged him close. "We'll get Noor back, don't worry."

He made a sound, completely forlorn, and she didn't think he'd heard her.

A hand landed on her shoulder and she looked into Quardi's grizzled face.

"We thought we'd lost you." Quardi's voice was gruff. "When Kas didn't come back straightaway, we knew things were bad." She turned to hug him, too, and he gently touched the side of her head. "You would have felt that."

She smiled. "It put me on my back for a few days. Meant Gaffri and Fek had to carry me through the mountains. It slowed them down."

Quardi didn't smile back. "Where are they now?"

She slid a look at Luca, who was hanging on every word. "They're gone," she said, and saw Quardi understood what she meant.

"That's a pity." He drew in a breath and shook his head. "What's this about getting Noor back?"

"We can't leave Eli and Noor up there. We can't leave anyone up there. They've got fifty Kardanx, twenty of our own. We have to go get them."

Pilar raised his head as if what they were saying had finally penetrated. "What's this? Go back? To Shadow?" He looked like someone who'd just woken up and found the whole world changed.

"There's enough room for everyone they've taken to fit into one sky craft," Taya said, and met his gaze. "And we have one sky craft."

Min made a sound, and crouched down. "Taya, I know we have to go back but . . ." She shared a look with Quardi. "I am afraid for you."

Taya slid an arm back around Luca. "I'm afraid, too. We'll need to plan it. But there is one thing that's good about it."

"What?" Min looked like she couldn't think of a single thing.

"I can get some more shadow ore for myself." If they were going up there, she would take as much ore as she could. Their sky craft was already beginning to bubble with rust, and it wouldn't last forever. The day would come when it wasn't going to be safe to fly, and then her chance of getting more ore would be gone forever.

"There was some shadow ore in the Dartalian Range. I could feel it. But it wasn't concentrated, it was just a tiny proportion of the other minerals there. This is an opportunity to get as much as possible, with very little effort."

Quardi was looking at her with a thoughtful expression. "We'll need wooden boxes."

"Anything that holds water without leaking, but yes, the wooden boxes worked."

"Luca," Quardi turned to her nephew. "Spread the word, I need people to help Taya. Tell them to come here for instructions."

Luca's face split into a grin, and he turned on his heel and ran out.

"I'll go talk to Garek, then I'll come back to help, too." Pilar all but ran out the forge.

"Taya, I'm going to ask you for a favor." Min looked down at the ground, cheeks flushed red. "Please, don't let Kas go with you. He can barely think straight, he's so tired. And Luca . . ." She closed her eyes. "Luca shouldn't lose him a second time."

THIRTY-THREE

TAYA EVENTUALLY WON THE FIGHT.

Garek had tried, but he realized he should have given the floor to Taya from the beginning.

It hadn't even taken that long.

She had simply walked up to Kas, taken his hand and leaned against him, and whispered in his ear.

Kas had closed his eyes, dropped his cheek onto Taya's head, and given a huge sigh. And just like that, the battle was over.

"Who will you take, then, if not me?" he asked as he raised his head and Taya stepped back.

"Me."

They turned, surprised, and Jerilia lifted her chin angrily. "I'm as good as any."

"It's not that," Garek told her. "I didn't think you'd want to go back."

She deflated a little. "I can't get it out of my head. It keeps whirling round and round when I close my eyes. Sometimes even when I don't close my eyes. I want to do something to hurt them. I feel like going back and beating them again is the only way this will stop."

"We have to be able to count on you," Garek said. "When I give an instruction, I need to know you'll follow it through. That you can do it."

She gave a sharp nod. "I give you my word."

"I'm going." Pilar made it a statement, not a request.

Garek nodded to him. There was no way he would stand in the way when it came to Pilar and Noor.

"I want to go, too." Lynal stepped forward. "Eli watched out for me on Shadow, kept me positive. I owe him."

Lynal had run with Kas all the way to Gara looking for Taya, and for that, Garek would forever be in his debt.

"You heard what I told Jerilia?"

Lynal nodded. "I give my word, too."

"What's the plan?" Kas asked, seeming more centered now that the decision had been made.

Garek hesitated. If he could, he would try to persuade Taya not to go. He felt a terrible, yawning pit in his stomach at the thought of her back on Shadow, of her back in the sky raiders' hands. It made it hard to think clearly about anything else.

"Taya and I both need to sleep, even if just for a few hours. We've had a grueling few days." He needed time to reason with her. And in truth, he really was exhausted. Night had fallen an hour ago, and he couldn't remember the last full night's sleep he'd gotten.

"Quardi is organizing boxes for me, anyway." Taya pushed a few tendrils of hair off her face. "We can't go until they're ready. We can use the ones we made on Shadow, but I'd like a few more as well."

"Boxes?" Kas asked.

"To bring back more shadow ore for me."

Garek nodded slowly. Why not? More ammunition against the sky raiders, more of Taya's element to sustain her. But she didn't have to be there to supervise getting more ore. It was piled in a heap outside the mine.

"We need food and water, enough for everyone they've abducted, and the boxes should probably be filled with water in advance, so we're sure they don't leak by the time we get to Shadow. If you can organize that while we sleep, Kas, then we'll leave at dawn."

"You only want to take three of us?" Jerilia asked.

Garek shook his head. "I need to let Aidan know what we're doing, and I have a feeling some of the guards in Juli might consider this trip an unmissable experience."

For the first time, Kas relaxed, and Garek realized he'd been afraid they were going with too small and inexperienced a force.

"We can only take at most another four," he reminded them. "But the Juli guard master, Vent, is sure to have some well trained volunteers."

That decided, they all went their separate ways.

He led Taya to his room behind the forge, which his father had set more or less to rights.

Quardi had filled the small tub with the hot water he always had to hand, and they took turns bathing, and then, naked, clean, and alone at last, he drew Taya onto his bed.

"Something is worrying you," she said as she tucked herself against his side.

He hesitated. "You going to Shadow worries me."

She was quiet, giving him time to explain.

"I know all the reasons why you should come, but I don't want you to. I want you safe here."

"Last time you left me safe here, I was taken away."

Her words made him flinch.

She tilted her head up to look at him. "I'm not saying that was your fault, I'm saying nowhere is safe until this is over. I'd rather be with you, and using my Change to help, than sitting here worrying about you, just as, you have to admit, you will be worrying about me, even if I stay right here in Pan Nuk."

She *was* right, and yet . . .

"Don't ask me to stay, Garek. Understand staying here, worrying about you, would be torture for me. And there are as many dangers here as on Shadow, but at least on Shadow, we'll have each other."

He had no answer to that. And he had to admit, while fear for her still twisted him up, something in him also relaxed at the idea of her being right beside him.

He pulled her closer, trying to enjoy the fact that they were here together, warm, safe, and comfortable.

Tomorrow, they would be none of those things.

AS THEY FLEW toward Juli Taya realized Pilar, Lynal and Jerilia had never seen the water city before.

Even when approaching the city by road—something she'd done a year ago to attend Aidan's sister's wedding—it was breathtaking, but coming in from the air, its full magnificence was revealed.

The way it rose out of and above the cliff, the way Corinnda's Hair fell in two waterfalls on either side of the city, tumbling and roaring down into the massive lake below.

All three of them leaned against the window and pressed their faces closer.

Garek, face still grim, still tight with unhappiness, landed them lightly on the massive palace wall, and Taya put out a tentative hand to touch his shoulder.

He brought up his own hand, curled his fingers around hers, but it didn't ease the worry on his face.

She didn't think anything less than her staying behind would do that, and even then, he would worry ceaselessly about whether she was safe here, too.

She tightened her grip for a moment, unable to offer any other comfort, and then looked out the window to see who would come up to greet them.

Dom and Vent.

And about ten guards.

Dartan brought up the rear. He looked as if he'd aged since they'd last spoken to him, only a day ago. His chiseled features looked stark, now; the grooves on either side of his mouth deeper.

Again, Aidan was nowhere in sight.

Garek opened the door, but he made no move to leave, so she stayed where she was, too.

It forced Vent and Dom to come to them.

"Someone out there is a traitor," Garek said. "I'm not saying anything where it can be overheard."

She hadn't even thought of that, but it was true. Someone in Juli had told the sky raiders when the Kardanx were leaving for home. And in a city full of suspects, Vent had her and Garek as an alibi, and Dom was the last person who would have done such a thing to his own people.

Vent climbed in, looking angry. Dom was just behind him, but he was harder to read. His hands were restless, though. He rubbed them together, gripped them, twined his fingers together. It was the only part of him not utterly still.

"Don't let Dartan in," Garek said to Vent, and the guard master's head came up in outrage.

"We know you and Dom are not traitors, but he could be. Every time I think of his reaction to the information about Habred having a deal with the sky raiders, I wonder why he took it so badly."

Vent opened his mouth, closed it, and leaned back out the door.

Whatever he said, they could all hear Dartan's protest.

"Move away from the door," Garek said, and Vent pulled in, turning with a look that said he'd had enough of orders.

Garek closed the door and shot the sky craft up to hover over the river.

"There, now there's no way he can listen."

Dom and Vent gaped at Garek, but Taya grinned, and Lynal, Pilar and Jerilia didn't bother hiding their amusement, either.

"You're serious in suspecting him?" Vent's anger turned to a scowl.

"It was as if he felt a physical blow at the news yesterday." Taya had also thought the liege's advisor's reaction had been unusual.

"If he's in league with the sky raiders, he would know about their deal with Habred, though," Jerilia said.

Taya shook her head. "Why would they tell him who else they were dealing with? If he thought he was the only one, then finding out Habred had a secret deal, too, would have come as a nasty shock. It might have occurred to him that the sky raiders are playing the states off against each other, and the only winner is going to be them."

Dom was watching them with his mouth open. "You think Dartan told the sky raiders when my people were leaving?" He looked out of the window, down to the palace wall, where Dartan was staring up, fury in every line, and his features hardened. "If it is true . . ."

"If it is true, he's betrayed the whole of West Lathor, as well as your people." Vent's voice was firm. "He'll be punished."

Dom didn't look as if that answer satisfied him, but he kept quiet, hands curled into fists now and still at his sides.

"So what did you want to say out of Dartan's hearing?" Vent turned back to Garek.

"We're going to Shadow to get everyone back. They took about twenty people from Pan Nuk, as well the Kardanx. There should be enough room for everyone in the back of this sky craft."

Dom turned slowly. "You're going back for them?" His voice was low, and strained with emotion.

"Of course we are, Dom." Taya stepped forward, put a hand on his arm, and Jerilia touched his shoulder.

The Kardanx bowed his head, and Taya saw him swallow hard.

At the news, Vent was silent for a long beat. He looked them all over with that cold, assessing gaze of his. "This is who you're taking?" His comment was to Garek, but he was looking at Taya and the other three when he spoke.

"If you've got up to four guards who'd like to come along, we have room for them."

"Oh, I have them." Vent turned to face Garek again. "I'm going to be one of them."

"So am I," Dom said. "Besides the fact that they're my people, and it's best to have at least one Kardanx in the rescue team, I can help you fly the sky craft."

Garek looked between them, then focused on Vent. "You'd be leaving the city in the hands of someone who might be a traitor."

Vent lifted his shoulders. "I have no proof. We could be wrong. And there is no way I'm giving up an opportunity to see Shadow."

"This is about rescuing people, not a holiday." Dom's voice was sharp, harder than Taya had ever heard it.

Vent blinked in the shock at the attack from such a soft-spoken quarter. "I'm the guard master of Juli," he said, voice equally cold. "I know exactly what this is. But this enemy is not going away any time soon, and I want to see them up close."

Silence settled in for an uncomfortably long time.

"As long as you understand I'll be giving the orders," Garek said eventually, "then I'll be happy to have a guard of your experience along."

Vent stiffened at the idea of taking orders from Garek.

"I've been there, I planned the last rescue. Either agree to follow my lead, or don't come."

Eventually, Vent inclined his head.

"Do you have two others who will want to come?" Taya asked him to diffuse the tension that was thick in the air. "What about Aidan? Where is he?"

He looked at her, face pinched in disapproval. "Aidan is tied up with his father. I've got a whole barracks of guards who would want to come. It would be better if you and your friends stayed behind, and others more qualified took your place."

"You really don't know how qualified we are," Taya said, and Dom's lips twitched. He caught her gaze for a moment, and she saw a gleam in his eyes.

"Taya doesn't answer to you, and she has her reasons for coming."

Garek looked like each word was spoken around a rock in his throat. He would love to take up Vent's suggestion, and leave her behind. She could see it. But not because he thought her incapable, like Vent did. Because he feared for her. Wanted her safe.

She decided to forgive him because of that.

"Everyone in this craft has the right to be here. More right than you." She spoke to Vent in her calmest voice. "Now, you can choose two guards to come, or we can go right now. It's up to you."

"Set down, I'll get two guards. But Dartan will want to come up while we wait for them, what do we tell him?"

"I'll tell him I want to speak to Aidan, that I've been over the border again, and there is a group of Fabre guards moving toward West Lathor. That we want to check it out."

"He'll want to know why I'm coming with you," Dom said.

Taya shook her head. "As you said, you can help Garek with flying."

Vent nodded. "It's as good an excuse as any. Maybe send these three to the back," he pointed to Lynal, Pilar and Jerilia. "No need for him to see them. Their presence makes the incursion into Fabre less believable."

Garek looked over at them, and with a tight nod, Pilar led the way to the back.

"You, too," Vent said to Taya.

She hesitated. "No. He knows Garek and I have just found each other again."

"He won't believe a guard like Garek would take someone who isn't a guard into a combat situation. I can't understand why Garek's letting you go to Shadow. No matter how much you dress up as a guard, it doesn't mean you've had the training. You shouldn't be allowed to wear that." Vent flicked a hand at her guard's trousers and shirt, his words intended to cut.

"This was what I had available to wear on Shadow," Taya told him, her voice even and quiet. "And I fought the sky raiders, along with everyone else, when we escaped. I've fought them since I got back, too. I've faced more sky raiders in combat than you."

"Enough." Garek gaze snapped to Vent. "Accept Taya will be coming, or again, we can take someone else other than you. As for Dartan, I'm happy to tell him I'm dropping Taya at home in Pan Nuk before we set out, if you think that will make him less suspicious."

Vent threw his hands into the air. "Fine. Put us back on the ground, and I'll get my two guards. And prepare to deal with Dartan at his most irritating."

As Garek lowered the sky craft, Taya guessed that Dartan in a snit would be no more pleasant than Vent.

She glanced at Garek, and saw the unhappiness had given way to worry.

She felt the same.

The Aidan she knew would be up here, in the thick of things—curious to have all the information she and Garek brought with them first hand.

Maybe he was tied up with his father. Or maybe he was in trouble.

THIRTY-FOUR

IT WAS A RELIEF TO LEAVE.

Garek streaked away from Juli with a deepening sense that all was not well with Aidan.

There was little he could do about it, though. So he'd have to trust that the princeling could take care of himself for a while.

Dartan had huffed and puffed, but he couldn't find a good reason for them not to investigate the lie Garek told him about the Fabre incursion, and he was unwilling to push too hard against it, afraid, Garek was sure, that he would be ignored, which would leave him stripped of authority.

Garek recognized the two guards Vent had picked as being from the Day Command, Nostra's team, who'd run all the way back from Pan Nuk to report on Taya's abduction.

They were introduced as Lena and Fen, and when they'd learned their true destination was Shadow, not Kadmine, they had been thrilled. With Nostra in Garamundo, Garek guessed they had the option of joining her there, or vying to replace her as Day Commander.

This trip would give them an opportunity to shine.

They both watched Taya with interest, and Garek wondered if they'd spent enough time in Pan Nuk to have heard about the Change she could call. If they had, they hadn't told Vent, but it was possible they didn't realize their guard master didn't know.

Keeping it from him had been part of the overall strategy of keeping it secret from everyone, exacerbated by his dismissive attitude toward Taya. But they would have to tell him when they made their plan of attack.

Garek's lips lifted a little at the corners.

The thought of Vent having to swallow his words when it came to Taya made him want to smile.

DOM FLEW to give Garek a rest, and Taya walked over to keep him company while Garek slept.

"You seemed to be closer to the Kardanx men who were leaving Juli than you were before." She hadn't expected such a personal response from him when he'd ridden out of the city to help.

His lips twisted in a sardonic smile. "Some of them."

He leaned back in the pilot's chair. "My father left straight away, he didn't wait for anyone. He tried one last time to get my mother to return to him, and when she refused, he disappeared. But I reached a peace of sorts with the others."

"They decided to stay?"

He nodded. "Aidan offered us a permanent place in Juli if we wanted, or to put us up for a few weeks to get back our strength, and make preparations for the long journey home. My mother and the other women all decided to stay in Juli." He paused. "Aidan offered me a position as Kardanx Liaison to West Lathor." He gave a humorless smile. "My plan is to write the whole of our story in a missive, send it to the *haidai* council and let them know all communications between Kardai and West Lathor must now come through me."

He sat in silence for a moment, and Taya could see he was enjoying thinking about the consternation that would cause.

"Most of the men chose to return home, more because it's what's familiar. They made peace with those of us who wanted to stay—they knew why. What happened—killing all the women—and then seeing the living proof of how it could have been if they hadn't done it by looking at your and Luci's people . . . it has shaken them all. Fayda keeps to himself these days, he isn't a leader of the group any more. I think he feels the weight of the blame."

"Was he one of the ones who was retaken?" Taya couldn't remember seeing the Kardanx elder among the men lying in the road after the sky raiders had left.

Dom nodded. "He wasn't on the road, so he must have been."

Jerilia and Lynal had come closer while Dom spoke, listening to his story, but the two guards and Vent sat against a wall, dozing. Pilar sat by the window, looking out at Shadow, getting closer and closer.

Maybe too close.

She walked through to the back, crouched down beside the pallet where Garek was sleeping, and hesitated, her hand hovering just above his shoulder.

His eyes opened, completely aware and awake. "What is it?"

"Shadow's getting close." She let her hand drop down, smoothed it over his shoulder, and he caught it, bent his head and kissed her palm.

She stepped back, hand still in his, and pulled him up. For a moment they stood, tight in each other's arms, and then Garek pulled back reluctantly.

"I better go see."

They walked into the pilot's chamber, and as they entered, Vent rose up, as alert and awake as Garek, although Taya would have sworn he was almost asleep before.

"What is the plan?" As Vent spoke, his two guards, Lena and Fen, rose up as well, seemingly ready for anything.

Garek looked out at Shadow, and gave a nod. "We hit the mine first, like we did last time. If we time our arrival to just before shift end, they may simply assume we're a little early."

"And when the real transporter arrives?" Vent asked.

"If we can take it, we will. Dom can fly it back."

Dom shook his head. "I was serious when I said I never wanted to fly one again. It's different when you're helping me, and the journey between the planets is all right, but half the time when we fled Shadow, I *know* I wasn't in control of the craft. I thought I was going to kill everyone in a terrible crash from the moment we got to Barit, and I never want to go through that again."

Garek nodded. "Then we destroy it."

Vent's lips thinned. "We should take it back."

"Then you can fly it, if you like," Dom told him. "I won't."

Vent grunted, but not in defeat.

Taya had the feeling he planned to work on Dom and try to wear him down, but he had the sense to realize a confrontation now would only make the Kardanx dig his heels in deeper.

"How do you know when shift end is? Where the mine is?" Lena asked.

"We worked shifts in the mine for four months," Pilar said, still sitting unmoving beside the window. "We know."

There was silence at his words.

"So, you pretend to be there to pick up the miners," Vent said, to prompt Garek to continue.

"We come down the ramp like we're the shift change," Garek said, "and as soon as Taya is far enough away from the craft, she takes her knife out of the water pouch, and she sends it straight to the guards on watch."

"Why her? Either Lena or Fen would be more accurate."

"No," Garek said, and there was a hint of laughter in his voice which had her looking across at him. "There were two guards last time, if there still are, then we'll need Taya, because once she hits the first guard, she can send the knife to the second one immediately, without having to fetch it back."

"How can she do that?" Vent's tone was incredulous.

"She calls the Change with shadow ore."

Vent stared at Garek, then swung his gaze to Taya. "You call the Change with shadow ore?" His voice was locked down, completely calm. "What does that mean?"

"It means I can manipulate it. Direct it through the air."

He said nothing more, but she shivered, feeling the anger radiating off him.

"You were so sure you knew everything about her," Garek told him, and the humor was gone from his voice. "We never said anything about her abilities publicly, because Aidan and I were afraid she would be in danger because of it. And we were right, it's why Habred had her abducted. You feel foolish because you've tried to ridicule her, and now you discover she has a rare power. If you'd been less confrontational from the beginning, more curious and less derogatory, we may have chosen to trust you. As it was, you gave us no reason to do that."

Vent's face flushed, Taya couldn't tell whether from embarrassment or fury, but eventually he gave a curt nod.

Garek nodded back, and then continued as if their little aside had never taken place.

"As soon as Taya throws the knife, we need to split into three groups. One to grab more shadow ore from the stockpile to use against any sky raiders at the mine site and to later load into the boxes we've brought. Another group needs to get into the mine, round everyone up and get them to the entrance, and the last group needs to make sure the guards die and don't have time to call for help."

He looked up. "Dom, you and Pilar go into the mine. Get everyone out."

Taya saw Pilar relax at the order. He'd want to see if Noor was working in the mine. No one would be more motivated to get the workers out.

"Jerilia, you take Lena, Fen and Lynal to the stockpile. Vent, you come with me, and we'll take down the sky raiders as soon as Taya destroys their helmets' air function." Garek looked around at every-one. "All clear?"

There were nods of agreement, but Taya noticed the two who knew Vent best, Lena and Fen, edged away from him.

He was still angry.

He'd have to channel it at the sky raiders.

THIRTY-FIVE

GAREK CAME DOWN from on high, dropping like a stone toward the mine.

Taya told him the sky raiders had always done that when she was on Shadow, spending as much time as they could off the planet as a way to prevent contact with the air, which caused a rapid breakdown and rusting of their sky craft.

But as he came down, he knew something was wrong by the way both Taya and Jerilia suddenly stiffened as they stood by the window.

"What is it?"

"They've moved the camp to the mine." Taya turned to him, eyes wide. "They don't need a sky craft for shift change, because everyone is living right next to the mine."

They were almost at the landing area, and Garek ran through his options. They had lost the element of surprise. And given that, they would have no better chance to pull off a rescue than right now.

Just before he set down he saw the tattered, sad camp cobbled together from pieces of the old camp, and saw, too, that the sky raiders were ready for them.

Either they'd made plans for the possibility of attack, or they were just very quick on their feet, but there were four of them, ranged around the landing area in the big, mechanical suits they used on Shadow, already firing white lighting at the sky craft.

The white lightning didn't affect the craft itself, but it would be impossible for anyone to climb out.

Garek made as if he was going to set down in the landing area, but at the last moment he called his Change and slid the sky craft to the right, knocking one of the sky raiders over.

There was a grating sound of metal on metal.

The other three hastily moved back and spread out a little wider, two in the front, one disappearing around the back.

They started shooting again as Garek lowered the craft to the ground.

"They have us pinned." Vent stood at the window, nudging Jerilia aside as he took in the stark, arid landscape.

"What do we do?" Pilar was staring out, face pinched and pale.

"We have to break the standoff." Garek was only too aware of what Pilar must be feeling with Noor out there somewhere. "We're not going to get another chance to rescue them. It has to be now."

"If you lower the back a little bit, I could squeeze out the side. Especially if the others made a noise on one side, and I slipped out the other." Taya studied the sky raiders with cool eyes.

"They looked well trained." Vent was studying them, too.

"Maybe you think we should go home?" Pilar was looking at Vent with narrowed eyes.

"No, but I don't think an untrained village girl is going to best them."

"I don't see you offering to go out there." Garek felt the hot, corrosive burn of anger in his gut. Vent was turning into a problem.

"We have to get out onto the ground." Taya ignored Vent completely, her eyes solemn as she looked at Garek. "I'm the best bet. I'm small enough that they might not realize the door is open wide enough for anyone to get out, and I can quickly take one of those suits out of the fight from a distance."

He hesitated. Then nodded. She was right. This was their only option other than going home.

Which they would not do.

"I need you to make it work," he told her—more a plea than an order.

She locked her arms around his waist, and he kissed her hard and fast, his hands twined deep in her hair.

"The worst that can happen is I get hit with white lightning again," she whispered in his ear as she pulled back.

"Dodge," he told her, squeezing her one last time before he let go, and she forced a smile for him.

Pilar, Jerilia and Lynal went with her as she headed for the back of the craft, and Dom took up position just inside the door to the back.

Vent stayed where he was, looking out the window, and Lena and Fen, after a moment's hesitation, stood with him.

"Now," Dom called, and Garek gently lowered the door, sliding the tip of his finger along the dial on the arm of his pilot's chair.

He heard noise from the back, the sound of something being banged against the wall as Jerilia, Pilar and Lynal set up their distraction.

"Stop!" Dom's shout had him lifting his finger up, and the noise at the back intensified.

"She's out." Dom's whole attention was on the back, his body quivering, and Garek rose up, tried to angle his body to see if he could catch a glimpse into the back area and through the thin crack of the opened door.

And hoped he hadn't just sent Taya out to die.

TAYA FELL BADLY.

Pain shot up her left shoulder and arm as she hit the hard-packed earth and she had to blink back tears and breathe through it as she rolled away from the sky craft.

She hadn't realized how big a drop there was to the ground, and sliding out sideways had meant she couldn't break her fall.

She scrabbled to a crouch when she thought she was far enough away and glanced back, wishing she could have rolled under the craft, with its deep cover, instead of away from it, but she couldn't work with the shadow ore knife anywhere near it.

She needed to protect their only way home.

Just ahead of her was the sky raider Garek had knocked over when they landed.

The mechanical suit lay in a crumpled heap, emitting an insistent, annoying sound.

She ran toward it, crouching down when she reached it to use whatever cover it could give her.

The other sky raider covering the back of the craft had been drawn to the side where Jerilia, Pilar and Lynal were making a noise, and she carefully rotated her shoulder as she worked out her best angle of attack.

The noise from the mechanical suit she was hiding behind made her jumpy and grated on her nerves, and she pulled the knife out of the water pouch she'd attached to her belt, and pressed it to the top of the darkened glass of the suit's bulbous head.

She held it there and counted out the seconds.

When she got to two, the suit made one last buzzing noise and then died.

The silence was noticed.

She could see the legs of the sky raider investigating the noise on the other side, and they went still when the beeping stopped.

Then the sky raider started moving around the back towards her.

No time to get up her courage. She had to *move*.

She stood and ran to meet him, the knife already airborne by the time the sky raider rounded the back corner.

She threw herself forward and rolled as he shot, the white lightning hitting the ground behind her.

She discovered she needed a lot more practice with shadow ore, because the distraction of diving out of the way lost her her connection to the knife, and it missed the suit and dropped to the ground.

She came up in a crouch and called her Change in panic as the sky raider readjusted his aim, slamming the knife against him with no thought to placement, so long as it was making contact.

She dived again, committing at the last moment and only just missing being hit, her gaze still fixed on the knife.

There was no third shot, and she winced as she forgot about her shoulder and put weight on her arm to push herself up. Favoring her hurt side, she rose slowly, never taking her focus off the enemy.

The sky raider remained still.

She looked at it more closely, and saw the mechanical shell was badly corroded, a result of being exposed to the air of Shadow for too long.

She wondered if that was because she and Garek had destroyed so many of the suits when they'd escaped, they'd forced the sky raiders to overuse whatever they had left.

She waited one more beat, just to make sure the suit was truly dead, and then left her knife beside it before she ran back to the gap in the door. She could see a slice of Jerilia's face, pressed up against it, trying to see out.

"I did it."

Jerilia turned and gave a shout, and the door started to lower, the edge catching the sky raider's mechanical shell and knocking it over.

The camp lay to the left of her, and someone tall darted out from the shacks, arm raised and back, and then threw what looked like a stone.

Eli!

She scooped up her knife and ran toward him, saw the rock he'd pitched at the sky raider at the front of the craft hit the torso area of its mechanical body.

The white lightning it was shooting at the sky craft stopped abruptly.

Suddenly, a horde of people ran out from the camp, and the air became a hail of shadow ore.

She caught hold of it with a spike of joy that almost overwhelmed her, and rained it down on both sky raiders in the front.

The second sky raider had turned when Eli ran out, and had gotten a single shot off, but shadow ore deflected some of it, so it only brought down three people before his suit was struck by multiple pieces of rock and he stopped moving.

Taya flew across the ground and threw herself at Eli. He was standing next to the sky raider he'd downed, tears tracking through the mine dust on his cheeks, arms wide open.

"We didn't know," he said, voice cracking as he swung her around. "We didn't know it was you until I saw you dive out the way of the sky raider at the back. I told everyone, no matter what, this is our only chance to attack." He heaved in a breath, his whole body shuddering. "We've been stealing shadow ore since we started work again, keeping a pile of it hidden, waiting for our chance."

"You knew we would come," she said as he set her down.

"I hoped. Noor and I hoped. But we didn't know when. We didn't even know if you were still alive." He straightened, his face working as he got back control.

The ramp had finished lowering while they spoke, and Garek ran down toward them.

Eli caught him in a tight hug and then stepped back, grinning. "You got Taya back, and then you came to get us. You'll never live this down, now."

Garek hooked an arm around her, and she felt it quiver along her back, as if he was a spring released from pressure.

He pulled her close, bent down, and kissed the top of her head. "I didn't do any of it alone." He squeezed her tight.

She ran her hand up and down his back, stroking him, and his breathing evened out.

Eli watched them, eyes bright. "You didn't do it alone, but my guess is, you'd prefer to."

Then he turned, his face changing from one moment to the next as he looked down at the sky raider lying on the ground. "He'll still be alive in there."

"For a bit," Garek agreed.

Taya sighed. She didn't like this part.

She hadn't liked watching it happen outside Luf, when she'd sat on the roof of the sky craft and waited for the sky raiders to choke and die.

She hadn't liked it before, when they'd killed their guards at the camp when they'd escaped Shadow, and she didn't like it now.

"Where's Noor?" Pilar ran up to Eli, eyes wild with panic.

"Down the shafts," Eli told him, hand going to Pilar's shoulder to hold him back when he tried to spin in the direction of the mine entrance. "She's safe, Pilar. She's okay."

He shuddered in a breath.

"Why don't you take Dom, go in the mine and get everyone like we planned," Garek told him, and with a nod, Pilar raced off.

Jerilia passed him, moving out of his way. She gave Eli a cheeky grin hello. "Should I get the boxes out the back and load them with ore?" she asked Garek and he nodded.

"Get the guards and Lynal to help."

"I'll help them choose which ore," Taya said, and then flicked her gaze to the fallen sky raider. She wanted to be far away from them while they died.

"You're allowed to feel sorry for them."

She looked up and saw Garek was watching her. He brushed a finger down her cheek.

"I don't know why you do," Eli said, nodding in agreement. "But you're entitled to your own feelings. Leave them to us. I don't think either Garek or I have any problem making sure they're dead."

She looked between them. They were both being honest.

With a nod of relief she turned toward the pile of shadow ore near the mine entrance.

It was much smaller than it had been.

She turned and walked backward so she could speak to Eli. "They took some of it away?" She didn't think that could be good.

Eli lifted his shoulders. "They must have. The pile looked like that when we got here."

It made sense they would have taken it. After all, it was their reason for being here, but she didn't like the idea that they'd gotten what they came for.

She wanted them thwarted in every way, because otherwise, they had reason to return.

As she headed for the stockpile, she noticed Vent had moved to the mine entrance, following behind Pilar and Dom as they disappeared inside. He turned to look at her.

"This is where you worked?" he asked.

She nodded. "Every day for four months."

"What's in there?"

"Tunnels, some of them close to collapse, and some with broken down digging machines in them. They learned the hard way the shadow ore broke their machines."

He paused before he stepped into the mine. "A word of warning. I don't like being made a fool of. I don't like being kept in the dark about your abilities. You and Garek are very friendly with Aidan, and I can see he thinks a lot of you, too, but you can't count on him forever. If you're looking for an easy ride to the top, understand I'll oppose it all the way, and I'm still the guard master of Juli."

Taya was aware her mouth was agape. Had he not *seen* Garek fight?

And then it occurred to her, no, he probably hadn't.

He'd arrived after they'd tried to stop the sky raiders taking the Kardanx, and maybe he'd only heard stories about everything else.

Even the way Garek had called his Change to knock the first sky raider over just now was difficult to understand if you didn't know how the sky craft worked. She barely knew herself, but she'd seen the way he'd gone slightly blurred at the edges as the craft had slid sideways, and she understood the power it had taken.

"You seem surprised." He was looking at her strangely.

"I didn't realize how ill-informed you were. There is no one better than Garek. There is no such thing as an easy ride to the top for him. He is the top. I was just trying to work out if you had never seen him fight."

"I saw him take down the guard master in Gara. I was impressed, but Utrel was clearly promoted above his competence level by the town master because they were conspiring together."

Taya met his gaze with her own, and shrugged. "You're wrong, but you'll find that out in time."

"We'll see. I notice you didn't contradict my impression of you."

Taya crouched beside a big rock, thick with shadow ore, and reached out a hand to touch it. She sucked in a breath, and then looked up at him. "I'm completely untrained, as you'd expect from someone who only found their calling in adulthood. Why would I deny the obvious? Almost any guard has better training than me."

He grunted, surprised, and then turned and walked into the mine.

She stared after him for a beat and then went back to the rock under her hand.

As Jerilia and Lynal came up, straining under the load of the water-filled box, she turned to them with a smile and held up her find.

"Let's get loading."

THIRTY-SIX

GAREK LEFT Eli and some of the other prisoners the job of smashing into the sky raiders suits and making sure they were dead. Instead, he walked toward Taya, watching her interaction with Vent with a frown.

"You all right?" he asked her when he got to the stock pile, and she looked up and nodded, then went happily back to choosing the most ore-rich rocks to take.

Garek stepped into the mine.

He'd never been in here before.

There had been no time when he'd arrived with Aidan to rescue everyone, and while they had no time now to indulge his curiosity, he decided to see what Vent was up to.

He was impressed with the smooth tunnels, and the lights attached to the walls, but the tunnels seemed to meander with no purpose, and there were numerous offshoots.

From down the main tunnel, he heard a whoop of joy, and then shouting, and guessed that Pilar and Dom had reached the ore face.

The sound of a boot scuffing against rock came from one of the side tunnels.

It was dark and rather than go down it, Garek waited, arms folded, in the light.

Vent reemerged a minute later.

"Find anything interesting?"

The guard master started, and then pursed sour lips.

"Couldn't see much, but there was a broken down machine, just like Taya said. Imagine what we could do with a few of them?"

"Whatever we did, we'd have to do it fast. They wouldn't last long in the air of Barit."

Vent went still, and then frowned. "The one I saw down there was pretty rusted, too. This happens to all their things?"

Garek nodded. "The sky craft won't be an advantage for West Lathor for long. If we're going to use it, we may have to force Harven, Fabre and Kadmine's hand."

Vent rubbed a hand over his head. "I had forgotten that."

Garek could hear the sound of feet and loud talking moving toward them. "While we're still alone, where is Aidan? And don't tell me he's held up with his father."

Vent hesitated. "I didn't think you'd accept that excuse." He looked down the tunnel, in the direction of the noise. "He disappeared."

Garek couldn't find a response for a moment. "What do you mean, he disappeared?"

"He was on his way back to Juli from Gara. I sent one of the guards with him, and when they were a day away from home, they set up camp. When morning came, Aidan was gone. His pack, his pallet, everything was still in the camp, but no Aidan."

"The guard didn't hear anything?"

Vent shook his head. "I've questioned him over and over. He's well-trained. If Aidan was taken against his will, they did it without making a sound."

"So why are you telling everyone Aidan's with his father?"

"Because no one sees Valtor anymore. Dartan and I are hoping everyone assumes the two of them are finally negotiating the handover of power away from prying eyes. We can't let it get out that Aidan's missing. It means West Lathor is effectively leaderless."

If anything would propel an invasion, learning West Lathor had no liege would do it.

Before he could reply, the miners came sweeping around the corner.

Those in front came to a hard, stumbling halt at the sight of him, which created a logjam.

"Garek." The Kardanx in the front group stepped forward, face relaxing. "You rescue us again."

"Jona." Garek remembered the Kardanx as the man who'd stepped up as leader of the Kardanx camp when they were making plans for the first escape.

"Everyone, please get in the sky craft as fast as you can. We need to go as soon as possible."

Jona nodded, and as the mixed group of Kardanx and Illy streamed past, he was touched, kissed or had his shoulder slapped in gratitude.

Noor slid her arms around him for a quick hug.

"Taya?" she asked.

"Outside, loading more shadow ore."

He started moving toward the entrance with Pilar and Noor, and then paused and looked back to find Vent trailing behind him.

He waited, and as Vent passed him, he shot out an arm, caught Vent's forearm in a tight grip. "I saw you exchange words with Taya before you came in here. You don't have to like her, but you'll treat her with the respect she deserves, or I'll leave you here."

Vent's eyes widened, and Garek spun away, and jogged up the tunnel.

It was time to go.

THIRTY-SEVEN

KARDAI WAS LUSH.

It lay on the other side of the Valley of Tears, the deep, terraced chasm that undulated with waterfall after waterfall from the high ground of the Illy to the lower, warmer climes of Kardai and the countries of the south east.

It was strange for Taya to see houses and buildings that looked like they could be found in an Illian village or town, surrounded by dark green ferns and thick bushes with bright flowers.

Jona stood beside her, looking out as Garek followed the river down toward Pinaru, the centralized city for the whole of Kardai.

"We can't expect the same reception here we got in Illy," she said to him. "Where will it be safe for Garek to land?"

Jona stared out, his gaze fixed at a point in the far distance.

He turned toward Garek. "I think a point needs to be made." His gaze flickered to Vent and then away. "Kardai has been happy to insult the Illy, but also happy to let West Lathor be our buffer against the other, more aggressive Illian states." He looked back out the window. "I think it's time we chose which side we're on."

"What does that mean?" Vent leaned back against the wall. He'd been quiet since he'd come out of the mine with Garek, neither engaging with her, or even looking directly at her.

"It means the more flamboyant our arrival, the more my story will be believed. And the more support I'll get for a promise of support from Kardai to West Lathor."

"You think you can get something like that?" Garek raised a brow in a grim face.

He'd rested a little, and Dom had taken over for him, but as soon as they came into the air around Barit, Dom had ceded the pilot's chair to him, and he looked tired.

She wanted to help, but she couldn't, and so she did the most useful thing she could instead—watched out the window for any sign of sky raiders.

"I'll try." Jona raised his shoulders. "My father is a *haidai's* son. I'm known to some in the Chamber."

There was silence as they all thought about it.

"What do you suggest?" Garek lifted the sky craft a little higher as they approached a town nestled on a bend in the river.

"There's a tower that rises out of the central palace in Pinaru. It has a small garden at the top, a place of contemplation. The stairs up to it take at least half an hour to climb. If you land up there we can get out and you can fly away, before any guards could reach us." Jona suddenly grinned, as if imagining the chaos such an arrival would cause. "The tower also has the benefit of being visible from every point in the city. Everyone will see us land. There will be no way to deny it."

"Will you be safe?" Dom asked. He was sitting on the floor, head leaning back against the wall. "They won't arrest you for conspiring with the sky raiders, or something like that?"

"We have Fayda with us," Jona said, his gaze flicking to the door to the back of the craft. "He's an elder. His word is his bond. They'll have to take what he says seriously, and with the rest of us all telling the same story, I don't think they'd have the guts to silence us that way. Especially not if we make such an entrance."

Taya wondered if one of the reasons he was suggesting this option was fear that if they were dropped off somewhere obscure, they actually would be in danger of being arrested for saying they'd been returned in a sky craft from Shadow.

"I'll also be talking about how we were saved by Illians who call the Change. How we had to be rescued twice."

Taya remembered that some of the Kardanx from the camp, especially the younger ones, had been chafing against the law against anyone who could call a Change in Kardai. They looked at the Illy, and saw the strength they could have had if they'd nurtured those with a calling, rather than wiped them out.

Dom snorted out a laugh. "Maybe they'll listen now, but I doubt it."

"Again, all I can do is try." Jona's voice carried an edge. "At least I'm going to try. You're staying in Juli."

"As the Kardanx liason." Dom looked up, and Jona's mouth fell open.

"Kardanx liason?"

"Aidan has given me an official role." Dom held Jona's gaze. "So you can tell those in the Chamber that any communications with West Lathor will now have to come through me."

Jona blew out a breath. "That will be an interesting discussion." He suddenly laughed. "A very interesting discussion."

The look he and Dom shared next was friendlier.

"I think Pinaru is coming up," Taya said, seeing the towers in the distance.

Garek lifted the sky craft even higher and Jona went into the back to let everyone know what was happening.

When they spiraled down toward the center of the city, Taya saw what Jona had meant.

The tower rose like a stem from amongst the tall buildings and smaller towers of the palace, the bulbous top shaped like the petals of a flower open to the sun.

The garden at the top was a circular lawn with benches and

chairs and filled with the exotic plants she'd seen on their journey over the landscape.

"I hope the plants survive our landing." She glanced over at Dom as he joined her at the window.

"Better they don't. More evidence we were here." He shrugged, cynicism in every line of him.

Garek set them down, and when the doors opened, Taya could hear bells ringing far below.

The warning had been sounded.

The Kardanx scrambled out, and Taya walked through to the back to stand with her fellow Pan Nuk villagers and see the garden.

There was a heavy mixture of scents in the air from the flowers and leaves crushed by the sky craft, and flanking the ornate door to the stairs of the tower were two sculptures, both abstracts of trees.

Something about the color and sheen of them rang bells in her head, and she risked stepping out and running over to them, past the Kardanx gathered in a group to peer over the side of the tower.

She noticed Vent, Lena and Fen had taken the chance to have a quick look over the side, too. Most likely they'd call it reconnaissance.

She touched one sculpture and then the other, and felt the zing of shadow ore—it wasn't pure—but there was enough for her to be able to wield it.

"Taya?" Garek looked out at her from the open pilot's door. The *what in the Star?* was unspoken but clear.

She called her Change and lifted one of the tree sculptures up a little off the ground to make him understand why she'd left the craft.

There was a gasp to her left as she did it, and she saw two old men, in the robes worn by the elders of the Kardanx Mother religion, crouched in hiding behind a massive flower pot.

Garek twirled his finger in the signal she knew was guard short-hand for 'let's go'.

With one last touch, Taya skirted the old men and ran back to the ramp behind Vent and his guards.

She turned to look one last time at the gardens and the group of

Kardanx standing in a tight group, waiting for the chaos and confusion created by their arrival to descend.

A few raised their hands in farewell, and then the ramp closed. When Garek turned the sky craft around to face them, they waited only a few minutes before the doors burst open and guards dressed in bright colors spilled into the garden.

She saw the surprise and fear on their faces, and then the shock as they registered the presence of their own countrymen.

"Did you see? There was shadow ore in those sculptures." She looked over at Garek, touching her fingers to her cheek as she remembered the feel of the smooth metal against her skin.

Garek hovered them in the air just above the garden. "Was it really necessary to touch them?"

She glanced over at him, saw his mouth was set in a grim line. "Now we know the Kardanx either mine, or have access to a mine, with shadow ore."

He inclined his head. "True."

He said nothing more, and she sighed as at last he lifted them higher and rose above the city.

"You're annoyed I left the sky craft." She slid a hand along his shoulders.

His jaw bunched a little. "Yes."

"I'm not used to checking in with someone else. I'm sure you're not, either."

For a beat he said nothing, then he shot her a rueful smile.

"True," he said again.

She laughed, leaning into him, and then he dipped the sky craft left and turned for home.

THIRTY-EIGHT

IT WAS JUST after dusk when the sky craft reached Pan Nuk.

The sound of the engines changed as Garek came in to land and everyone in the pilot's chamber began to stir.

Taya had dozed, lying on his pallet near the pilot's chair.

Dom had fallen asleep leaning against the wall, and Vent had looked asleep, too, but he came to his feet as if he'd been wide awake the whole time.

Lena and Fen came through from the back, Fen covering up a yawn as they presented themselves to Vent for orders.

"We have a lot to do," the guard master said, peering out the window, then he spun back to Garek. "This isn't Juli."

"I never said it was. The whole point of the rescue was to bring back the people of Pan Nuk." He concentrated on landing lightly at the end of the main street, but kept the engines running.

Taya had stumbled to her feet. "What would you like me to do?" She smothered a big yawn.

"Get everyone out. I'll go set this down where we hid it last time."

She nodded, giving Dom a hand up, and then walking through to the back without acknowledging Vent or his scowl.

Garek lowered the ramp, heard the shouts of happiness from outside as everyone worked out their people were home.

"You need to get out, too," he told Vent. "I've got a hiding place for the sky craft, and it's a little way from the village. Kas will find you somewhere to sleep."

Vent looked like he was going to argue, and Lena and Fen held still, waiting.

"Why can't we drop them off and go on to Juli?"

"Because I'm tired, and this is my village. Taya will want to see her family, and we all need a rest."

He held Vent's gaze, and with a huff of ill grace, Vent turned on his heel and stalked out, Lena and Fen slouching behind him.

There was a clatter of feet running up the ramp, and Taya came into the pilot's chamber with a few Pan Nukkers.

"They're going to help cover the sky craft and stand watch," she said, walking over to his chair and resting a hand on his shoulder. "The doors are all still there for you to land on."

This sky craft was becoming a millstone around his neck, Garek realized as he set it down in the valley. He was torn between doing what was safe—spending the night under it like he'd done before—or walking back to the village and a comfortable bed with Taya.

"I almost can't wait for it to fall apart," he said staring up at it, his arm hooked around Taya's shoulder.

"It's a burden," she agreed. "And a huge advantage." She slid her arm around his waist and turned them in the direction of the village.

"You don't think I should sleep under it again?"

She lifted her head. "If we have to, but after dinner. I don't mind where we sleep, as long as we have a little privacy."

And just like that, he didn't mind, either.

THE GUARDS CAME JUST after dinner.

Vent stood when they appeared suddenly in the flickering light of the fire, and Taya saw his surprise.

She stood herself, and Kas, Garek and Eli rose, too.

"What is it?" Vent asked them, and she noticed at last that they were in Juli guard uniforms.

Garek was watching Vent, rather than the newcomers, a frown on his face. "Who are these people?"

Vent hesitated. "Members of the liege's special protection unit."

The liege's bodyguards, in other words. Why would they be here?

"How did you know we'd be here at all?" Garek asked them, and Taya remembered that of course Dartan thought Garek and Vent were off on the border with Kadmine, spying on an enemy camp.

The leader of the group of four studied them all, his gaze skipping over the men and lingering first on Min, and then on Taya, the action deliberate and somehow threatening.

He finally turned back to Vent. "Dartan wanted us to leave a message for you, in case you came back here rather than returned to Juli." He paused. "As I see you have."

"We just arrived a few hours ago," Vent said, and there was a defensiveness to his tone.

"Where's the sky craft?" The guard looked past the camp fire, toward the village.

"Hidden." Garek was suddenly beside him, and the guard stepped back in surprise. "What's the message?"

"For Vent's ears only." The guard's mouth formed a mulish line and he straightened his jacket. He looked around at them, as if expecting them to leave their seats so he could talk with Vent privately.

No one moved.

Vent shook his head. "Come on, then. Let's move away a little."

He moved down the path the guards had come in on, and with a flare of his nostrils, the guard strode after him.

The three left behind spread out a little, as if blocking the path of anyone who might try to follow them.

Taya heard Vent exclaim, and then go quiet, but he moved back to the fire almost straight away. "We need to fly back to Juli tomorrow."

Garek said nothing, his expression neutral.

"We'll catch a lift back with you," the guard said.

Vent glanced over at Garek, and Taya thought she saw him wince.

"I didn't catch your name." Kas spoke for the first time, stepping closer to the guard. "I'm Kas, the town master."

The guard didn't look like he was going to answer for a moment. "Ewen."

He didn't introduce his three companions and after an uncomfortable silence, they each offered their own names.

As Kas invited them for dinner and kept their attention, Garek crossed over to Taya's side.

"Let's go," he murmured, his lips brushing the shell of her ear.

She looked over at Quardi, gave a little wave goodbye, and he blew her a kiss from across the fire.

The guard, Ewen, watched the byplay, ignoring Kas as her brother made a suggestion about where they could pitch their tents for the night.

"Are we going back to the sky craft?" Taya had to half-jog to keep up with Garek as he towed her by the hand.

"No. I'm going to trust it's hidden well enough. I don't like these new guards. We know there's a traitor in Juli, betraying us to the sky raiders, so I'm not leading anyone I don't know or trust anywhere near it."

"Vent doesn't know where it is, either, so he can't tell them."

Garek hummed in acknowledgment. "True, but I don't think he would anyway. It doesn't seem like he's even in control of Ewen and his team. It's as if they're outside his command."

Taya had picked that up, too. "Maybe they only report to the liege."

Garek had led her through the warmth of the forge, through the smaller opening into the enclosed courtyard, and into the small room he'd always had as his own at the back.

She could hear laughter and loud voices from the homes around them, but it was a good sound, a happy sound, that embraced, rather than excluded. The sound of a homecoming.

They didn't turn on a light.

They didn't need to.

With the door off its frame, part of the landing pad for the sky craft, moonlight filtered in.

Garek stood in front of her and slipped her jacket off her shoulders, throwing it over the chair beside the bed.

He worked the buttons of her shirt, and she reached up and did the same to his.

When they both stood with buttons undone, he leaned forward to rest his forehead against hers.

"I didn't want you to go out alone to confront the sky raiders on Shadow."

He reached a hand through the flaps of her shirt, and she shivered in reaction as his warm fingers caressed her ribs, just below her breasts.

"I know."

She saw his lips lift in a quick smile. "You didn't show it."

"It was the only option. And we didn't have time to waste."

He lifted his hands off her body and used them to push back her hair, to lift her face to his. "I don't like it when the only option is for you to risk yourself."

"We'll have to make sure the odds are better next time, then." She leaned forward, kissed his chin, and then placed tiny, quick kisses along his jaw as she unbuckled her trousers and pushed them down her legs.

When she kicked them free, she saw he'd done the same, and they stood for a moment, naked in front of each other, neither touching.

Taya drew in a deep breath. "I love you."

He lifted her up, and turned as she hooked her legs around his waist, setting her down on the bed, and lowering himself over her.

"When I was walking the walls of Gara, I never thought I'd hear those words from you again. I thought you'd be tired of waiting for me, tired of the silence. And instead, you wrote to me, sent me presents, waited. Everything I could have wished for." He held himself above her, placed a kiss on her breastbone. "I don't know what I did to deserve you."

She lifted her hands and reveled in the smooth, hot feel of his skin as she swept them down his sides. "I'm sure you can figure it out." She grinned up at him, and saw him go from serious to wicked.

"Maybe I can."

She laughed as he tickled her, clamping him closer so he couldn't get access, and then went still, looking into his eyes.

"If this whole mess didn't include the safety of West Lathor, if Pan Nuk wasn't going to be affected, what would you do?"

"It was always going to include Pan Nuk," he said, as serious again as she was. "The sky raiders face no real opposition, so they were always going to keep coming back."

She felt like her energy for the fight had been drained away, but he was right. Until they got rid of the sky raiders, there would never be an end to it.

"Then we have to keep fighting." She closed her eyes, tried to find the well of determination and anger she'd been using to fuel her resistance up until now.

"We do." Garek kissed her then drew back, and when she opened her eyes, she saw the wicked gleam was back in his. "But not right now."

THIRTY-NINE

GAREK WOKE COMPLETELY, lying in the darkness with the warmth of Taya pressed against his side.

The sound that woke him came again, the faint scuff of a boot on the stone flagging of the courtyard outside his open door.

He touched Taya to wake her, pressing a finger against her lips as her eyes fluttered open, and then easing from the covers to stand in front of the bed, ears straining for every sound.

The bed creaked as Taya rose off it, but although he winced, he decided it could have just as easily been the sound of a restless sleeper.

He looked over at her, the thin light of the moon just silhouetting her naked form. She made a face of apology and then lifted up her shadow ore knife to show him she was armed.

Her other weapons, her spears and her sword, were all at her and Kas's house, out of reach, but the knife was better than nothing.

"Ewen?" Taya mouthed, and he nodded.

It could only be Ewen. The question was, was it just him and his three companions?

It was possible they were only the front guard, scoping the terrain while more hid in the hills and waited for the all clear.

Or, and this was something he hoped wasn't so, the message Ewen had brought for Vent's ears only was an order to help Ewen capture either Taya or himself. Or both of them.

But he guessed it was Taya.

Hadn't he foolishly set this up by bowing to Vent's advice and telling Dartan they would be dropping Taya off in Pan Nuk before they went to the Kadmine border?

Dartan would have thought his guards would be able to take her with no resistance. It would have been a shock to them to find Vent and himself here.

And now he realized it shouldn't even be a surprise.

If Habred wanted her, why wouldn't Dartan want her too, if he was the one in communication with the sky raiders? The sky raiders wouldn't care who took her, as long as they had her.

And he could just imagine why they'd want her.

She was a living, breathing shadow ore finder. And they were here to find shadow ore.

He pointed to the corner of the room, the place of deepest shadow, and after a moment's hesitation, Taya complied, disappearing completely in the darkness.

He took up position beside the doorframe, waiting and listening.

Someone stepped into the room, a second person just behind them, and called an air Change. He felt the air compress and then expand rapidly over his bed.

He waited, wanting to see if there was anyone else coming before he committed, and in the faint light which seeped in through the door, he made out two figures outside.

All four of the liege's bodyguards would be in this plot. They were a team.

The person in the lead reached the bed and went very still, looking down at it.

"What is it?" The intruder behind him edged closer as well, his voice a whisper.

"They're not here."

"Shit."

They both turned, and as they did, Garek did to them what they had just tried to do to him and Taya.

He slapped the air hard on either side of them, then forced it away so fast, it almost made a vacuum.

The guard who was closer to him fell, screaming, but the one by the bed must have had a split second to build a protective layer of air over his ears, and while he staggered, he didn't go down.

Garek stepped closer, and pulled the air from the guard's lungs. He fell backward, half on the bed, half off, and Garek stood over him.

He sensed the two guards outside in the courtyard burst into the room behind him, but when he looked over his shoulder, he saw Taya's knife slashing at them, the shadow ore glimmering deep purple in the moonlight.

They stumbled back, frightened by the sight of a knife without a wielder, and Garek turned back to the man lying at his feet.

"What is it?" Quardi's voice bounced off the walls of the court-yard, coming from the forge, and he must have been holding a lantern, because a warm, yellow light spilled out and brightened things up.

There was more shouting and when he turned again, he saw Taya's knife was spinning in place in the open door, and the two guards had retreated to the courtyard. He just caught a glimpse of Kas and perhaps Min, before he turned his focus once again on the man lying at his feet.

Ewen.

He was wide-eyed, hands scrabbling at his throat, lips turning blue.

"Garek?" Taya stepped out of the shadows, and the light spilling into the room from outside gave her skin a golden glow.

She was glorious and gloriously naked.

She tipped her head in query at him, and he remembered Ewen.

He tore his gaze away from her and decided he wanted answers more than he wanted to see Ewen die, but only just.

He released his hold and Ewen turned onto his stomach, gagging and trying to suck in air.

Kas appeared in the doorway, and the knife spun up and over, into Taya's hand.

Kas lifted a hand over his eyes at the sight of his naked sister, and then cupped it so he could just see Garek.

"Why don't you two get dressed, and then you can tell me what happened."

THE VILLAGERS of Pan Nuk were tired of being attacked.

As Taya stepped back out into the courtyard after pulling on some clothes, she could see it in the way Eli and Lynal shoved Lena and Fen into the courtyard.

Vent was already there, he'd come running at the sound of fighting, and now he stood over the two guards who'd come into Garek's room, Ewen and Timu, his face a tight, neutral mask.

One of the other men who she'd kept back with her knife sat against the forge wall, bleeding from a slash to his face, but there was no sign of the other one.

"Where's the second man, the one—?"

Quardi had rolled his chair over to her when she'd stepped out and he reached over and touched her arm lightly, stopping her in mid-sentence. "Taya . . ."

She frowned down at him. "What is it?"

He sounded so worried.

"He didn't make it, Taya."

She tried to understand what he was saying. "I didn't try to kill them, just keep them back," she said, but her voice faltered toward the end.

Quardi lifted his shoulders. "That knife is incredibly sharp, and it got him in the throat."

She had slashed the knife with as much control as she could, but it had been dark, and she wasn't as precise as she had a feeling she could be if she only had a chance to practice.

Time to do that had been in short supply since she'd discovered her calling.

"I killed him?" She wanted to make absolutely sure she understood him correctly.

He nodded. Sighed. "I'm thrilled about it. Proud of you, even. But I know you're going to see it differently, so I'm sorry for that. They would have killed Garek, is my guess. Taken you." He tugged her sleeve, forcing her to look back down at him. "You did the only thing you could have done."

She felt as if she'd been shoved under water; her sense of the world around her receding a little, as if she was immersed in something thick and deep.

She saw Garek looming over Vent, in half-buttoned trousers and nothing else, asking him something with a snarl on his face, and she forced herself back into the present, to participate fully.

"What was the message he gave you?" Garek had lifted the guard master a little way off the floor, not with his hands but by calling his Change, and from the look on Vent's face, Taya guessed he was finally finding out first hand how strong Garek was.

"Nothing to do with this." Vent finally worked out the train of Garek's thoughts and he was shaking his head vehemently. "He told me a ransom note has been received for Aidan. It looks like it's from the Iron Guard."

Garek dropped him back down to the ground. "The Iron Guard took the princeling?" He was silent, thinking through the ramifications.

"And what about this lot?" Kas was another Pan Nukker who

sounded like he'd had enough, and his sweeping gesture around the courtyard transmitted pure contempt.

"Ewen is the liege's bodyguard. The others are in his team." Vent stared at them with weariness. "I've thought for a while they were up to no good. I've caught them out of the palace when they should have been guarding the liege, but they don't report to me, they report to him, so I didn't have cause to make a fuss about it. Dartan told me they were following orders and the liege was happy, but now . . ." He looked at them one by one. "What happened tonight isn't the liege's order, and even if it was, they would know it wasn't legal."

"So whose order was it?" Eli glared at Lena and Fen, but Lena raised her hands in a gesture that communicated both disbelief and innocence, and he must have believed her, because he turned instead to Timu and nudged him with his foot. "Whose order was it?"

"I can do what I did to you in the bedroom all night," Garek's voice was pleasant as he looked down at Ewen, so pleasant his words sounded like a lover's promise, rather than a threat, but the effect on Ewen was immediate.

"Dartan."

"Just to be clear, Dartan ordered you to . . .?"

"To take the girl, take you." Ewen shifted on the cold hard floor and looked down at his feet. "If you were too difficult to control, I had permission to kill you."

"But not Taya?" Kas's voice was not steady.

"She's too valuable to someone. Dartan was getting a lot to hand her over."

"You know who that someone is?" Taya asked, unable to stand being spoken about as if she wasn't present.

Ewen looked over at her, face blank.

"The sky raiders. Dartan was going to hand me over to the sky raiders."

The look on his face told her he didn't believe her.

"It's true." Vent slumped against the wall. "I don't want it to be, but it's true."

"They want you," Quardi said, his voice slow. "They want you to find shadow ore for them. And now they know you exist, they're not going to stop until they get you."

Garek leaned against the wall and crossed arms thick with muscle over his chest. "That's why we're going to get them first."

FORTY

"I WANT to go find the Iron Guard."

Garek looked over at Taya, lying beside him in the meadow above the village, and forced himself to focus on her words rather than the gentle touch of the Star's light on his skin, and the feeling of contentment that had settled over him.

"Why?"

"Because I want them to teach me how to control my Change."

This was about the dead guard.

He reached out a hand and traced a fingertip down her arm. "That makes sense, but they don't seem to be the most sympathetic of groups."

She was silent for so long, he thought she'd drifted off to sleep. "When you took Vent back to Juli with Ewen and his team, he told you he was going to arrest Dartan, but that means there's no one in charge of Juli. Not really. So who's going to negotiate with the Iron Guard for Aidan's release?"

That had worried him, too. He shook his head. "Vent, I suppose."

"Let's offer to go instead. If they're hostile, I'll have to make another plan, but if they aren't, if there's something else going on with them, something we don't understand yet, then it's possible they could help me control the shadow ore. Teach me things it might take me years to learn on my own."

He had wanted to go looking for Aidan. Was going to suggest it to Taya in the next few days. "You'll need to bring some of your shadow ore weapons with you."

"Your father is almost finished the new armor he's made me with the ore we brought back. And he's made some arrowheads out of it for me, too. So I don't have to worry about throwing so much as directing."

"He showed me." That Taya had to have weapons made for her, that she had to become a warrior when she was so clearly not one by inclination, made him angry every time he thought of it.

He could be her shield, though. Her buffer in the new reality they found themselves in. That would be the best use of his skill he could think of.

She reached out to him. "If I have more control, I'll be safer, and I can protect everyone better."

He nodded. Rose up on an elbow. "Then let's wait for my father to finish making what you need and we'll go look for Aidan."

And if the Iron Guard weren't amenable, he would help them change their mind.

ABOUT THE AUTHOR

Michelle Diener is an award winning author of historical fiction, science fiction and fantasy.

Michelle was born in London and currently lives in Australia with her husband and two children.

You can contact Michelle through her website or sign up to receive notification when she has a new book out on her New Release Notification page.

Connect with Michelle:
www.michellediener.com